WINTER'S END

BARBARA PRONIN

Black Rose Writing | Texas

©2025 by Barbara Pronin
All rights reserved. No part of this book may be reproduced, stored in a retrieval system or transmitted in any form or by any means without the prior written permission of the publishers, except by a reviewer who may quote brief passages in a review to be printed in a newspaper, magazine or journal.

The author grants the final approval for this literary material.

First printing

This is a work of fiction. Names, characters, businesses, places, events, and incidents are either the products of the author's imagination or used in a fictitious manner. Any resemblance to actual persons, living or dead, or actual events is purely coincidental.

ISBN: 978-1-68513-599-7
LIBRARY OF CONGRESS CONTROL NUMBER: 2024950589
PUBLISHED BY BLACK ROSE WRITING
www.blackrosewriting.com

Printed in the United States of America
Suggested Retail Price (SRP) $21.95

Winter's End is printed in Minion Pro

*As a planet-friendly publisher, Black Rose Writing does its best to eliminate unnecessary waste to reduce paper usage and energy costs, while never compromising the reading experience. As a result, the final word count vs. page count may not meet common expectations.

PRAISE FOR *WINTER'S END*

"Taught and gripping, *Winter's End* is a page-turner filled with honest characters who capture your heart and soul."
–**Bestselling author Faye Kellerman**

"A highly recommended read for fans of emotive drama and wartime action."
–*Reader's Favorite*

PRAISE FOR EARLIER NOVELS

"Emotionally gripping. I loved it from the first page."
–**Mary Higgins Clark**

"My kind of book. A neat, suspenseful plot about people you worry about."
–**Tony Hillerman**

"Tantalizing. Hooked my interest from the start and never let me go."
–**Phyllis A. Whitney**

"A must-read. Pronin had me from word one."
–**L.C. Hayden**

For Larry, my brother, my friend –
And for Steve, who left us far too soon.

WINTER'S END

"Man cannot discover new oceans unless he has the courage to lose sight of the shore."
–Andre Gide

PROLOGUE

Fairfield, New Jersey
April 2017

It was one of her better mornings. Her legs felt steady, and her hip complained only a little as she rose. She was bathed and dressed and making tea when she heard Anneke's key in the door. It was just past seven.

"Oma?" The voice was full-throated, full of cheer. "Good morning!"

"*Goedemorgen*, my little one! A splendid day!"

"Yes, I can see that. You're up and moving all on your own!"

She smiled, setting the teapot on the stove. "Why do you talk as though I am an old woman? I am not yet ninety. Breakfast?"

Anneke laughed, taking her grandmother's hands. "There are roses in your cheeks, Oma. You're excited!"

She had four great-granddaughters, all accomplished, all beautiful – but looking at Anneke was like looking in the mirror into a faraway past – turquoise eyes in a round face, blonde hair, fine as silk, tucked behind her ears.

"On such a day, why wouldn't I be excited?"

Anneke grinned, releasing her Oma's hands, a quick glance at her watch. "I can squeeze in some tea and toast," she said, dropping into a chair by the kitchen window, drawing the curtains wide. "I have a history class at eight – and a quiz."

The old woman nodded, pouring tea, putting wheat bread into the toaster. "You'll be finished by two, yes?"

Anneke fetched lingonberry jam from the fridge. "Oma, I promise you, pinky fingers, cross my heart and hope to die, I will be at the airport by two."

"Don't say hope to die."

"Sorry."

"Flight 458."

"Arrives at 2:55. I know."

She passed her granddaughter a plate of toast. "I made *speculaas* cookies yesterday," she said. "Would you like some?"

"Does a frog jump?" Anneke sipped tea. "No wonder the house smells like cinnamon. Who could say no to your *speculaas*?"

The old woman smiled, turning.

"Sit, Oma. Eat your toast. I'll get the cookies before I go."

She sat, lightly, and wondered how she would endure the hours until Anneke returned from the airport.

But then, she had been well-schooled in waiting, skilled at keeping the angst from her smile no matter the wait or the circumstance.

Morning sun splayed across the table, Anneke's profile etched like a sculpture against the blue New Jersey sky…

PART ONE

Haarlem, The Netherlands
November, 1944

EVI

Evi Strobel watched the three German *schnellboat*s race quickly toward shore.

"Evi, hurry your breakfast, *ja*?"

She glanced across the small barge kitchen, saw Mam packing powdered milk and tins of sardines into a brown leather satchel. Another poor soul fleeing Hitler's wrath would soon be secreted in the hold of the old yellow barge.

She returned her gaze to the approaching *schnellboats*, sleek and fitted with torpedoes. They neared the shore in perfect precision. Her breath stopped in her throat.

They have no reason to board, she told herself. But she watched, rapt, the swell of the River Spaarne rising under her as they veered north, away from the pier. Only then did she let out a ragged breath.

Mam, apparently, had not seen or heard the commotion.

"We will need you at the Dans Hal this afternoon, Evi. Right after school. You won't forget?"

Evi nodded, though she barely heard the words. The *schnellboats* would likely tie up a few kilometers up shore – a restricted wharf where Nazi seamen would unload provisions the likes of which Hollanders had not seen or tasted in years.

Her mouth watered at the remembered taste of *stroopwaffel* and *chocolat,* and her mother's delectable puff pastry in the days before sugar became a prize. She was not sure which she hated more, the constant fear that any day could be your last on this earth or that the Nazis had been slowly starving them to death for four long years.

The bastards would likely drive the lot to the old vegetable market in the *stadsplein,* in the city center, which the SS had long ago commandeered for their headquarters. Evi had watched them once, unloading cured hams tied with string, and big sacks of flour and sugar.

Her stomach rumbled. Air raid sirens had brought her awake more than once during the night, and it was harder and harder to go back to sleep when her stomach ached with hunger.

"Evi, did you hear me?" Lotte's voice was sharp.

"I hear you, Mam. I'm ready."

She swept crumbs into her teacup – the last few bits of a tasteless cracker Mam had managed to concoct from rolled oats and water.

"All right, Mam, I am on my way. I will see you later at the Dans Hal."

That she was needed meant there were underground messages for her to deliver to Resistance volunteers – altered identification papers, perhaps, or packets of stolen ration cards. It irked her that she was not doing more vital work, but it was the one good thing about looking younger than her sixteen years. Even with contraband stowed in her schoolbag, she was less likely to be stopped at a German checkpoint.

"*Goed*, then," Mam waved distractedly. "Be off then, *lieveling.* Try to have a good day at school."

Grabbing her book bag from a hook by the door, Evi ducked slightly to exit the narrow doorway of the barge and climbed the three steps to the pier. A stiff breeze, cold for early November, sent a shiver through her small frame. She hoped the gray wool sweater she had chosen would see her through the afternoon.

She blended into the crowd of students, merchants, and fishermen jostling for space along the narrow walkway, off to pursue whatever passed for normal in the midst of daily chaos.

She glanced at the street lamp where, for so many mornings, she had met up with Sissi Weissbauer. She stared for a moment, then moved on.

She had been nearing her fourteenth birthday, three years ago in February, when the world fell off its axis. The Germans had begun purging thousands of Jews from all over the Netherlands, whole families disappearing into Nazi hell – as though barring them from nearly everything and making them wear yellow stars on their clothing were not enough to torment them.

But Sissi....

Evi had held out hope for many mornings, one day walking past the Weissbauers' shuttered tailor shop, peering through the dusty glass. But it was silent inside...and dark.

She remembered the uproar in that winter of 1940, the riots in the streets as thousands went on strike to protest the round-up of their Dutch Jewish neighbors. But the Germans had only multiplied their sweep, openly shooting dissenters in the street, and sending trains full of Dutch Jews to near certain death.

She moved more quickly as the crowd dispersed, making her way around an ugly, bombed-out crater near the turnoff to the old school road that had not been there the day before.

Nothing in that long ago February had shaken Mam's decision to deepen her commitment to the Resistance – nor had it stopped Papa from leaving them because of it – and it hadn't stopped Evi from siding with Mam, no matter that it put them both at risk.

She walked past a pair of SS lieutenants standing to the side of a horse chestnut tree, their black boots half-buried in an avalanche of dried, fallen leaves. In their brown tunics and field caps, faces half-hidden by deep visors, the Germans seemed indistinguishable one from the other. They nodded stiffly as she passed.

She was past them when she heard her name.

"Evi!"

Annemarie Haan came up swiftly on her left. "*Goedemorgen*, Evi! May I walk with you?"

She shrugged at the lower-level student, a skinny, freckled, redhead whose mother helped assemble *Het Parool*, the underground newspaper, at the Dans Hal.

"Quickly, then," she said.

Annemarie scowled. "You heard the air raids last night…"

Evi nodded.

"More holes in the streets, and the guards pay no mind. They scare me, those Germans. I hate them."

"You are young, innocent, and not Jewish, Annemarie. They are not apt to bother with you."

"Still. I hate them."

"There is reason to hate them. Just don't be shouting it about."

The first bell sounded from the brick-fronted schoolhouse looming just ahead of them, small clusters of students jostling toward the entrance.

"Walk faster," Evi said. "We'll be late."

With school buildings all over Haarlem commandeered by the Nazis, the school once meant only for upper-level students now took up the overflow of younger children with nowhere else to go. AnnMarie hung back the last few yards.

Sophie Van der Oost, in her old blue corduroy jumper, gestured wildly near the entrance. "Evi, you are nearly late."

"I know. I did not sleep well last night – and Annemarie slowed me down."

"Who can sleep with sirens blaring – and bombs going off half the night?"

The second bell sounded as they stepped into the building. Annemarie took off down the hall.

"Did you hear?" Sophie lowered her voice. "The Germans are cutting gas usage to two hours a day!"

Evi shrugged. Mam had told her so last night.

"How are we to keep warm with winter coming on?"

"Likely they will cut the power again as well."

Sophie groaned.

"*Shh*. Keep your voice down. There are spies everywhere. Even here."

She hoisted her bookbag over her shoulder and hurried down the hall, wondering why she bothered when classes were hit-and-miss at best and surely there was more important work she could be doing...

ZOE

It had been a busy morning. By half past eleven, Dr. Zoe Visser had treated an ear infection in a squirmy little beagle pup, diagnosed kidney failure in a cat with a distended stomach, and performed emergency surgery to repair the hind leg of a little dachshund who hadn't been fast enough to get past the wheels of a moving car.

The dachsie was resting comfortably and would likely be fine, Zoe reflected, scrubbing out of the pet *kliniek's* OR. Medications were hard to come by these days, but the cat was young and otherwise healthy enough to survive, and perhaps even to reverse the kidney failure.

In all, the outcomes had been mostly positive, and she was more than ready for her lunch break. Shrugging off her white jacket, she slipped into the old gray coat she had taken with her to university.

"I will be back in an hour, Lise," she told the receptionist.

"Not a problem," the girl said. "Short of another emergency, no appointments until one, and Dr. Mulder should be back soon from Amsterdam. He went in this morning for supplies."

Zoe paused, pulling a woolen cap over tawny curls. She had not been aware that Daan had gone to Amsterdam. There would likely be work for her to do tonight.

• • •

Walking into the wind, she put her hands in her pockets and made her way past a deserted playground to the other end of the *stadsplein*, the heels of her practical black oxfords sounding dully on the cobblestones. She walked quickly, past the frankly appraising stares of the SS officers standing about, and turned into a market street hastily put together after the Nazis had commandeered the old market hall.

Two more shops, she saw – a juice vendor and a *kaffie* shop she'd patronized over the years – were closed and boarded up. Zoe felt the air sucked out of her. More food shops forced to close because they had no goods to sell.

She passed the green grocer's, glanced at half-filled crates of carrots, potatoes, and beets, a few winter melons, and wilting heads of cabbage available to those who could afford them. More than four years into a war thrust upon them had made more and more Hollanders – even those like her parents, who had never before put a hoe to the soil – dependent on what they could grow themselves, or catch.

Zoe shivered in her woolen coat. With the cold descending, the Nazis commandeering the lion's share of food, and spring planting months away, the last of even these meager crops would soon be gone. *God help us,* she silently mouthed the words, *to survive till winter's end.*

Sighing, she ducked into a small café situated between the struggling produce market and a fish vendor. She chose it not because the food was good or plentiful – nothing was plentiful these days unless the shopkeeper had forged an arrangement with the Nazis – but because it was well-suited for her purpose. Pulling off her cap, she stuffed it into a pocket, then wriggled out of her coat and found a place for it high on the crowded coat rack.

She chose a small table near the kitchen and looked up at the young man waiting to take her order. He was tall, slim, and fresh-faced, not much older than she, Evi guessed. He set a glass of water in front of her and smiled in a way that told her he could be interested in more than what she wanted for lunch.

At twenty-four, Zoe knew she was pretty. She was also one of the youngest veterinarians in Haarlem, if not in all the Netherlands, having graduated from high school at sixteen and finished her veterinary studies just before the rowdy student protests against the Nazi invasion had triggered university shutdowns. She loved her work, and her work for the Resistance, but it left little time for a social life.

She turned her attention to the paper menu, crossed through with black marker where choices were no longer available.

"I will have a herring sandwich on pumpernickel bread," she said. "With butter if you have it," she said. "And coffee."

The young man looked as though she had given him a gift. "Straightaway, mademoiselle."

Zoe smiled at his use of the French.

She kept her head down when her food arrived, and ate the sandwich quickly, leaving her guilders on the table before the waiter appeared with the check.

Making her way back to the coat rack, she stood with her back to the café's diners and fussed about with her left hand as if to adjust the scarf around her neck. All the while, her right hand moved quickly from pocket to pocket among the jumble of outerwear on the rack.

She was stuffing two small leather cases into the pocket of her coat when she heard the call from behind.

"Mademoiselle!"

She felt the blood drain from her face.

"Your earring!" the server called, coming up behind her. "It was on the floor beneath your table."

Zoe closed her eyes and wrapped her coat close around her. She was not wearing earrings.

"Not mine, I fear," she turned to face the waiter, touching her naked earlobe. "No earrings today. It must belong to someone else. But thank you," she managed to smile.

He looked deflated. "Aah...yes, I see...Well...please do come in again."

On the street outside, perspiring in the cold, she took a deep gulp of air and fingered the leather cases in her pocket. It was what she liked least, of all the duties she had taken on for the Resistance, snooping through other people's pockets.

It was stealing, really, she knew it was stealing, there was no other word for it. But it was necessary, seizing identification papers that could be altered for Jews and other enemies of the Reich who were forced to run for their lives.

Still, she tried to even her breathing and kept her head down as she walked. Random German checkpoints could turn up anywhere, and SS observers might decide to stop you for no reason at all.

• • •

In her own small office, Zoe closed the door and slipped the two leather cases out of her coat pocket. One, she saw, contained a Swiss passport in the name of Josef Huber, born January, 1918 in Geneva. The other held a Dutch ID card in the name of Johanna Stoepker, born 1909 in Amsterdam. Altered and fitted with the photos of desperate escapees, they might help to save two lives.

Zoe hated that she needed to do this. But she hated the Nazis more, and the identification papers, she knew, could be replaced without too much fuss by their rightful owners.

She placed the cases in the bottom of her handbag beneath a jumble of keys, make-up, and other paraphernalia, intending to pass them on to Daan Mulder when he returned. She hung the bag and her coat on a peg behind the door, and put her white coat on over her dress.

Straightening, she opened the door.

MILA

Mila Brouwer whirled once before the tailor shop's three-sided mirror, watched the taffeta skirts of the lavender dinner dress dance against her legs.

"Very good, Gita" she said. "A quick press at the hemline and the dress will be perfect. I can come back for it if you like."

"No need, *Missen*, we will deliver it to your home by five this afternoon."

"Thank you."

Mila ran a hand over the smooth bodice with its deep vee-neckline, then slipped out of the dress and handed it to the dressmaker.

Mother will love it, she thought, slipping back into her navy wool – and father will not care how much he paid for it – not so long as she remained a lovely centerpiece for his visiting Nazi dinner guests.

She stepped into her shoes, grabbed up her handbag, and stepped out into the street, a bell tinkling overhead as she peered up and down the cobblestoned street. She headed north past the white-spired church and veered east through the empty playground, moving with purpose to avoid the roving eye of some German soldier just off duty. Bad enough she would have to put on the lavender dress and flirt with SS officers at her father's dinner table this evening. She had no wish to engage with one of them now.

At the far end of the street sat the old, red brick Dans Hal, once the heart of the city's social agenda. She did not come here often. Her work for the Resistance was accomplished by other means. But she stepped inside now, closing the door behind her, and surveyed the spacious front room.

Half a dozen children milled about, playing hide and seek among the chairs. At the far end of the room, she saw the girl she was looking for – Evi Strobel, bent over a table with her mother, Lotte, cutting something out of a roll of white paper.

The Dans Hal, and the low-key *dans* parties held there each Saturday evening, she knew, was one of the underground's more ingenious ploys. So long as they kept up the pretense, changed the décor from time to time, and turned out to dance in reasonable numbers, it was an invention the Germans largely passed over as a harmless Dutch custom that kept the local population in check.

How shocked – and how furious they would be to know that right in this hall, under their ugly noses, in a small room blocked off behind the strings of lights and the cut-out paper stars, were the radios and typewriters and mimeograph machines at the heart of the local Resistance.

In another corner, several people Mila did not know, were stringing garlands of small, white Christmas tree lights, although the Yuletide holiday was more than a month away.

"Mila!" a voice called. "Over here."

Glancing back at the Strobels, she stepped toward the voice, recognized her father's wine and whiskey vendor.

"It's good to see you, Mila," Finn Stoepker said. "This is my wife, Hanna. Hanna, this is Mila Brouwer"

The woman was spreading a cloth across a table. She looked up and waved. "It's good to meet you, Mila. Thank you."

Mila was not sure what the thank-you was for. She hoped it was for her father's patronage, which was liberal, because anything else she did in support of the Resistance was not common knowledge. At least she hoped it was not.

She smiled. "You are most welcome….It looks as though you are preparing for another party."

"On Saturday evening," Hanna nodded. "Perhaps you will join us."

"I will do my best," Mila nodded, although she knew, even if Hanna did not, that her presence at her father's table would be far more valuable in the end.

Daan Mulder, the owner of the pet *kliniek* and second in command of the local Resistance, hailed her as she turned.

"We rarely see you here, Mila," he said. He put a hand over his heart. "But your presence is deeply felt. Thank you."

At least she knew what Daan's thank you was for. She returned the gesture. "No need, Daan. I only wish communications were more consistent."

"We are lucky to have what we've cobbled together," he said. "At least we are certain that what we do have is secure – and we are working to improve things all the time."

She held his gaze. "My father is hosting dinner guests tonight."

"Ah," Daan's smile was genuine. "Let us hope the evening is productive."

Mila nodded, moving toward the far table where the Strobels bent over their craft. Jars of paint and glue littered the table. Mila had seen Evi here on one of her rare visits – had observed the girl's confident gestures, the graceful way she held herself, in spite of her youth.

Hallo, Lotte," she said.

The girl's mother looked up. "Mila, hallo!"

"I understand your cousin Johann is visiting friends in Belgium," Mila fingered a painted paper cut-out. *What a world, she thought, when even here in the Dans Hal, information was mostly conveyed in a sort of code, lest it find its way to hostile ears.*

"But it appears," she went on, "that his young friend was unable to join him."

Lotte met her gaze, and Mila knew she understood. *An escapee Lotte had recently harbored in the hold of her barge was safe past the Belgium border. But his daughter, a frail university student, had not survived the harrowing last leg of the journey.*

Lotte closed her eyes.

"We do what we can," Mila paused and turned her attention. "This is your daughter, Evi, yes?"

The girl looked up. "Hallo."

"How old are you, Evi?"

"Sixteen. Seventeen in February."

Mila glanced at her schoolgirl attire. "Yes, I thought as much."

The girl followed her gaze, brushed at her schoolgirl skirt. "I dress like this and put my hair in pigtails so that I look younger when I am – running errands," she said. "I mostly manage to escape the notice of the Germans."

"Ah, clever." Mila pondered. "You're a brave girl, Evi."

"I try to be." The girl stood straighter. "I hate the Germans. I wish I could do more for the Resistance."

Mila nodded. The girl could be perfect for what she had in mind – if Lotte could be persuaded to let her do it.

EVI

It was past three when she hurried down the wharf, the wind pushing at her back, and made her way along the row of dingy houseboats tied up at the pier. Finally, she let herself into the familiar yellow barge, shivering in her grey sweater.

She stood for a minute and listened. It was quiet in the barge, the kind of light quiet, the way it felt to her when there was no one inside but her. It was different from the heavy quiet she felt when there was another human breathing beneath her feet. She guessed that whoever was to be smuggled into the hold had not yet been delivered.

What if the day came when a pair of SS men blustered in...would they detect the heavy quiet of someone living and breathing beneath their feet?

The thought sent ice chips down her spine.

She changed her grey sweater for a warmer blue one and pulled on heavy stockings beneath her plaid wool skirt. She ran a brush through her fine blonde hair, then stood before the mirror and braided it into two long plaits, which she tied with ribbons.

She looked at her image and made a face at herself. The braids, along with her small frame and pale complexion made her look more like twelve than her nearly seventeen years. She loathed that, almost as much as mourned the barely swelled chest under her sweater. She wished she could trade it for Sophie's ample bosom...

On the other hand, as Mam was quick to point out, her petite frame was a virtue – a blessing when she bicycled across the city with sensitive materials stowed in her battered book bag.

Buttoning a jacket over her sweater, she took a last, forlorn look at herself. Then she searched under the sink, where Mam sometimes left paperwork for Evi to transport. She found an envelope with her name on it, stashed it between the books and drawings in her bag, hefted the bag over her shoulders and swung herself up out of the barge.

She unlocked the shed, retrieved her bicycle, and pedaled off toward the Dans Hal.

ZOE

"Ah, you're back," Lise called from the reception desk. "Dr. Mulder has not yet returned, and a patient is already waiting."

Zoe glanced at her watch. It was not yet one, but a young boy and his mother sat at one end of the waiting area, a freckle-faced springer spaniel pup draped across their laps.

"Hello there," she smiled. "I am Dr. Visser. "And who is this?"

"This is Bella," the boy volunteered. "Back for her four-month shots."

"Ah, yes," Zoe said. "I thought she looked familiar." She beckoned them into the first examining room. "And how has Bella been behaving?"

"She is *wonderbaar* – very good," the boy put the pup down, holding her leash in one hand, and looked up at his mother. "Right, Mam?"

"Mostly," his mother agreed. "She has got the hang of housebreaking pretty well, *lieve god,* but she is chewing on just about everything."

Zoe grinned. "Normal for the age. Keep your shoes and house slippers out of her reach for a while, and be sure she has something of her own to chew on – a toy, or an old sock – while she is still teething."

She lifted the Spaniel pup to the table, ruffling her black and white coat. She felt the pup shiver, and ran a soothing hand down her back. "You will be fine, Bella, I promise," she assured her canine patient. "This will all be over sooner than you think."

In short order, she injected the pup with the vaccines she needed, all the while talking softly and sending reassuring smiles to her young master.

"There! All done," she said, setting Bella on her feet on the floor, laughing as the pup shook her little body as though she were shaking off water.

"She is good to go," Zoe laughed. "No need for me to see her again until she reaches her first birthday."

She watched the family troop out to the desk, wondering as always that even now, when most families had little enough to sustain themselves, they managed to provide for their pets.

She turned and washed her hands, put fresh paper on the examining table. Of course, the *klineik's* accounts receivables grew longer by the month, and vaccines were increasingly harder to come by, but neither she nor Daan would think of turning away an animal in need so long as they were able to help.

It was nearly four before she heard Daan's voice, talking animatedly to Lise.

"You are back," said Zoe, hands in her pockets. "How was Amsterdam?"

The owner of the pet *kliniek* was bent at the supply cabinet alongside Lise, systematically filing syringes, nail clippers, and other supplies into compartmented bins.

"Ah," Daan said, rising. "It was as we expected," he told her, a meaningful look in his eyes. "Busy day, traffic heavy as ever, but all good to go, Zoe. Good to go."

Zoe nodded, interpreting his message. Tonight. The transfer was a go.

"Good," she said. "Everything is in order. I may need to leave a bit early."

Daan Mulder rose to his full height, an unimposing five foot-eight, a stocky figure with unruly blonde hair and a pock-marked face that belied both his inner and outer strength. He had recently married the love of his life, Ilke, a busy attorney with no time for the Resistance but with no opposition to Daan's commitment. Zoe trusted Daan's instincts completely.

"You may leave any time you like," he told her. "It is going to be a long, cold night."

MILA

The lavender dress arrived at five, as promised, just as Mila stepped from the shower. "Put it on the bed, Reit," she called to the maid. "I will be out in a moment."

Hondje, her little Maltese ball of white fluff, waited at the foot of her bed. Poor Hondje. She hadn't had much time for him of late. She smiled and ruffled his top knot.

Toweled off and powdered, she brushed her red-blonde hair into a loose chignon and put on the amethyst earrings her father had given her weeks ago for her twenty-fifth birthday.

She put down the brush and slumped for a moment against the mahogany dressing table. Her father. What was she to do about the growing chasm between her love for him and her passion for the work of the Resistance?

Millions of their countrymen were making do with wilted vegetables while her father's table groaned under the finest delicacies, thanks largely to the Germans who dined with them. Her father was a businessman, a smart businessman, a man who'd spent years building the shipping company that had kept her family in silks and satins long before the war made them scarce. It was not his fault that the Germans needed his shipping routes. How else could they move the goods, and the machinery, that kept the Nazi machine functioning? And how else could he keep his business running?

She pulled on silk stockings – a gift from a recent *dinner guest* – and drew a lacy slip over her shoulders. Four years into this bitter war, fewer than a quarter of Holland's Jewish population was left, and those mostly in hiding – and as more Jewish families feared the threat of deportation, many were children placed reluctantly with willing Dutch hiding families.

Was her father a collaborator? Of course, he was. The thought made her blood run cold.

As would his blood run cold, she knew, if he had any idea what his only daughter was up to each night after those endless, wine-soaked dinners.

EVI

Evi heard the stifled cry.

She looked up from her homework. "Mam?"

Lotte had been hunched over the banned radio receiver, listening to the illicit *radio Oranje*.

"Nothing that concerns you, *lieveling*," she said. "More student protests in Amsterdam."

University students had raged against the Blitzkreig from the moment it had smashed across the Dutch border. This was hardly news.

"Mam, what is it really?"

Lotte sighed. "Two students were shot this morning by a Nazi firing squad in Amsterdam. They said it was in retaliation for the death of an SS officer - not that these Nazis need a reason. Any excuse to flaunt Herr Hitler's power."

Evi slumped in her chair. With the universities long since shuttered, too many students with time on their hands became the targets of Gestapo scrutiny.

"Six months," Lotte murmured, stowing the radio in an empty cereal box in the cupboard. "Six months since the Allies landed at Normandy, and still, God knows if we will survive long enough to see liberation."

Evi sat straighter in the worn wooden chair. This was, perhaps, a good time to take advantage of the moment.

"Mam," she began. "I am nearly seventeen. I want to do more for the Resistance."

She looked into her mother's face, thinner than she remembered, and creased with lines Evi had been slow to notice. "I'm not a child. I can do more than pass out leaflets and transport paperwork. I want to do something that matters."

Lotte ran a hand across her face. "*Lieveling*, everything you do matters. The papers you transport are saving lives."

"But Mam, I am smart, you know I am, and careful," Evi persisted. "I know my way around all of Haarlem, and I know how to get by without attracting attention. There must be something more I can do – some sort of reconnaissance, perhaps."

Her mother looked at her. "Reconnaissance, Evi? Do you even know what that is?"

"Of course, I do. It's observation. I can bicycle around the city, perhaps, and watch for German troop movement."

"And then what, Evi? To whom will you report this – troop movement?

"I do not know for certain, but I know people do this, to help our own soldiers plan their strategy."

Her mother sighed audibly.

Evi knew as well as Mam that the Dutch Army had been ill-prepared against the Germans from the start, clinging to some idea of neutrality and taking orders from the queen who fled to London the day after the Germans breached their border.

"I don't think so, Evi," Mam said. "The Dutch army does not need or want your service."

"The police then."

Mam threw up her hands. "Evi, half the Dutch police force is collaborating with the Germans. You know that. That is how they survive."

"Not all of them," she argued, though of course it was impossible to know which half could be trusted.

Silence.

Evi tried her most persuasive voice. "Mam, I'm young. I'm healthy. I learn fast. There must be more I can do."

Lotte reached for her. "We will see, Evi. Let me think about it. For now, pray this will be over soon, that the Allies are near to ending it…"

If only, Evi thought. Mam was right. Ever since Normandy, there had been constant speculation that liberation would come soon. But the months rolled by, and hope along with them, and still it was at best a dream.

"There is tea," Mam said into the silence, a hand on Evi's cheek. "I found some in the market place at Leiden when I delivered the *Het Parool.* "

Evi sighed, reminded of the German *schnellboats* – afraid to think what might happen to Mam if they found stacks of the *verboden* newspapers onboard the barge.

Before she could answer, Mam leaned toward her and put a finger to her lips. "I will give some thought to what you might do for the Council. Meanwhile, if all goes well, a *guest* will be delivered tonight for safekeeping."

Evi turned and went back to her homework, but the algebra equations swam before her eyes. She put her hands under her arms to warm them. It was cold on the barge, even before the cutback of power had rendered the heater mostly useless. She pulled one of Mam's crocheted blankets across her lap.

How she missed the house they had lived in before the Germans came – the spacious rooms, the big porcelain bathtub, the brick fireplace smudged a deep, smoky black in the winter time. Another blow dealt by this war, the move to the barge after Papa left.

Cheaper to live in, Mam had said, with a hold big enough for hiding refugees and reason to be navigating up and down the coast when she needed to.

Evi studied the worn-thin braided rug that lay under the coffee table and over the hatch in the floorboards.

Once, she recalled, they had harbored a whole family in the hold – an anxious young mam, a dark-bearded papa, and their child, a thin little boy with huge blue eyes who had been well-schooled in the need for quiet.

She remembered the day she came home from school with a small packet of candy corn – a rare prize she had won in a spelling competition. She had clambered down the narrow ladder to share the sweets with little Johann, only to find the hold empty of all of them.

She focused her gaze on the worn carpet, wondering suddenly what had become of the three of them once they had been moved from the barge?

She closed her eyes, took a deep breath, and blew out a thin stream of air. This was how it was now, Mam in danger and herself helpless, making do in this old yellow barge with its cramped spaces and its tiny shower, on this busy river with its creaky drawbridges and the vast North Sea beyond.

If there is a God, she tapped her pencil on the table, *please let the Allies come soon...*

ZOE

There had been air raids again the evening before, and grenades whistling, but tonight, *lieve god,* it was still and quiet at three o'clock in the morning. Zoe could see her breath, and smell the mist that rolled in over the river bank.

She pulled her coat close around her, counting the scant handful of stars strewn high in the inky darkness. It was a night perfect for their purpose.

She tapped one foot against the gravel, mostly out of sight on a flat strip of land below the level of the river, anxious as always during these wee hour transfers. Narrowing her eyes and peering into the distance, she could make out no human shapes.

She turned, checking in every direction, and waited.

Finally, the sound of a motor idling, movement she sensed before she saw it. She strained to see human forms emerging – one, then a second, bent low and moving fast.

"Zoe?"

The taller of the two figures reached her, his eyes sweeping the landscape. She had met him before – Johan Steegen, a history professor who had narrowly survived the bombing of Rotterdam and now owned an auto repair shop in Haarlem.

"Johan, yes."

"This is Max Leibmann, the concert pianist," he whispered, as the second figure came into view. "World-esteemed, but a German Jew hunted by his countrymen."

Zoe studied the gray-bearded Leibmann, whose recordings had come with her from her dorm room in Amsterdam to her small apartment in Haarlem. "It is a pleasure to meet you, *Meneer*."

"Arrogant pigs, these Nazis," Leibmann whispered. "They have no respect for the artists whose music lies deep in the bedrock of Germany."

Zoe nearly smiled, surprised to encounter a Jewish escapee with some fight apparently left in him.

She turned to look around them, then back at the older man, who was bareheaded and wearing a light trench coat. "We need to be quick and quiet," she said, handing him a dark woolen scarf. "Our walk will be less than two kilometers, moving well below this berm, mostly unseen from either the river or the roadway. But it well past curfew. We must be very alert and try to stay out of sight."

"Godspeed," Johan Steegen said, melting back into the night.

Zoe took the older man's hand and helped him down a short slope. Scanning the landscape once again, she tucked her arm into his and led him slowly forward.

Zoe broke the uneasy silence. "You have new identification papers, *ja*?"

"I received them this morning in Amsterdam. They say I am known as Claude Zeller, a Swiss national. A bank clerk."

Zoe wondered if the originals were among the ID papers she had pilfered from a coat rack in Haarlem.

"Then I shall call you Herr Zeller. That is who you are now – and that is how you must be known, at least until you reach your destination."

Another silence, deep, thoughtful, their footsteps crunching gravel.

Zoe's gaze again swept the landscape as far as she could see. German troops were mostly off duty and sound asleep at this time of night, and the river front was quiet – but there were sometimes a few soldiers, mostly noisy and drunk, still roaming the streets.

"You have family waiting for you in Belgium, Herr Zeller?"

"In France," the man answered. "My wife left Germany in 1939, entirely at my urging. I stayed to finish a concert tour, and then the Nazi crackdown came, and it became impossible for me to leave."

Zoe could not imagine how the old man had remained so long in hiding. "Now, *lieve god*, it is near the end of your journey. Your wife will be overjoyed to see you."

"*Alevai*," he murmured. "It is a Yiddish expression. It means, 'may it be so.'"

"Indeed," Zoe said. "We will do our best to make it happen. But best, in the meantime, to keep Yiddish expressions to yourself."

They moved on in silence, the dim lights of the barges and houseboats moored along the river coming into view.

"What is your profession by day, if I may?" the old man asked.

"I'm a veterinarian, "Zoe said.

"A veterinarian?" He reared back. "So young!"

Zoe shrugged, a finger to her lips. "A protégé, my parents called me."

"Where are they, your parents?"

"In Enschede," she said. "That is where I grew up."

He nodded.

"May I ask why you do this?" he said after a moment. "Why do you risk your life to help an old Jewish piano player escape the Nazi purge?"

Zoe debated. Not a question often asked anymore, by her comrades or by those who were escaping.

"I had a child minder when I was young," she said. "My parents are both physicians. They worked long hours, odd hours sometimes, and so I went after school and sometimes in the night to Frau Didi, who lived just across the road from our home. Like you, she was a pianist, Frau Didi, though not nearly as proficient, of course. She gave piano lessons, and she sang when she talked, and she baked the most wonderful butter cake."

The sweet, spicy smell of Frau Didi's kitchen was real and deep-seated in her memory.

"One morning when I was home on a break from university, I woke to a great ruckus. From our front window, I saw two burly SS men carry Frau Didi down the front steps of her home and throw her into the back of an SS van."

"Ah, she was a Jew, your child minder…"

Zoe nodded, alert to any sound or movement. "And proud. I did not hear her scream, not even once as the door of the van slammed shut and the two SS men, cool as could be, got into the van and drove away. But *I* screamed. I screamed as I crossed the road and watched the truck drive out of sight. I screamed at the sight of Frau Didi's blue front door, gaping open on its hinges."

She paused a moment, the memory of the moment etched into her gut.

"Alas, we are not safe anywhere," the old man murmured.

Zoe shook her head. "I knew that night I would never see her again," she said. "I can only imagine where they took her."

She paused, again sweeping the landscape, moving closer to the shoreline.

"I went back to school, and finished my studies. But I always knew that when the time came, I would fight on the side of the Resistance."

The old man was silent.

"You were passed to my employer in Amsterdam this morning, yes?"

The old man nodded. "Somehow, God help us, a man wearing a German uniform took me across the border into Rotterdam. It was just before dawn, during a change of the guard. I have never been so frightened in my life."

Zoe nodded. A *marechaussee,* no doubt – a Dutch Resistance fighter wearing the stolen uniform of the Royal Dutch Military Police to help make such passages possible. They were thankfully growing in numbers these days, under the unwary watch of the Nazis.

The path before them narrowed and more lights came into view as they approached a line of cargo-carrying barges.

"Stay close," whispered Zoe. "We will soon enter the *Blijjde Tiding.* It means, literally, *Happy Tidings.* It is the name the owner chose for the barge."

She hoisted herself down, knocked twice, and held a hand out to help the old man.

"*Godzijdank,*" Lotte Strobel said, holding the door wide. "Thanks be to God. Welcome."

"Lotte, this is – Claude Zeller," Zoe said in the semi-darkness. "Herr Zeller, this is Lotte Strobel."

Lotte clasped the man's hands.

"Herr Zeller is a Swiss bank clerk," Zoe said, emphasizing '*Swiss.*' "He has the proper identification papers. He will stay with you, Lotte, for perhaps two days, until the next link in his journey is in place. Then you will take the barge down river, where an escort will help him to Tilburg and, God willing, out of harm's way across the Belgian border."

"I understand," Lotte said, fully aware that the route could change if the Germans were watching, sometimes even to a long slog across the Pyrenees and into Spain. She doubted the old man could survive such a journey. But there was no point in further distressing him.

"Herr Zeller" she said, "there is little comfort anywhere in the Netherlands these days. It is cold below in the area where you must stay. But there are plenty of blankets – and first, you must have some tea, *ja?* Evi, fill the teapot. Zoe, will you stay for a cup?"

"*Dank je,* but I cannot," Zoe said. "I need to get some sleep tonight before I go back to the *kliniek* in the morning."

Impulsively, she hugged the old man. "*Goed geluk*, Herr Zeller. Safe journey."

MILA

Mila counted the empty wine bottles sitting on the sideboard – six of them. Her mother had claimed a headache and excused herself from the table hours ago, but at half past ten, the overstuffed SS lieutenant and his sallow-faced young companion showed no signs of flagging.

Worse yet, he and her father had been mostly focused on the finer points of Dutch and German football, and the half-drunk blowhard had yet to offer up anything that made it worth her sitting here.

Lifting her glass, she looked over the rim and directed her gaze at the older German, who picked up her glance like a radio signal and turned at once to face her.

"*Fraulein* Brouwer," he murmured, "you are a quiet presence, albeit a lovely one. Thank you for putting up with our chatter."

His fleshy face, two small, dark eyes like raisins in a bowl of pudding, made her want to retch. She forced herself past it. "My pleasure, *Obersturmfuhrer*, she cooed. "It's a joy to listen to your stories."

Her father shot her a look, but she ignored it. She had long ago taught herself perfect German, and it served her purpose well. "You have a way of adding interest to any topic, *Obersturmfuhrer*, even an ordinary day's work. Today, for example. I am sure you were incredibly busy, and still you made the time to visit with us."

She saw the man's gaze slip to the low point in the vee of her neckline, then reluctantly travel back to her face. "*Ach*," he muttered. "I did nothing of the slightest interest to the beautiful and gracious *fraulein*."

She looked directly into his eyes.

"Oh, I doubt that, *Obersturmfuhrer*. I am. In fact, very interested. The Reich expects much of its finest officers. You have a difficult agenda, *ya*?"

"*Ya, und* tomorrow – the younger man broke in, his sharp beak of a nose in the air.

The *obersturmfuhrer* gave him a silencing glare. "Nothing of importance tomorrow, *Fraulein*. A rather pedestrian agenda."

Mila offered an encouraging smile.

She leaned forward to fill his glass, the man's gaze returning swiftly to her bosom. That, and the abundance of free-flowing wine, appeared to loosen his tongue. "Tomorrow I am charged with overseeing the collection of – equipment for shipment to Berlin," he told her.

Moving war materiel out of the Netherlands? Mila's expression never changed. But she knew her father's Berlin route included a stop in Utrecht, and it was information Resistance leaders might find useful.

She offered up her most coquettish smile. "Rather inconsequential work for someone of your rank, is it not, *Obersturmfuhrer*?"

The pig never looked up from her neckline She could sense his rising desire.

"Surely such a task as gathering and shipping goods could be accomplished by an underling, *Nein*? Someone with more brawn and less intelligence?"

"Mila –" her father broke in. "That is impudent and none of your business."

That lowered the level of testosterone. "Sorry, father. My apologies, *Obersturmfuhrer*. That is quite true. It is not my business."

The moment was over, but she had gained a tidbit that could be helpful. More than that, she was more than ever convinced that her plan for Evi Strobel could be managed.

The spell was apparently broken, too, for the evening's guests. The fat-faced lieutenant heaved himself out of his chair, all *danke scheins* and boot-clicking *wunderbars* and silent signals to his underling, and almost before she knew it, they were headed for the Brouwer's massive front door, her father close behind them.

He was an imposing figure, her father, tall, slim, with his manicured beard and a full head of greying hair. He faced her now in the mirrored hallway, eyes blazing, the door firmly closed and locked behind him.

"What kind of game do you think you are you playing, Mila, flirting with a high-ranking member of the Reich?"

"I was hardly flirting, Papa," she held her head high. "I was merely underscoring his importance to their cause. You know every one of them loves having his ego stroked."

He was not mollified.

"These dinner party meetings are important, Mila, important to my business, as you very well know, and your presence adds grace to our evenings. But while you are most welcome to participate in discussions of music and the arts, let me make it clear that you are more to be seen and less to be heard from, unless you are spoken to directly, especially when it comes to matters of business. Do you understand?"

Mila flushed. In her twenty-five years, she had never felt so rebuked by her father – or so undervalued. But, of course, he had no way of knowing that her presence at these dinner parties was more important than he knew.

She unclenched her jaw, managed a smile. "I understand, Papa. It will not happen again."

• • •

In her bedroom, Mila threw off the lavender dinner dress and tied an old silk robe around her waist. She stepped into her oversized clothes closet, closed the door behind her, and drew a wireless device from behind a shoe rack.

Sitting on the floor of the closet, her back resting against the skirts of dozens of day and evening dresses, she entered a familiar set of digits. She had never met the man who received her communiques. She knew him only as Pieter. He had contacted her some months ago, through Daan Mulder, as news of her father's dealings with officers of the Reich became known to the Resistance Council – and she had been eager to be able to help.

She waited as the digits she entered passed through a secure line. After a moment, she heard a response.

"Pieter here."

"Good evening, Pieter." She did not identify herself, nor did she need to. "It appears there will be a movement of supplies out of Haarlem tomorrow, through Utrecht en route to Berlin. Troop movement will be minimal, I think, and the route should be easily accessible."

"We had heard something similar, Mila, but confirmation is good."

Each understood the implication. Having advance notice of movement by the Germans offered a target for Resistance bombers. Only a week ago, they had blown up a German transport on its way to The Hague. As payback, the Germans had shrunk weekly rations, but the gain had been worth the punishment.

"On another front," Mila said, "I would like to move forward with the plan I put forward to you a week ago."

There was a pause. "That might be a dangerous undertaking even for you, never mind for a school girl."

"She is eager to help," Mila said." I will instruct her myself, and I believe her mother will be amenable. I know you understand how much there is to be gained, Pieter. What we need from you is the – the physical support the project would require."

A longer pause. "I understand. But you must recognize the risks of an operation like this," Pieter said. "The girl must understand them, too… But if you have her agreement – and her mother's consent – we will provide the support you need…

He paused. "Be sure the girl is well-prepared for this, Mila. There is no room for error here…and a misstep could be fatal."

EVI

Evi gathered the bedclothes for washing and collected what was left of the food in the hold now that Herr Zeller had been moved.

Not that there was much to share. With rations less and less dependable, the greatest prize in their larder, as far as Evi was concerned, was the last few bits of the ham that Mam had managed to preserve last summer. But Jews did not eat pork, and so for the escapees, there were whatever vegetables Mam could find, plus some oats or beans, a bit of bread, and a very occasional egg. It was not much. They were all wasting away. But somehow, Mam made the rations stretch.

Evi had been sound asleep yesterday morning when the motor turned over and she was awakened by the movement of the barge. It was not yet fully light, and Evi had guessed they were bound for Middleburg, where Mam would pass Herr Zeller into another pair of hands, then rummage through the marketplace for whatever she could find to purchase.

She hoped the old man would be safe.

This morning, she felt the familiar empty quiet, the hold vacant and Mam at work – and with school cancelled for Nazi troop maneuvers, the day stretched ahead of her. She would take the laundry to the *wasserette*, she decided, and then, perhaps, bicycle to what was left of the book exchange and bring home something to read.

She ate one of Mam's homemade oat crackers topped with a tiny dollop of what was left of the orange marmalade, then took up the laundry bag, swung out of the barge, and took her bicycle out of the shed.

Even dressed in a coat over a sweater, with a grey wool cap pulled low over her ears, she felt the wind bite her face. She blew out air and saw her breath. It was going to be a cold winter, she could tell, perhaps even more snow than usual – just what they needed, with two hours of gas and power a day and no end in sight to the misery.

•   •   •

She found herself alone in the *wasserette* on that early Friday morning. She was moving the laundry from the washer to the dryer when she heard the shattering of glass. She spun around to see, through the open doorway, two SS officers reaching into the display window of the silversmith's shop across the road.

Glass lay everywhere, heavy boots trampling over it as the Germans hauled out silver trays, candle sticks and whatever else they could grab from the showcase, stowing armfuls of the stuff into the trunk of a Mercedes Benz automobile emblazoned with the SS insignia.

Evi backed up against the row of dryers. The SS took whatever they wanted, she knew - and not only from the Jews. She and Mam knew people whose cars, even their homes, had been *'requisitioned'* with no recourse. But she had never witnessed anything as brazen as what she was seeing now.

She watched as a white-haired man in a denim apron slowly emerged from the shop. Before she could tell if there was a yellow star on his apron, the two intruders battered him to the ground and walked over him into the shop.

Eyes wide, breathing hard, Evi ducked behind the row of wash machines. *What if they had seen her watching?*

Her glance darted to the restroom door, a full twenty feet away, then to a door marked, 'employees only' not much closer to her. Paralyzed, debating whether to run or not, she heard the slamming of doors and a motor starting up and the screech of auto tearing away.

In the silence that followed, she felt her heartbeat slow. She huddled against a washer, unable to move until she heard the sounds of people gathering.

Slowly, she brought herself to her feet, peered over the washer, moved slowly toward the doorway. She saw a small crowd murmuring over the downed shop keeper, who lay pale and still on the sidewalk.

She could pick out the occasional word – *politie... ambulance* – but as she moved close enough to see blood pooling at the curb, she knew with grim certainty that it was far too late for either.

ZOE

It was a two-hour trip from Haarlem to Enschede, and never a guarantee that a bus or a train would run as scheduled. But she had been promising her parents for months that she would try to come home for a visit, and with the pet *kliniek* closed on Sundays, and no pressing work to do for the Resistance, Zoe thought perhaps this was the day to make the effort.

She sat, sipping tea, in the only comfortable chair in her flat, an old broad-backed armchair covered in flowered chintz that Lotte Strobel had helped her lug up the stairs when she'd moved into the tiny studio.

"We have no need for it on the barge," Lotte had assured her. "It is old, but I think you will find it comfortable – and you will do us a kindness to take some of these extra dishes and cooking pots that have plenty of life left in them."

It was one of the things that had most surprised her when she had taken the job in Haarlem – the solidarity of the Resistance community, the way they looked after each other with the same intensity that they poured into fighting the Nazi scourge.

She took the last few sips of her tea and decided that yes, she would try to get to Enschede and get back to Haarlem before curfew.

She packed a bottle of water, a hard roll with a bit of gouda cheese – her reward for standing two hours in line with her ration card – into a canvas shoulder bag along with a photo of her with a beautiful English Spaniel, gifted to her by the Spaniel's owner in lieu of payment.

Of late, some of the smarter women in Amsterdam had begun wearing trousers, Zoe knew. She wished she had a pair now against the cold. But she put on warm stockings and her trusty grey coat over a well-worn sweater and skirt, wrapped a red wool scarf around her neck, and headed out for the walk to the bus station.

• • •

In the depot, four SS guards with bored expressions surveyed the comings and goings. But the rifles at their sides sent a chilling message, and most passengers kept their heads down as if they had no other business but to study the octagonal pattern of the grimy, black and white-tiled floor. But to her relief, there was a bus to Enschede scheduled to leave in thirty minutes.

Zoe paid for her ticket and boarded the bus, surprised to find it nearly full. Scanning the rows of seats, she found one toward the back, next to a middle-aged woman who edged closer to the window and smiled at her as she sat.

"Do you have enough room?" the woman asked.

"Oh, yes, thank you. This is fine," Zoe stuffed her bag underneath the seat in front of her.

"Do you live in Enschede?"

Zoe turned. "No. I am going to visit with my parents."

"How nice!" the woman exclaimed. "A pretty girl and a devoted daughter. Your parents must be proud."

Zoe smiled.

"You live in Haarlem, then…"

"Yes. I do."

"My name is Fiona. It's a Scottish name. My father was Scottish."

Zoe nodded. "Zoe."

"I came to Haarlem yesterday from Gronau to visit my sister," Fiona said. "It's difficult to live here, is it not – what with power only two hours a day?"

Gronau was in Germany, just over the border, where there was far less rationing, Zoe guessed. She looked straight ahead. "It is."

"Not that there is much to cook here, in any case."

What was she to say to that?

But her seatmate was relentless. "They are saying the power may be cut altogether. Have you heard?"

The prospect had hung over the city for weeks. "I hope not."

A short pause, then Fiona leaned in. "But they say the Allies are getting close. My sister's brother-in-law has a son in the Dutch Air Force. He told them as much, just this morning."

That rumor, too, continued to pass from ear to ear, but there was little evidence on which to pin their hopes. "We can only pray he is right," Zoe said, leaning back in her seat as the engine noise ramped up finally, and the bus lumbered out of the station.

• • •

Enschede, for all its distance from Amsterdam, had been bombed by the Germans a year earlier – a fright that had roiled Zoe's stomach for days until she was able to contact her parents. But she saw little evidence of the destruction here on the walk from the bus depot to her parents' house.

Patches of green defied the cold, and gable-roofed houses that had been there for generations wore an air of quiet resignation. Everything seemed the same, and all of it somehow different, but Zoe found her smile growing wider with every step she took, and her mother's happy cry when she came to the door filled her with unbridled joy.

"Henk, Henk," her mother bellowed. "It's Zoe. Zoe is here!"

Still basking in her mother's embrace, Zoe felt her father's arms come around them both. The three of them stood together in the narrow entryway until her father finally broke away.

"Food, Emma, food! The girl is wasting away! Look how skinny she is!"

Zoe laughed. "Not so much! And you, Papa. Are you well?'

His bald spot had widened, Zoe saw, and the paunch that had once lay over his belt buckle had all but disappeared – and her mother's rounded cheeks now verged on hollow. But her eyes were bright and, altogether, they looked well. Zoe bubbled with an excitement that verged on tears.

She ate her mother's spinach and potato pie, the vegetables harvested from their own garden, and relished every bite of the sausages her father had wrested from the butcher in exchange for a few machine tools.

"I thought the other night about Frau Didi –" she began.

Mam shook her head. "We have never heard a word. The house remains empty."

They ate in silence for a moment.

Zoe told them as little as possible about her work with the Resistance, and steered clear of making promises she could not keep about staying out of harm's way.

She toured what was left of her parents' winter garden, and accepted the sack of potatoes and beets that Papa packed for her with care. Sooner than she wished, before the sun set so that she could get home before curfew, there were aching goodbyes and more hugs and more kisses at the door.

• • •

The bus to Haarlem was not as full as it had been on the morning run. She chose a seat midway down the aisle and hoped the companion seat would stay empty. Love, fear, hope, despair – emotions she had worked so hard to control all day now bobbed and collided within her. She wished for nothing more, in the two-hour ride home, than to close her eyes, perhaps nap for a bit, and try to recapture the calm she needed to do what she must do every day.

The empty seat next to her was, happily, still unoccupied when the motor came to life. Zoe leaned back in her seat and adjusted her bag and the precious sack of vegetables at her feet. Her last conscious thought was of her father's regret that he could not drive her to the bus station. His eight-year-old Volkswagen still sat behind the house, but of course there was no petrol to purchase even if there had been extra funds.

She was reflecting on that, her eyes heavy, when the bus lurched to a stop, pitching her forward so abruptly that her head hit the seat in front of her. Parcels flew out of overhead bins. People jostled and shouted.

The bus crept forward, pulling to the curb, and everything went quiet until the doors screeched open, the lights flickered on, and two Gestapo officers – she thought she recognized the Gestapo insignias – stepped up into the interior.

"*Ach tung!*" the larger of the two shouted, his face a menacing red. "Stay in your seats and be silent." He moved forward, followed closely by his smaller cohort, took a folded piece of paper from his breast pocket, and read.

"Johan Gruber… Gerda Gruber…Stand, *bitte*, at once."

The 'please' was token only, Zoe realized, because the two clearly meant business. They advanced up the aisle, looming larger as they neared. Passengers cowered in their seats.

"Johan Gruber…. Gerda Gruber," the German said again. "We know you are aboard *zis* vehicle. Stand up and identify yourselves or we begin to hurt others until you do."

There was faint murmuring, a craning of necks. Zoe sat frozen in her seat.

With no warning, the larger Nazi reached for the passenger just across the aisle from her. He yanked the man up out of his seat, held him with his left hand as though he were a rag doll, and with his right hand punched him squarely in the face.

The man, barely conscious, from what Zoe could see, grunted, and sank into his seat. For an instant, the silence was palpable.

The German stepped backward to the seat just in front of her, held up what looked like a heavy baton, and thrust it downward with force. Bones cracked, the sound unmistakable, and a man howled in pain.

The German reached for his pistol, held it over his head. "Who is next?" he shouted, yanking a small child out of her seat. "Perhaps this pretty little *fraulein*?"

The child's mother shrieked, people stirred and mumbled, the man with the broken bones groaned louder.

"No!" Zoe found herself shouting. "Put her down. She is an innocent child. Choose someone your size, please, *mein Herr, bitte*!"

Releasing the child, the big man moved forward, stopped directly in front of Zoe, and shoved the pistol in front of her face.

Terrified, Zoe sat wide-eyed.

A long moment passed.

"Stop!" someone behind her shouted. "Stop! I am Johan Gruber."

The Nazi slowly holstered his pistol and strode toward the back of the bus. "Johan Gruber, you have been named an enemy of the Reich. This is your *frau*, Gerda Gruber?"

There was a shuffling of papers, the sound of handcuffs clicking into place, and muffled sounds as the Germans half-kicked, half-dragged the man and his kerchiefed wife down the aisle, down the steps, out into the pearly gray darkness. The flashing lights of a German Kubelwagen lit frightened faces red and blue as the doors of the bus wheezed closed.

Outraged cries, tears, shouts. Zoe heard it all, her heart still racing, loudest to her ears the moans and groans of the injured passenger just in front of her. The driver was pleading for people to return to their seats, but before the bus pulled back onto the roadway, Zoe was out of hers.

She stopped briefly to assess the passenger across the aisle, a middle-aged man in a suit and tie with bright red bloodstains on his clean white shirt. Palpating his bloodied nose as gently as she could, she noted with surprise that it did not appear to be broken.

"Apply pressure," she reached into her coat pocket and handed him a lace-trimmed handkerchief. "I will be back in a moment," she told him, moving to the seat in front of her.

A glance at the keening man's bloodied trousers told her the sound of bones breaking she had so clearly heard had been the fracture of his right knee cap when the German's baton smashed into it. There was a jagged tear in the woolen pant leg and the knee appeared to be swelling.

"My name is Zoe Visser," she told him in low tones. "I am a veterinarian, not a medical doctor, but I think perhaps I can help ease your suffering a bit until you can be seen by a doctor."

All around her, there was chatter, shouting, the sounds of people sobbing.

"Help, please."

"My daughter needs help!"

"I can't find my medication!"

Zoe bent to her patient in the low light, gingerly palpated the knee.

"Aah!," the man groaned.

"What is your name, sir?"

"Hans...ah, it hurts!"

"I know, Hans. Take a deep breath. I will try to fashion some kind of tourniquet."

Glancing around her, she spied a towheaded child clutching something that looked like a wooden cribbage board.

"*Behagen*," she bent to the boy's level. "How would you like to be a hero today, and let me use your cribbage board to help that man whose knee was broken?"

The boy looked at her, blue eyes wide, and silently held out the board.

It was small for her purpose, but placing it beneath the man's shattered knee cap, she pulled the wool scarf from around her neck and wound it tightly around the makeshift splint.

A small crowd had gathered behind her.

"Back in your seats, please," the bus driver shouted. "For your safety, please, back in your seats!"

The mother – perhaps grandmother – of the little girl who had been threatened, pulled a pin out of the lapel of her coat. "Can you use this?"

Zoe accepted the pin. "Perfect, *bedankt*. Thank you. *Ja*."

Pinning the scarf into place around the injured knee, she gently lowered the man's leg onto the seat. "This will help to keep your knee immobile, Hans, until you can be seen by a doctor."

She looked around her at the slowly dispersing crowd. "Does anyone have some aspirin?"

A packet of aspirin was thrust at her. She offered two tablets to Hans.

"*Bedankt*," he grasped Zoe's hand.

"No need," she said. "I hope this will help you to feel a bit better. We will see that you have help when we get to Haarlem."

She crossed the aisle to check the bloody nose.

"It's better, I think," the man drew the handkerchief away. "It's only bleeding a bit."

Zoe nodded. "But there is swelling," she said. "And I would not be surprised to see your eyes blackened by the time you wake up tomorrow morning."

"*Verdoemde* Nazis," the man growled

Zoe sighed.

He moved the handkerchief back to his nose. "Thank you so much for your help."

Zoe sank into her seat, closed her eyes, and although she fought against the image, she vividly re-lived the stark terror of that pistol shoved into her face....

MILA

It was more than just audacious, Mila told herself, her footsteps loud in her ears on the worn boards of the wharf. It was perhaps reckless, as Pieter suggested, to ask so much of an inexperienced girl. But she had fine-tuned the details and discussed them at length with both Daan and Pieter, who reluctantly agreed that, given the proper training and back-up, the benefits might well outweigh the risk.

At the very least, she told herself, keeping an eye out for the *Blijde Tiding*, Lotte would listen and then decline. Mila might do so herself, she thought, if she were a mother and such a plan was suggested for her only daughter.

On the other hand, Evi was clever and strong-willed, and eager to help the Resistance.

Spying the barge, Mila descended the stairs and knocked softly, careful not to sound urgent enough to inspire fear inside.

"Who is there, *behagen*?"

"It is I, Mila Brouwer. Hallo!"

The door swung open. Lotte's tense face relaxed into a smile. "Mila, what a happy surprise! Do come in!"

The light was low, what little there was provided by a small kerosene lamp next to an armchair and another on the table where Evi was bent over her books.

"Thank you, Lotte. I hope all is well."

Lotte pointed downward. "As well as can be – for all of us. And you?"

Mila nodded her understanding. Someone was hidden in the hold. "I've brought you something," she said, reaching into her handbag.

Evi stood.

Mila set two jars of cherry jam on the table, along with a packet of dried beef, a jar of yeast, and a small bag of flour. It was as much as she felt she could offer without appearing to condescend – or worse yet, to be bribing the two to come onboard with her plan.

"We are lucky to have supplies in our cellar that were stored years ago," she lied, unwilling to disclose that her father's German dinner guests provided more than they needed. "And our cook has been managing to stay below our rations."

"Are you sure --?" Lotte began, as Evi surveyed the treasure

"*Behagen*, there is nothing more to be said," Mila shrugged. "These days, we must share what we can."

"Ah, *dank u*, Mila, thank you." Lotte gestured to a chair. "Sit, won't you? Will you have some tea? I found fresh peppermint tea leaves at a market stall in Middleburg."

"Wonderful, thank you!" Mila sat and removed her gloves. "It is cold, and not yet December."

"We have battery power on the barge, and kerosene – but we are careful to ration their use," Evi told her, pulling her chair next to Mila's. "We are already collecting as many candles as we can find."

Mila nodded. Power, or the rationing of it, was one of the topics she broached now and then to her father's Nazi dinner guests. To date, she had elicited no useful information. But she guessed the power they did have would be cut off even further when – if – the Allies neared and the Reich looked to tighten its control.

Evi pushed aside her books as Lotte set a tea tray on the table, and there was sudden quiet after a murmured round of 'please' and 'thank you' and, "ah, the tea is so fragrant!"

It was Lotte who broke the silence. "Mila, we are pleased you have come – and thankful for your generosity. "But I am guessing you have not come all this way for a social visit. Perhaps you have some news to share?"

Mila hesitated, took a sip of tea, and steeled herself. "Not news, exactly, but I have put together a plan with the Resistance Council to eliminate a few of the Reich's despicable officers – and at the same time, help us to acquire a few Nazi uniforms and credentials that can be used as cover for our police *marecheussees* and volunteers."

She measured the look that passed between mother and daughter.

"I realize, Evi, you are not yet seventeen. But you are a pretty girl, and I think that with some make-up and suitable clothing, you could pass for older, *ja*?"

Lotte's eyes narrowed. Evi sat straighter in her chair.

Mila took a breath. "There are German officers here in Haarlem who are attracted to our beautiful young Dutch women – the younger the better, in many cases. They regularly patronize a few of our taverns – mostly taverns in quiet areas, far from the *stadsplein*, away from prying eyes."

She leaned in. "These Nazi pigs are looking to – shall we say, to connect with the young Dutch beauties they find in these taverns, some of whom are happy to comply."

Both pairs of eyes stared straight at her. "Collaborators," Evi whispered.

"*Ja*, sometimes, in return for German favors. But the operation I propose – which has the full support of our Resistance leaders – has a very different purpose."

She leaned in closer.

"The plan calls for one or two of our pretty young women to patronize these taverns and deliberately catch the attention of German officers."

Two mouths dropped open. Mila expected as much. She laid out the rest of the plan, the protections that would be put in place.

There was total silence when she finished.

Evi was the first to recover. "Are you asking me to be one of these young women?"

"I would do it myself," Mila said. "But I have already met with too many of these Nazi officers. I am afraid my face might be too easily recognized."

"*So, you are asking me to…?*"

"*Ja*, Evi, if you are willing to be trained, and if your mam will allow it."

Evi clasped her mother's hands. "Mam, you must say yes. You must! I can do this. I know I can!"

Lotte's gaze went from Evi to Mila. "You cannot be serious, Mila. This could be far too dangerous -"

Mila sighed. "We all take risks every day, Lotte – hiding refugees on your barge, *ja*? Transporting them down river in broad daylight right under the nose of the Germans."

Mila lowered her voice. "There is danger in so many of the things we do – but in this instance, a pair of Resistance volunteers will be in place…bodyguards, ready to defend Evi if she needs it, and put these Nazi officers in the ground."

Lotte paused. "What happens when these officers are discovered missing?"

Mila shook her head. "They will not be missed. The war has stretched on far too long. German soldiers desert the Reich Army every day."

Lotte looked at her daughter. "But the violence –"

"I have seen more than my share of violence," Evi burst out. "Innocent people shot in the street. Nazis leaving a shop owner for dead, his blood dripping into the gutter…"

Mila spoke quietly. "She is right, Lotte. You have seen these things for yourself. You risk your life – and your daughter's life – every time you transport a fugitive."

She could see Lotte's mouth working.

"These Nazi bastards have been getting away with murder from the moment they crossed our border," Mila said. "We work daily to sabotage their phone lines, bomb their transports, keep innocents from dying at their hands – but they never lack for new ways to torture us."

She paused. "Lotte, this is a chance for Evi – your beautiful, brave Evi – to help us eliminate one *verdoemde* Nazi at a time."

In the silence, Evi locked eyes with her mother. "I have to do this, Mam."

Mila saw the defeat in Lotte's face. "…What, exactly, would she have to do?"

EVI

The kerosene lamp flickered and died early on a Thursday night – all at once, without warning, plunging them into darkness as they sat eating a dinner of cold cabbage soup.

Mam burst into tears. Evi rose silently, carrying their dishes to the sink. She reached into a cabinet with a steadiness that surprised her. "We have candles, Mam," she said. "We will be fine."

"I'm sorry, *lieveling*," Lotte sniffled. "I am the mother. I should be the brave one. It is only that …"

"You *are* brave," Evie murmured, setting two fat candles in a pair of brass holders. "I hope I can be as brave as you have been from the moment the Germans stormed in."

She struck a match and set the candles alight, bringing an eerie, dancing light into the cabin.

"It is fortunate the hold is empty," Mam's face was half in shadow. "It will be pitch dark down there."

She paused. "Evi, Zoe asked me yesterday if we could manage to shelter two little children – Jewish orphans from Germany who saw their parents shot to death by Nazis as they watched."

Evi's eyes widened.

"Resistance forces are trying to spirit the children out of Germany and deliver them to relatives in Portugal," Mam said.

"Portugal?"

"Yes. From Belgium into Southern France, then though Spain and into Portugal – which is still, *Godzijdank*, a neutral country."

But the danger in such an extended route was daunting, Evi knew. "How old are these children?"

"I believe they are four and six."

Evi shivered, not just from the cold. Her mother's face looked older in the flickering light. "Mam," she said, "children that young cannot possibly be in the hold by themselves."

"I know. I know that, Evi, but neither can they be turned away. Most of the hiding families in Haarlem are already caring for more children than they can feed – and we are at least able to transport them down river to be moved along to other hands."

Evi washed and dried the few dishes by candlelight. "When are the children scheduled to arrive?"

"If they arrive. We can never know for certain, you know that, Evi – but perhaps in the next few days if God is good to them."

Evi took a deep breath. "We may as well go to bed now, Mam. Tomorrow, in the light of day, we will talk about what we can or cannot do."

· · ·

First light came late as winter stole more of the daylight. Evi had been awakened by air raid sirens during the night and once she thought she had heard the scream of a grenade. She climbed out of bed just after seven and dressed in the murky darkness.

With no way to light classrooms as the days darkened, she was fairly sure school would be closed. But all was quiet, and she missed her friends. She decided to find out for certain.

She scribbled a note for Mam, who was still asleep, pulled a wool cap over her ears, and hoisted her book bag over a shoulder. In moments, she blended into a smaller group than usual heading toward the main road. She was not surprised. Without power, fewer businesses could operate, and there were fewer places for people to go.

She paused at Sissi's lamp post, then shivered in her coat and turned toward school. She walked past the SS guards with barely a nod, burning more keenly than ever to play her part in the plan Mila had proposed.

• • •

To her surprise, she saw for a full block before she reached the building that the school doors were wide open. Clusters of students stood chatting in the cold, a smattering of teachers walking from group to group.

She spied Sophie, her blond braids pushed up under a green wool cap, waiting on the top step. She picked up her pace, walking through clouds of her own cold breath.

"Evi!" Sophie ran down the stairs to meet her. Fat tears were running down her cheeks.

"What is it?" Evi rummaged for a handkerchief but could not find one. "What happened?"

As if the sight of her friend had fueled the spigot, Sophie cried even harder.

"Are you hurt?"

Sophie shook her head.

"Then what?"

Sophie worked to gain control. "It is Lukas."

Evi reared back. "Sophie, you scared me half to death. What about Lukas?"

"He is…" Her friend took a shuddering breath. When she spoke, her voice was a whisper. "Lukas is quitting school. This is his last day, he told me. He is joining the Royal Dutch Police."

Evi stared. "Surely not on the side of the –"

Sophie leaned in close. "No. He is joining so he can wear the uniform and be out and about after curfew. There are plenty of Royal Dutch police, you know, who are not collaborating with the Germans."

"I know that, Sophie. So, Lukas will be a *marechaussee* – working for the Resistance."

Sophie nodded and wiped away a tear, her expression a mix of pride and sorrow.

"But Sophie, that's wonderful!"

She was fairly bursting to tell Sophie that she, too, would soon play a new role for the Resistance. But Mila had sworn her to silence about the plan, and she knew she must keep her word.

"Be proud of Lukas," she whispered. "Think of it! He will surely save innocent Dutch lives. And, surely, he will not drop out of sight. He knows where to find you, Sophie."

"I know." Sophie kicked a stone at her feet. "But not to see him every day!"

Evi looked ahead at the last group of students climbing the steps to the entrance. "We must go inside. It is late."

"I do not think it matters," Sophie fell into step beside her. "With the power cut, and the days so short, my English teacher told us classes will be held for only two hours a day."

"Two hours! It hardly seems worthwhile."

Evi followed her friend up the stairs, but her thoughts were already elsewhere.

ZOE

For two nights, Zoe woke with vivid nightmares, reliving the bus ride home from Enschede – the brutality of the Nazis boarding, the pistol trained on her face. On top of that, the air raids had been increasing – whether because the Allies were getting close or because they were being repelled, she did not know. In any case, she felt as if something in her was slowly turning to steel.

She dressed quickly, nibbled around a half-rotted apple, and locked her apartment door behind her. She would make the time this morning to talk with Daan.

With the power out for much of the day, the hours and services at the pet *kliniek* were necessarily being cut. Medications were hard to come by, surgery by daylight alone was difficult if not impossible, and it took electricity to power the X-ray machine and the autoclave where their surgical instruments were sanitized.

She was turning her key in the lock to the office when Lise came up behind her, and by the time she shed her coat and scarf and donned her white coat, she heard Daan speaking to the receptionist.

"Zoe, *goedemorgen*," he said, smiling when he saw her, but it seemed to Zoe that the vigor was gone from his voice.

She peered at him. "*Goedemorgen*, Daan. Can we make some time today to talk?"

"Of course. Yes. My office at noon. Now, if I may, a short meeting about what we must do here at the *kliniek*..."

It took less than ten minutes to review their appointments, charge Lise with cancelling those they could not accommodate, and get on with the business at hand.

Zoe dressed a couple of post-surgical wounds, inoculated a four-month-old schnauzer, and took fluids to process from a listless little pup with a fever. By then, it was getting close to noon.

She knocked lightly on Daan's closed door, entered at his murmured, "Come in."

The stress in his face was unmistakable.

"Are you alright, Daan?"

His voice was quiet. "As much as I can be, I suppose. Lack of sleep. Not enough to eat. You heard the air strikes last night?"

"Of course."

Daan sighed. "I am keeping Lise on for as long as I can pay her. With business this slow, I do not know how long that might be."

Zoe nodded.

"*Verdoemde* Germans..."

She took a seat in front of the desk. "I had my own brush with the Gestapo on the bus coming back from Enschede." She shivered. "There is nothing more motivating than a pistol in your face to put some steel in your spine."

Daan's lips pursed. "We will need all the steel we can muster, Zoe. "Those grenades we heard last night were clearly targeted…and they did not miss their mark. The football club stadium was fully demolished, and what was left of the Haarlem Synagogue."

Zoe closed her eyes.

"And that is not the worst of it." Daan ran a hand though his thinning hair. "The Germans are building a new defensive line, cutting through the north of the city. We think they are preparing to protect against the Allied invasion."

She blinked. "Does that mean –"

"We cannot be sure, Zoe. "We can only guess when the Allies will push through. But we do know the Germans are grabbing up land. Dozens of families are being forced out of their homes, including some who have been hiding Jewish children for many months."

It hurt Zoe's heart that so many German-Jewish parents, in the years since Hitler's rise to power, had been forced to make the wrenching decision to send their children to those who would take them in the hope of keeping them alive.

"*Lieve god*," she breathed. "Where will these families go?"

"That is the issue we are facing, Zoe. There are few places they *can* go. To other family members, for a while, perhaps, some to the homes of friends. But even that may not be a long- term solution – not when food is already scarce and winter is coming on fast."

Zoe waited for what she knew was coming.

"We need to find places to house the families who are being forced out of their homes. There must be someplace they can go to have a chance of survival."

MILA

Evi's pretty face, as Mila examined it in the small bathroom mirror of the barge, was perfectly made up for the mission. Her lightly rouged cheeks and heavily-lined eyes, her blonde hair smooth and sleek around her shoulders, gave her an air of sophistication.

She was dressed in one of Mila's revealing black sheath dresses, but there was no mistaking her youthful innocence – and that, Mila thought, was what would help to draw her prey.

Evi's gaze was fastened on her image in the glass, as though she did not recognize the face she saw.

"They are not stupid, these German officers," Mila told her for the tenth time, demanding Evi's full attention. "They will want to bed you, but only if they are confident that you are who you say you are, and that you are as eager as they are."

"Yes, we've been over this again and again." Evi met Mila's gaze in the mirror. "I am nineteen years old. My parents are dead. I live with my little pussycat, Arabella, in a small house in the woods, and my boyfriend has just left me. I am so very tired of young boys. How very nice it is to be with a man."

"Yes, but you will likely have a choice of German officers to target. Choose someone who is already a bit drunk," Mila said, "and spin your story slowly. Gain his confidence, and do not rush the moment. Let the German take the lead. Flirt with your eyes – yes, like that!"

She showed the girl how to hunch her shoulders to make the most of her cleavage.

"Play a little with the hairs on his hand," she said. "Push out your lower lip – yes, like that. But do not invite him to come home with you until you sense that his – his lust to bed you is stronger than his sense of caution."

Mila felt a pang of uncertainty. How do you teach an innocent girl to recognize the urgency of a man's desire – or was it something she would naturally understand?

"You worry too much, Mila," Evi said, as though she read her thoughts. "I will know what to do and when to do it."

• • •

In the small living area, Lotte sat stiffly, drumming the fingers of one hand on the frayed arm of her chair.

Evi took her hand. "Mam, please try not to worry. Resistance men will be on guard, and I know precisely what to do. I will be home before you know it, I promise."

Mila watched her young charge, who looked cool and confident in the low-necked dress she had chosen for her. Evi was far from big-bosomed, but the right brassiere and the right moves teased just enough to be enticing. In all, she looked older than her not-yet-seventeen – and Mila felt confident she had done everything in her power to prepare her for her assignment.

EVI

The tavern sat in a wooded area on the outskirts of the city, a dimly lit building between a shuttered grocery store and a row of dark and silent houses. Evi wrapped her shawl around herself, trembling as much from anticipation as from the cold.

They had arrived, to her complete astonishment, in a Royal Dutch Police vehicle driven by an officer who left them half a kilometer from their destination – a *marechaussee*, she thought. She did not see his face, but perhaps it was Lukas. She wanted so much to share that with Sophie, but she knew she dared not do so.

Behind her, two burly Resistance volunteers retreated into the woods, just out of sight of the tavern. Mila stood in the shadow of a giant fir tree. Evi waited for her signal.

Finally, in the silence, Mila held up a hand. Evi took a deep breath and moved toward the darkened back door.

It was smoky inside, and dimly lit, and Evi heard laughter and booming voices. She made her way to the curved bar, where there were several open bar stools. She chose one near the end, hopped up on the stool, and waved to get the attention of the pot-bellied bartender who was chatting with someone she could not see.

Taking a lipstick out of her purse, she went through the motions of applying it, willing herself to look down the length of the bar at the customers chatting each other up.

As Mila had promised, there were more than a few German officers laughing, toasting, and drinking. They were loud and brash, and mostly big, a few not much older than she. *What if they paid her no mind?*

The bartender appeared, narrowing his eyes, scrutinizing every part of her upper body. He wavered for a moment, his moustache twitching. She was terrified he would hear her thrumming heartbeat.

Hoping she looked calmer than she felt, she popped the lipstick back into her purse and looked directly at him. Finally, nodding as though he had made up his mind, the bartender spoke.

"*Goedenavond,* young madame. I have not seen you here before."

She took the moment, sat tall in her seat, gave him her most convincing smile. "Alas, I am forced to try someplace new this evening. I will never go back to the tavern near the *stadtsplein* where I went with my cheating boyfriend."

The bartender seemed to appraise her again. "Ahh…and what is your name, *behagen?*"

Her name! It was something she and Mila had not discussed. "Emma," she blurted. "My name is Emma."

The twitch of moustache. "*Welkom,* then Emma. You will perhaps make some happier friendships here. What may I serve you tonight?"

For that, she had been well prepared. "Amstel, *behagen*." It rolled off her tongue. She smiled.

• • •

She was not prepared for the bitter taste of the beer, and it took every bit of will she had to choke it down without gagging. She ordered a second, and was fingering the glass, trying to figure out how to drink without swallowing when she felt a heavy presence behind her.

She turned to see a ruddy male face attached to a broad-shouldered body looming over her shoulder. He was dressed in uniform, but without his tie, an SS insignia on his collar. Evi forced a smile.

"*Goedeavond, Fraulein*," he said in a mix of Dutch and German. "Is a beautiful girl like yourself unaccompanied?"

"*Ja*," she said sadly, inclining her head, trying to determine his rank.

He saved her the trouble. "*Untersturmführer* Hans Vogelmann, *fraulein*. May I sit with you?"

Again, Evi shyly inclined her head. "*Ya, bitte*," she said, pleased to toss off one of the dozen German phrases Mila had drummed into her.

The brute smiled, slipped onto the stool next to her, and placed his cap on the bar. His face was flushed, and she was startled to see sweat beading on his broad brow in spite of the cold in the tavern.

Steeling herself, Evi played out every nuance of the script Mila had prepared for her. She told her sad story, flirted outrageously, pretended to sip from her stein of beer. By the time the SS underling ordered his fifth beer, and another for the beautiful *fraulein*, he was half-sitting in her lap.

"*Untersturmführer*," she murmured, taking his big hand in hers. "I think that perhaps you like me a bit, *ja*, and I like you, too. Perhaps you would like to walk with me to my lonely little house just near here?"

Leaning in, he planted a sloppy wet kiss on her cheek, tossed some guilders on the bar as he slipped off the stool, steadied himself, and clapped his cap on his head. "*Ya*, beautiful *fraulein*. It would be my pleasure."

Evi's heart hammered, but she hung onto the German's arm as he crashed through the tavern's back door, clearly so drunk that he had trouble navigating on his own. With his arm heavy across the back of her neck, she struggled to remain upright, but she murmured softly into his ear as she led him toward the dark of the woods.

When they arrived at the clearing Evi had been shown, she moved to untangle herself from his grasp. The big man stumbled and fell, and tried to right himself, but it did not matter because the moment Evi was clear of him, she heard the pop of a pistol.

The German lay sprawled on the leaf-strewn groundcover, eerily still, silent. Evi was horrified, fixed on his body, hypnotized as blood pooled under his head.

Before she could respond, big hands reached out to grab her, and Mila appeared at her side.

"Good girl, Evi," Mila whispered, holding her close. "You are good?"

Evi nodded stiffly in the darkness, looking into Mila's face.

"Good" Mila smiled. "You did well, Evi. You are a very brave girl. Come. We will take you home at once."

PART TWO

HAARLEM, THE NETHERLANDS
DECEMBER, 1944

ZOE

November slipped soundlessly into December, the days short, the nights pierced with pangs of hunger and the sounds of Luftwaffe air raids. In the midst of a sleepless night, Zoe began to wonder how many innocent Dutch had been already sacrificed to Hitler's war – how many brave men lay, maimed, in hospital on this very night.

The idle thought made her sit up in bed, suddenly inspired and counting the hours until first light.

Telephone service was at the whim of the Germans, but she was able to reach Daan at home that morning, telling him only that she would not be at the *kliniek* until noon.

She debated trying to call her cousin in Heemstede, but decided that an in-person visit was safer and more practical for her purpose. She was dressed, her face and tawny curls half obscured by a woolen scarf, and out the door before eight.

She could easily walk the few kilometers from Haarlem to Heemstede, she thought – another reason why her plan could work. But the commuter bus was still running. It would save her some time, and there was less chance she would find herself walking into a Nazi roadblock.

She sat sipping ersatz coffee in the depot until she could board the bus. There were Germans everywhere, imposing, watchful, even on this daily commuter run. Zoe shivered, that pistol in her face forever etched into memory, then boarded the bus, withdrew into her scarf, and passed the time with her eyes closed, a worn paperback novel in her lap.

There were two short stops, passengers out, passengers in, nothing out of the ordinary. Zoe was one of the first to get off the bus when the Heemstede stop was called.

• • •

It was an old hospital, brown-bricked, five stories tall, overlooking a post office and a shuttered glass factory. Zoe went to the front desk and asked for Dr. Gerrit Visser. To her vast relief, she was summoned almost immediately to his office on the second floor.

An airbrush of cheeks, a quick hug. "Zoe! What a surprise! You are well?"

Gerrit, like everyone, had lost some weight, and his posture was slightly bent. His hairline, like his father's, was receding early, making him look older than his years. But his brown eyes were as warm as ever, his short beard neatly trimmed.

"I am well, cousin, yes, *dank u!*,"

He settled her in a chair across from his desk and took a seat behind it.

"So, Gerrit," Zoe began. "My mother has kept me informed over the years. But tell me, how does a shy little boy from Enschede become the head of a hospital in Heemstede?"

Gerrit laughed. "He muddles his way through school, grows a dapper little beard, and somehow, he manages to fool people smarter than he into thinking he is a brilliant administrator. And you, Zoe? You are a veterinarian, yes? In Haarlem?"

"Yes, and yes. It is a perfect job for me. My patients never question my diagnoses."

Gerrit chuckled.

The two had lived kilometers apart in the first ten years of their lives, playing in the park nearly every afternoon, learning to swim, to skate. They had not seen one another for nearly as many years, but she was happy to feel that there was still an easiness between them.

"You are well, Gerrit?"

"Mostly. Like everyone." He paused. "Do you remember Jaan Voelker?"

"Of course. He used to play soccer with us."

Gerrit sighed. "He was killed last month in a German bomb strike. He was working to repair a blocked sewer line at the time. Wrong time, wrong place…an innocent – "

"Oh Gerrit, I am so sorry."

She told him about her encounter with the Gestapo on the way home from visiting her parents – the blatant cruelty, the pistol inches from her face. "It is the reason why I work for the Resistance, Gerrit. We all must do what we can."

He nodded sadly, and it was time, she knew, to tell him the reason for her visit.

She repeated Daan's concern for the Haarlem families losing their homes to the German outpost.

"Think about this, please Gerrit," she said. "Several of these families are hiding Jewish children. Now they have no place to go."

She paused. "This is a public hospital, cousin, an established hospital, and not one the Germans are apt to search without reason. Do you think you could find a way to house these people here?"

Gerrit met her gaze. When he spoke, his voice was quiet. "We are at this moment, Zoe, hiding more than a few Jewish doctors in this hospital, as well as three downed Allied airmen who were grabbed by sympathizers and brought here for care so they would not be found by the Germans. They are posing here as hospital patients and medical personnel. We are hiding them, as they say, in plain sight.."

Zoe brought her hands to her face. "Oh, Gerrit..."

"But whole families, Zoe – and children...I don't see how..."

"We are skilled at moving people, Gerrit." She leaned forward. "We can bring them here in small groups, take circuitous routes so as not to draw attention. Only as many as you can manage to accommodate, cousin...It is *urgente*. These people are desperate."

Gerritt rubbed the back of his neck. "I know."

He got up and paced across his office. "Perhaps the basement. It is where our morgue is housed. But there is not much light or open space down there. It would not be a decent space for children..."

He paced a moment more, then turned to face her, his hands resting on his desk. "Waits...I have another idea...."

He sat. "Before the war began, we had started to renovate the top floor of the hospital. Our hope was to create a ward expressly for cancer patients – and a research lab to ...well, no matter. We abandoned the project when the funds ran dry after the German occupation. Part of the floor is still unusable because it is only half-renovated."

Zoe leaned forward. "If we could insulate it, Gerrit – keep it masked from entry as though it still being renovated..."

"I don't know..."

"We could dress some of the men in work clothes, cousin." Zoe leaned forward. "Give them paint and some building materials they could pretend to use if they needed to..."

Gerrit stood, resumed his pacing. "Yes, but even if we could manage it, Zoe, I'm not sure how we could feed these people. Our kitchen is struggling now to feed our patients."

"*Lieve god*, Gerrit, we are all hungry. We hear rumors that tulip growers are plowing over their fields and eating the bulbs... "

She touched her cousin's shoulder. "I can promise you the Resistance Council will do its best to find food for these people. But first we must keep them off the streets."

Gerrit ran a hand through his beard. "All right" he said at last. "We will find a way."

Zoe allowed herself to feel excited on the short bus ride home. Moving numbers of people into the hospital unnoticed would present its own challenge. But the prospect of protecting all those families and children would make it more than worth the risk.

She thought of the two Jewish orphans Lotte Strobel was reluctant to harbor because they could not be left alone in the hold of the barge. At the hospital, there would be daylight and space to move around, and plenty of people to look after all the children.

She burst into Daan's office at the *kliniek* without bothering to knock.

He was bent over a ledger, pen in hand.

"Daan, you will never guess what happened." She closed the door behind her, took a seat in front of him. "I have truly wonderful news."

She told him of Gerrit's agreement to mask off a floor of the hospital in Heemstede, to hide as many families as they could manage.

Daan pounded a fist on his desk. "Brilliant, Zoe, I do not know how you made this happen, but may God bless you – and your cousin! There is already panic, especially among the hiding families who have only days to evacuate."

He reached for the telephone. "I will let Pieter know at once. How soon can we begin the transfers?"

Zoe thought. Increasingly, the Germans were withholding food to keep the Dutch in line. Even with rations, most of the country relied mostly on bread and root vegetables – boiling potato peels for soup to fill their bellies.

"There is an issue, Daan," she said. "I promised Gerrit we would find a way to provide food."

Daan did not appear to be deterred.

"Not all the news is bad, Zoe. One or two of our civic-minded public servants are embezzling the occasional batch of ration cards. It is a risk, but you can tell your cousin not to fear. We will keep them supplied with food."

MILA

For Mila, it was a fait accompli. Evi had been brilliant, all had gone as planned, and a Nazi pig was in a shallow grave, his uniform and papers commandeered to help save innocent lives.

She was less sure when – or whether – Evi might agree to a repeat performance. The girl had been quiet on the way home, understandably anxious, and Mila had not pushed, only praised her for being so brave, and allowing her to gather her thoughts.

Tomorrow, she would pay another visit to the barge. Today, she had other things to do.

She brushed her hair, let it fall into place, caught up one side with a gold barrette. Strange as it seemed, in the year she had been repeating German dinner talks to Pieter from the privacy of her bedroom, she had never met him face to face. She expected he had a very good reason for wanting to meet with her now.

In the kitchen, she refused to eat the sausages her father's Nazi guests had brought, instead making do with a chunk of bread and a cup of tea.

"You are wasting away, Mila," Reit admonished.

"As are we all," Mila said. "Tell Mother I will be home in time for dinner – and if there is more food than you need for the table tonight,

Reit, please take some to the Dans Hal, where it will help feed those who need it more than we do."

Riet would grumble, but she would comply, Mila knew, and it gave her no end of pleasure to know that the Nazis who came to her father's table were inadvertently feeding the people for whom they held such contempt.

• • •

The address Pieter had given her was in a shabby, red brick building set between a barber shop and a shuttered camera store. Mila picked her way around a bombed-out crater in the cobblestoned street and crossed the road. The sign on the glass door read, *Van der Gruden Plumbing Supply*. Mila knocked gingerly and walked in.

The man sitting at the only desk in the room was blond and clean-shaven with the greenest eyes she had ever seen. He rose from the desk to greet her, and something in his smile caught at her heart.

"Mila, *ja*? Please, come in!"

Shaken, she worked to find her voice. "Pieter? *Ja, hallo*. It is good to finally see your face."

What a stupid thing to say," she told herself. '*Good to see your face!*'

But he did have a remarkable face, strong, compelling, intelligent. And how could he not be all these things, four years at the head of the Resistance movement in one of the largest cities in the Netherlands?

Pieter only smiled again, indicated a chair facing his desk, and waited for her to sit before he did. "It's good to meet you, too, Mila," he said in the resonant voice she knew. "And to thank you in person on behalf of the Council. Your contributions have been invaluable."

She took a moment to match her tone to his. "Thank you, Pieter, but hardly necessary."

"But it is. Some of the casual intelligence you have gained and shared with us has been more useful than you know." He paused. "Among other things. it has helped us to blow up a German storage facility, raid a stock of Nazi radio equipment, and commandeer more than one hidden store of food or supplies."

Mila offered a wry smile. "It is the least I can do, given that my father, willingly or not, is collaborating with our German enemies…"

"We all do what we must." Pieter shrugged. "And despite my misgivings, your scheme at the tavern the other night was a brilliant success. How is the girl? Is she willing to repeat, do you think?"

"I hope so. I will talk with Evi tomorrow. I think she may have been a little – overwhelmed. But she is strong-willed and committed, and I am hopeful she has been able to overcome her misgivings."

"Good," Pieter nodded. "It is a small-scale operation and it must remain so, but worth the risk, I think, for the uniforms and identification papers."

"I hope Evi decides so as well. And her mother." She sighed. "I only wish there was more I could do!"

Pieter leaned forward. "I hoped you would be thinking that, Mila…because it seems perhaps you can, if you are up to the risk."

She looked up.

"You were an art major in school, were you not?"

"I did some drawing, yes, mostly fashion…"

"The Allies have determined that the Germans are building more than just a new defensive line in the north. There is construction going on all along the coastline – machine gun nests, observation points, and more. We have been asked by the British to provide a map of the installations. But we need to get close enough to do so."

Mila listened.

"If we can send such a map through channels, we have reason to hope for a strategic raid by England's Royal Air Force – possibly even on German submarine facilities, which would severely cripple their nautical abilities."

She was unsure how she could help.

"Access anywhere near those military zones is highly restricted, as you might imagine, Mila – and to create even a rudimentary map would take an eye for detail, a practiced hand – and enough charm and quick thinking to maneuver past the SS guards."

She cocked her head.

"It is a dangerous task, Mila, with no less risk than you have assigned to Evi Strobel. You cannot be caught red-handed sketching behind enemy lines – and I am not sure how, or if, we could help you should you need it. But you speak excellent German, your background as an art student makes for plausible cover, and you are a beautiful woman with a proven talent for captivating officers of the Reich."

Mila was speechless.

"You would, of course, carry forged papers," Pieter said. "And we can provide you with drawings of the pre-war installations. You can study them as the baseline from which to work if you choose to do this."

Mila thought for a moment. It was indeed not any more dangerous than what she had asked of Evi.

Pieter did not press her.

She took a moment. "I cannot promise I can manage this, Pieter. I can only promise to do my best."

He nodded as though he expected nothing less. "Are you certain?"

"I am."

His green eyes studied her. "You understand the risk – and the danger."

"I do."

He watched her for a moment, as though she might change her mind, then reached into a drawer and brought out identification papers for a Trude Altenkamp, 28, born in Zurich, Switzerland. He slid them across the desk to her, along with a thin manila folder.

Trude Altenkamp. Mila memorized the name, glanced at the paperwork, slipped it all into her oversized bag. She held out a hand as she rose to leave, but to her surprise, Pieter came around the desk and took both her hands in his.

"You are a brave woman, Mila – and resourceful," he told her. "You are a credit to your countrymen....to all of us."

It was no more than she had told Evi Strobel. But it warmed her, nonetheless.

EVI

It was cold in the barge, as always. Evi pulled a green sweater close around her, examined her handiwork, and lit another match. There were enough bits of leftover candlewax to fashion into a new candle, and just enough of a length of wick. Mam would be pleased. "Waste not, want not," she had admonished so often that Evi heard it in her dreams.

She looked at the finished candle, reasonably rounded and sleek, marbled with the soft colors of candles past, and she remembered something. She ran to her sleeping quarters, rummaged through a drawer, pulled out a length of red grosgrain ribbon. Perfect!

She tied the ribbon around the base of the candle, wrapped it carefully in tissue. It would make a perfect Christmas gift for Mam.

She sucked in her breath, feeling tears ready to spring, as they so often did these days. She blinked them way, threw her hands over her eyes. It was hard enough to keep hunger at bay, never mind worrying over Christmas.

Still, the holiday was on her mind, and it was something to focus on besides that night in the woods with the SS officer.

She had been scared nearly out of her mind by the time they left the smoky tavern. She thanked God the German had been too drunk to notice how badly she was trembling. Then the gun shot in the darkness, the burly body of the drunk SS officer crumpling to the ground, nearly on top of her, literally before he knew what hit him.

She had no pity for the dead Nazi. He and his like deserved to die – and she tried not to picture him being stripped of his uniform, pistol and papers, or his body tossed into the waiting ditch as Mila led her away.

But the boldness of the mission – the sheer daring, and her own part in making it happen, had left her breathless. What if the German had been just sober enough to realize he was being tricked? What if the Resistance shooter had misjudged the rendezvous point? What if *she* had misjudged it?

She still was not sure how she had felt when it was over…Fear? Pride? Recklessness?

But after three days of thinking it through, she had mostly been able to put her doubts aside. She was ready and willing to do it again if she was asked.

Mam would be against it. She had been reluctant from the beginning, and although Evi had shared with her as little as possible, she knew Mam was anxious for her, protective, as though she were still a child.

Evi moved to the mirror above the bathroom sink, studied her serious face. She was not a child. Not anymore. Not after what she had done in the name of justice and what she hoped she could do again. She was still two months shy of her seventeenth birthday, but she was not a child anymore.

• • •

At four o'clock, it was nearing dark, and Evi began to worry. Mam had left this morning to work a shift in one of the only pharmacies still operating in Haarlem. But the pharmacy closed at three. Where was she?

Perhaps she had been needed to be at the Dans Hal – or she'd gotten word of new rations. They were living mostly on bread and potatoes, so anything new would be welcome.

The thought of food made her mouth water. Evi went back to her book, but she could not focus. Anything could happen in these dangerous days. Anyone could be stopped and harassed by German interrogators for no reason at all – and Mam took chances every day.

By the time she heard footsteps descending from the wharf, she was nearly frantic.

"Mam – are you alright?"

"*Ja, lieveling*, I am fine." Mam threw off her heavy wool cape, stepped out of her shoes. "I am sorry. I knew you would worry. Daan Mulder summoned me to the Dans Hal. It seems a major tulip grower outside of Den Helder has plowed up all the bulbs on his land and is giving them away for food. I will take the barge tomorrow, while you are in school. There will be food to share, Evi. Think of it!"

Evi felt her muscles go slack, knowing Mam was all right. But Den Helder… the air base…the bombings…it was a dangerous destination,

"But, Mam…"

"Never fear, *lieveling*, I will be careful. I will make the run in the early daylight, and be back here well before curfew."

Tulip bulbs…Evi wanted to protest. What if Mam was seen – and stopped? But people were starving, and the prospect of food – even starchy tubers – made it difficult to argue.

• • •

She was rinsing their soup bowls, daydreaming of sausages and fresh eggs, when she heard a light tapping at the door.

"Hallo? It is Mila."

"Mila!" She let her into the barge. "Come in."

Mila hugged her, but the look in her eyes when she pulled back was questioning.

"I am fine, Mila, truly," Evi gestured to the small sofa.

Mam greeted Mila warily, watching from her chair, where she sat unraveling an old afghan blanket for yarn that could be repurposed.

"You have a strong and clever daughter, Lotte," Mila sat. "You should be proud."

She turned to Evi. "I am proud, Evi. You preformed a great service in a time when we all must fight just to survive."

Evi sat next to her, on the edge of her seat. "If you are here to ask me to do it again, Mila, the answer is yes. I will."

"Evi, are you certain –" Mam leaned forward.

"I am as certain as you are, Mam, that taking the barge to Den Helder for tulip bulbs is worth the risk you will be taking."

ZOE

Radio Oranje was calling it the *HongerWinter* – the winter of hunger – and justly so, with the Germans consistently shrinking rations, and starvation threatening all but the most self-reliant.

The worst of it, Zoe thought, as she turned off the broadcast and hid the radio behind a stack of linens in the closet, was that many Dutch farmers were more than willing to share what little they could grow in the cold – but even moving the food from the countryside to the city was difficult under German watch because the bounty was often commandeered.

Since Gerrit had come through with his promise to house the displaced Haarlem families, Zoe and a cadre of Resistance volunteers had somehow managed to move people, never more than a few at a time, into the hospital in Heemstede.

Today, if all went well, Zoe would transport several more, as always walking a circuitous route to avoid German scrutiny.

Because the SS and the Gestapo frequently shifted checkpoints to take the unsuspecting by surprise, Zoe planned to walk the route once by herself before moving anyone else. Even if she needed to recalculate, she thought, she should be at the pet *kliniek* by noon.

• • •

There were two men, three women and two children under the age of five in the designated area of the park, huddled in heavy coats and scarves. Among them stood a uniformed Royal Dutch policeman. Zoe sucked in her breath as he approached.

"*Mevrоew* Visser," he said quietly. "My name is Lukas Jenssen. I have been sent to assist you in this transport."

He looked young to be wearing the uniform. "Who sent you here?"

"The thane of Cawdor."

She hesitated. They were the right code words, stolen from Shakespeare's Macbeth. But she needed to be certain. "And why should I trust you?"

"Because these people trust me. Because the Resistance Council knows that a Dutch police escort will lessen the chance of German interference."

Zoe relaxed. A *mareschaussee*…

A kerchiefed woman whose Persian cat Zoe had treated more than once rose from a nearby bench.

"Else Jenssen, Zoe," the woman laid a hand on the young man's shoulder. "Lukas is my son. We are proud of him."

"As you should be," Zoe stepped away. "Let us not tarry, then. I will leave it to you, Lukas, to get these people safely to the hospital."

• • •

She stopped briefly at her favored café, where she ate a quick lunch of boiled potatoes and came away with a Dutch driver's license and a French passport liberated from a couple of winter coat pockets.

Daan was waiting when she arrived at the *kliniek*. "A moment in my office, Zoe."

"Apologies for sending Lukas to your meeting spot unannounced," he said when they were seated. "Pieter tried to telephone you earlier, but the call did not go through."

She dropped the stolen driving license and passport on his desk. "I am always fearful of German roadblocks. But thanks be to God, nearly all our refugees have been transported."

Daan examined the purloined ID's. "*Bedankt,* Zoe. Two more lives perhaps saved."

In the quiet that followed, Zoe realized what was missing – the low thrum of barks and animal sounds that had once always emanated from the kennels. These days, with food and guilders short, overnight stays for doctoring their animals was out of the question for most.

"Are there appointments scheduled this afternoon?" she asked.

"Nothing I cannot handle by myself." Daan leaned forward and lowered his voice. Close the door, please.

Zoe did so, and dropped into a chair.

"Something has come up. An opportunity. It is urgent and dangerous, but worth the risk, we think – and we need all the help we can get."

She nodded.

"As you are well aware, Nazi troops have been sweeping through our farmlands, seizing produce and supplies. We think some of that food is earmarked for German troops in Poland, because much of it was seen being loaded onto a train that is scheduled to leave Haarlem for Krakow tomorrow evening."

Daan's voice was barely above a whisper. "We have the means in place to blow the train off the tracks in a forested area to the north," he said. "But we will need to take ownership of all that edible cargo – and quickly, before the German command gets wind of it."

"I understand."

"We need to have volunteers with handcarts and bicycles waiting in the woods just out of sight of the tracks. They will need to sift through the wreckage, strip whatever foodstuffs they can find, and transport the goods to the hospital loading dock in Heemstede. '

Daan paused. "Again, we cannot minimize the risk. It is an hour's bicycle ride from the blast point to the hospital, more if the Germans are quick to reconnoiter, so our volunteers must be hardy and shrewd. But if we are quick to get in an out, the reward is worth the risk. Can you help?"

Zoe wrestled for a long moment, weighing the image of the pistol in her face against the need to feed the hungry.

"We will need a map," she said, finally, "The volunteers must study all possible routes. But people here are angry as well as hungry. Perhaps they will welcome the chance to act."

MILA

Mila strolled just outside the restricted area early on a Saturday morning, her hair glinting red and gold in the cold December sunshine. An artist's portfolio full of drawings and charcoals was slung over her shoulder, and under one arm she carried an oversized sketchpad,

She had expected to find the place alive with German soldiers ready to stop and question her, wary of running into an officer who had sat at her father's table. In any case, she had prepared a cover story about needing to do a sketch of the old lighthouse for an art class.

But the whole area was bewilderingly quiet. Save for a few guards with rifles resting at their feet, there was little to impede her progress.

Opening her sketch book, she ventured casually beyond the orange-ribboned boundary, pulse quickening as she peered into the distance, sketching, listening for footsteps behind her.

She was prepared to flash a flirtatious smile, apologize for a stupid blunder, absorbed as she was in her work.

But to her astonishment, no one approached her, and she left as quickly and easily as he had entered, ducking under the orange tape with her sketch pad full of drawings stowed beneath her fashion drawings in her portfolio.

At home, puzzled, she tried reaching Pieter more than once from the relative safety of her clothes closet. But the secure line went unanswered, which left her even more uneasy. She dressed for dinner with equal measures of curiosity and dread.

Her parents and their guests were just being seated when Mila entered the dining room clad in a form-fitting, azure silk dinner dress with a neckline low enough to be noticed. She did not know either of the two SS men who rose as she entered, but she saw their gaze move to study her curves as she took her seat and offered a welcoming smile.

"Mila, please welcome *Hauptscharführer* Ludvig Schluck and *Oberscharführer* Heinz Pfeiffer, who will be dining with us this evening. *Mein Herren*, this is our daughter, Mila."

Mila studied them as she sat, the one bulky, straight-backed, with a Hitler-like moustache, the other with a bulbous, pig-like nose and blue eyes set too close together.

"*Mein Herren*," she gracefully inclined her head, amused as always at how her non-German speaking father managed to wrap his tongue around all those protracted German vowels.

Her mother offered low-key comments about the weather and the coming Yuletide, and there were short bursts of conversation as the dinner of pork roast and sweet potatoes was served. But apart from the sound of silverware clinking and wine being poured, these officers, like the guards she had seen this morning, appeared to be oddly distracted.

"So, *mein Herren*," Mila tried. "Will you be going home for the Christmas holidays?"

The pair of Germans exchanged glances.

"Alas, *nein*," the larger man said finally. "I am afraid we may be needed here."

His companion was absorbed in his food.

Mila leaned forward, revealing more bosom. "How awful, *Oberscharführer Pfeiffer*. And why is that?"

Her father cut her off with a comment about the roast – how succulent and perfectly spiced – and the Germans agreed, helping themselves to a second portion.

The conversation limped along despite Mila's effort to spur it on. Finally, as the fourth bottle of wine was emptied, the older German laid his napkin on the table.

"I fear, Herr Brouwer" he said, "with many thanks for your gracious hospitality, we must make this an early evening."

His companion rose, clicked his heels together in the Reich fashion, and bowed from the waist. "Our thanks to you as well, Frau Brouwer, and your lovely daughter," he said in passable Dutch. "The repast and the company have been a delight."

Her father rose. "Of course, *mein Herr.* "Perhaps as soon as tomorrow. Cook will roast the goose you brought this evening."

The pig-faced officer shook his head. "*Danke schoen,* Herr Brouwer. "I wish it were possible. But we are summoned to a Reich meeting at the Haarlem Cinema tomorrow evening, and there is much to do in preparation."

He rose and bowed again, first to her mother, and then to her. "Our gratitude again for this repast and your gracious company. We hope to see you soon again."

Mila was relieved, if still puzzled, when the two of them were gone. She said brief goodnights to her parents and hurried to the sanctity of her bedroom.

She locked the door and, without bothering to change out of her silk dress, sat down in her clothes closet and pulled out the secure line. To her great relief, the call was answered.

"Pieter," she began. "I was worried that I could not reach you earlier. I have the sketches you asked for, and I hope they are useful. But alarm bells are going off in my head."

She lowered her voice. "Both the few German guards I saw this morning, and our SS dinner guests this evening appeared to be oddly distracted – and it appears some sort of meeting is planned for German personnel tomorrow evening at the Haarlem Cinema."

Pieter took a moment. "Tomorrow morning if you can manage it," he said finally. "Ten o'clock. My office."

EVI

It was a different tavern, set far back from the street along the same small stretch of quiet highway just outside the city limits. The same arrangements had been made with the Resistance bodyguards, and Evi had memorized the path to the rendezvous point where she was to lead her drunken German victim.

Mila, for some reason, was not in attendance, but Evi told herself it made no difference. She felt alluring and confident in the emerald green sheath dress, and she was in good hands, she assured herself as walked through the tavern's rear door.

The interior was strikingly similar to the first, smoke-filled and dimly lit. She took a seat at the far end of the bar, and tucked a few stray hairs into her upswept chignon. The bartender took her order without hesitation.

She was nursing her Amstel, surreptitiously peering down the length of the bar to survey her prospects, when a voice whispered in her left ear.

"*Bist du allein, fraulein?*" He asked in German. "Are you alone?"

She turned on the bar stool, a smile on her face. The young SS officer was lean and clean-shaven, with startlingly blue eyes. He gestured questioningly to the stool beside her.

"*Ja, ja,*" she said, encouraging him to sit, and hoping he spoke at least a little Dutch.

He ordered two beers and another for the *fraulein*. She asked, in Dutch, how long he had been in the Netherlands, and he answered easily enough.

"*Drie yaren,*" he said in perfect Dutch. Three years.

She tried her most seductive smile. "That is a long time. Do you like it here?"

"*Eine* beautiful land *mit* many beautiful ladies," he murmured in a mix of languages, leaning close enough for her to smell the beer on his breath.

It was difficult to tell how drunk he was. He did not seem to be slurring his words, though his gaze seemed oddly unfocused.

"Where in Germany do you come from?" she asked.

"*Munchen,*" he said, smiling sadly. "Munich. Also, beautiful. Ach, *ya, meine* beautiful *Munchen.*"

"You miss your home, then?"

"*Ich vermisse mein familie.*" I miss my family.

She brought to mind one of the German phrases Mila had taught her. "*Unt deine freundin?*" she asked, smiling coquettishly. Your girlfriend?

The German downed his fourth beer and slung a heavy arm around her shoulder. "*Sie,* my beautiful *fraulein,*" he murmured. "You will be *meine fraulein, ya?*"

His fingers began to play with the neckline of her dress. Evi smiled. "*Een ander?*" She held up her nearly full mug. *Another?*"

The German had trouble snapping his fingers for the bartender. She took it as a welcome sign. After his fifth beer, as his gaze explored the cleft between her breasts, both his eyes and his smile looked decidedly off kilter.

"*Liebhaber* - lover - she said in German, her fingers playing with his belt buckle. "*Wirst du mit mir kommen?*" Will you come with me?

In answer, he tried a wet kiss, which Evi barely managed to avoid. He slapped a wad of Dutch guilders on the bar and slipped crookedly off his barstool.

Evi stood beside him, settled his arm over her shoulder. "*Ich lebe in der nahe,*" She whispered into his ear, silently thanking Mila for her language lessons. "*I live very nearby.*"

By the time they reached the back door, she was certain the Nazi would have difficulty navigating. But as they stepped outside, he found strength enough to turn and flatten her against the wall of the tavern.

"*Nein, bitte,*" she said, easing herself out from under him. "*Nein, liebhaber.* Better in my house, in my bed."

She stepped away, but he was stronger than he looked, and in one swift motion, he eased them both to the ground. He was heavy on her, clapping a hand over her mouth as his right hand searched for his zipper.

"*Bitte!*" – Please, she tried, mumbling into his hand. He was pulling her dress up with his free hand, grappling with clumsy fingers to pull down her underwear. She could feel him hard and pulsing against her. Panic rose in her throat.

"*Nein, bitte,*" she mumbled, praying for someone to exit the tavern door, pushing hard against the German's chest with every bit of strength she could muster.

He rose up slightly and, in that instant, she heard the pop of a pistol, and the German collapsed against her, the full weight of him pinning her firmly to the ground.

Evi gulped air, trying to ease herself out from under him, looking for the Resistance shooters. But the man who shoved the German's body aside was a complete and total stranger.

"Are you okay?" he asked in English – American English, Evi thought – as he helped her get to her feet.

"I – *ja,* I think so," she began, her heart beating against her chest. She heard the heavy pounding of boots against packed earth, and her bodyguards appeared out of nowhere and pinned the arms of her rescuer behind him.

"Who are you?" they demanded.

"Whoa," the man struggled to break free. "I'm an American. American. United States Army Flight Officer Jacob Reese."

There was no mistaking the American accent. The bodyguards loosened their grip. The airman began to back away, hands over his head. "My plane went down here in Dutch territory during a scouting drill, September fourteenth, nineteen-forty-four."

Evi stared at the tall American, dark haired, lightly bearded, broad through the shoulders and dressed in civilian clothing. Her bodyguards seemed uncertain. But there was no time for discussion, with an SS officer lying dead at their feet only steps from the tavern's back door.

The Resistance guards bent, each grasping one of the German's arms, and the American needed no instruction to grasp him firmly by the ankles. Together, the three moved quickly into the woods, and Evi, still shivering, chignon askew, put one foot in front of the other and followed.

She watched, coming slowly back to herself, as the German's body was stripped of all that was useful and tossed into the waiting grave.

As before, she had no idea if she might be asked to do this again. But she did know two things for certain. The first was that she might owe her life to this downed American airman.

The second was that she would demand a pistol of her own and she would damn well learn how to use it.

ZOE

With time of the essence and phone service unreliable, Zoe went directly to the Dans Hal. As always, there were women and children at work creating wall décor, chatting and laughing, creating a quite believable smokescreen in the event Nazi snoopers showed up.

She knew fewer than half of the women she saw, but she was greeted heartily by those who knew her.

"Doctor Visser, hallo!" called Leela Bakker, who printed underground communications for the Resistance, and whose rowdy little schnauzer had been a patient. "Are you here to help?"

"Actually, I'm here to recruit help," Zoe kept her voice low. "We need volunteers for tomorrow evening. Is there somewhere we can talk?"

Leela took her into the office, where they spoke above the noise of a mimeograph.

Zoe laid out what was needed. "The train will be detonated tomorrow after dark, at precisely five-twenty," she said. "We need at least a dozen people – strong people who can pedal for an hour and who understand the risk – to wait in the surrounding woods with wagons or carts secured to their bicycles. We will need to very quickly harvest food from the wreckage and take off in different directions, with the hospital in Heemstede as the end point."

Leela nodded.

"We cannot know how quickly the Germans will react, so speed and caution are critical. Can we do this?"

Leela did not hesitate. "We can."

She studied the map Zoe showed her and took it to the mimeograph to make copies.

"Again, Leela, we need to underline the danger…" Zoe spoke above the din.

Leela turned to face her. "The food on this train is food that was stolen by these Nazi bastards out of the mouths of our families. Every farmer in Haarlem will want to help A number of their wives are here right now. They can spread the word and I am quite certain we will have all the help we need tomorrow evening."

• • •

Zoe checked in briefly at the *kliniek*, assuring Daan there would be enough manpower for the mission.

He nodded. "I leave it to you to inform your cousin, to be sure they are ready at the hospital. I will meet this evening with Pieter and the Council. There is more news. Good news, I think."

It had been far too long since they had heard good news. Zoe prayed he was right.

• • •

She made her way home, where she soaked in a warm bath until the water cooled. At dawn, after a fitful night, she dressed for the walk to the hospital.

The streets were peaceful in the early light, almost eerily quiet, the rhythm of her footsteps on the cobblestoned sidewalks attuned to the beating of her heart. A yellow bird perched on a mailbox watched her as she passed. She took it as a sign of better days to come and increased the pace of her step.

She found Gerritt in his second-floor office and quickly apprised him of the plan.

"Glory be," he said. "The food will be a blessing. I will arrange for the loading dock to be open and have someone on site to help."

Zoe settled back in her chair. "So, dear cousin, how are you managing?"

"It's frantic," Gerrit said, running a hand through his hair. "With dozens of people secreted on one floor – including children being children – we have constantly to remind them to remain quiet or risk being discovered. Add to that the inconstant food supply, and I find myself lying awake even on rare quiet nights."

"I understand, Gerrit. But you are saving lives. I hope this food will help."

He nodded. "If you would like to see how our 'patients' are faring, Zoe, I can take you on a tour of the top floor – which, as I am sure you recall, is once more closed for renovation."

They took the service elevator to the top floor and wove their way through an intimidating jumble of stacked hospital beds, furniture, and medical equipment.

Midway down the corridor, ladders rested against a wall and paint cans were scattered about. Three 'workmen' in overalls chatted softly, seemingly on break from the job.

Beyond them, behind what looked like a solid wall, Zoe walked into another universe.

In the unthinkable event that the hideaway was discovered, the room needed to look as much like any other ward as possible. But the reality of so many displaced men, women and children living in such chaotic conditions nearly brought Zoe to tears.

A sea of cots sat close together, little more than inches between them. There was an antiseptic smell in the space, and a palpable, unnatural, quiet. A few people napped, others read, some sat staring at the grey sky outside the tall hospital windows. The 'patients' were dressed in dull blue hospital gowns, the staff, mostly Jewish doctors and nurses, Zoe guessed, wearing white coats much like the ones she wore at work.

In a far corner of the room, a lightly bearded man with expressive blue eyes was reading animatedly, if quietly, to a group of children of assorted sizes who sat silently at his feet.

Gerrit moved aside to speak to someone, and Zoe moved closer to the storyteller.

"But as spring came, the ugly duckling realized something quite surprising," the man read in accented Dutch. "He had become as beautiful a swan as any in the clear blue lake."

The children looked at the picture he displayed, seemingly mesmerized by the familiar tale and the mellow voice of the storyteller. Zoe smiled, watching the face of the reader, nearly as regretful as the children seemed to be when the story wound to a close.

"The end," the storyteller said, closing the oversized picture book. The children groaned, and the man put a finger to his lips. "Hush," he admonished. "Remember? We must be quiet."

He suggested a bathroom visit, and perhaps a glass of water before he read another story. One by one the children, some as young as three or four, rose and silently dispersed.

Zoe smiled. "You are the Pied Piper of Haarlem, it seems. He was always one of my heroes."

"Thank you, I think." He rose from his perch on the side of a bed. "I am not certain I deserve the title, but I would be honored to be your hero. Kurt Schneider." He held out a hand.

Zoe recognized the accented Dutch. Her eyebrows rose. *A German?*

He seemed to sense her surprise. "Yes, I am German – a fallen German, if you will, and an identified enemy of the Reich."

Zoe thought of Herr Zeller, the concert pianist. "You are not compelled to answer, but I will ask anyway. What did you do to earn the wrath of Hitler?"

He smiled, and the sun shone through his blue eyes. "My brother and I built yachts in Cologne, with a regular route into Rotterdam. Over time, we smuggled dozens of Jews and German dissenters like myself across the border – until the SS got wind of it and came after us."

Zoe studied the neatly trimmed beard, the slightly crooked smile. "You were lucky to escape with your life."

He raised his hands in a futile gesture. "My brother was not so lucky."

Zoe nodded. "I am sorry..."

He inclined his head. "Thank you. As am I."

"So," she went on to lighten the moment, "were you always a storyteller, Kurt Schneider?"

He found his smile. "Alas, no. But I do love children, and reading stories helps to keep them from becoming unruly."

Gerrit came up behind her. "Ah, Kurt, this is Dr. Zoe Visser. She is a veterinarian who works for the Resistance – and my very dear cousin. It was she who persuaded us to create this erstwhile hiding place."

"Our gratitude," Schneider said, putting a hand over his heart. "This is the second time I have been forced to flee from the Nazis. When I fled Germany, I settled in Haarlem, but my home is in the path of the defensive line they are rushing headlong to complete."

His gaze settled on Zoe. "Fortunately, the bastards who pounded on my front door and gave me twenty-four hours to evacuate seemed to have no knowledge of my previous brush with the Gestapo. But I would not be surprised, somewhere up the line, to find myself still in their sights."

Gerrit patted Schneider on the shoulder. "I will leave you, if I may," he said. "I have matters to see to. Zoe, can you find your way downstairs?"

"Yes, of course – and thank you again, Gerrit. I will see you soon, I hope."

Kurt Schneider bowed ever so slightly. "It is a pleasure to meet you, Dr. Zoe Visser." He smiled, and the room brightened.

One by one, the children trickled back. "More, *Meneer* Kurt, please?"

Zoe stepped back. "Do not let me keep you." She was embarrassed to find herself staring

MILA

Mila withdrew the drawings from her artist's portfolio and set them on Pieter's desk. She had done her best to project angles and distances, and she knew from the expression on Pieter's face as he examined them that he was pleased with what he saw.

"This is good work, Mila. Thank you for taking the risk. I will get these to London straight away."

"The strange thing, Pieter, is how remarkably low risk it was," she said, leaning forward across the desk "As I told you, the few German patrols I saw seemed totally uninterested. They were too busy conferring with one another to pay me any notice – and the pair of SS officers at dinner last night managed barely to sit through dessert. Apart from mentioning the meeting at the Cinema, they had very little to say,"

Pieter met her gaze. "It was more than good fortune, Mila. I think I may know why they seemed so preoccupied."

He kept his voice low. "Our intelligence tells us that some two-hundred thousand German troops and perhaps a thousand tanks were massed yesterday in the Ardennes Forest in Belgium. We think they are preparing to launch an invasion on the American front – some sort of payback, as it were, for their losses in Normandy last June…and perhaps a last-ditch effort, also, to turn the tide of the war in Hitler's favor."

Mila felt her blood quicken.

"We are doing what we can and we pray the American allies will prevail. If they do, it could mean an end to the war – and liberation."

"But if not…"

"We can pray, Mila. God knows four years of hunger and misery have been more than enough to bear."

His green eyes darkened.

"My guess is that news of the attempted siege is beginning to trickle down to the rank and file. The tension – and speculation about what is happening at the front – could account for this distraction you noticed."

Mila considered.

"It could also be the reason," Pieter went on, "why German officers will be meeting at the Cinema tonight. Undoubtedly, there is news to be shared, perhaps even a shuffling of troops."

Mila listened, excited to think an end to the war might be in sight, but reluctant to re-live the fading optimism that had followed the Normandy invasion.

She looked down at the drawings on his desk.

"In any case, thank you, Pieter," she said, "for trusting me with this assignment. God speed to the Allied forces. And if there is anything more I can do…"

Pieter smiled. "That is very like you, Mila. As if you have not already done so much," he tapped at the drawings."

Mila placed her hands on the desktop, surprised to find months of rancor rising to the surface. "Pieter, I am tired of being on the sidelines. That mission at the coast yesterday stirred my blood. I am capable and careful, and I am sick of this war and of an endless tide of Hitler's Nazis sitting on our graves. I pray the end of the war is near, but until it comes, I am ready to get my hands dirty. I ask again, what can I do?"

Pieter's green eyes bored into her.

"I am a trained marksman, Pieter, in case you did not know," she said. "I have trained at the shooting range, alongside my father, since I was twelve years old, and I daresay I can handle a firearm as well as anyone – and better than most."

Pieter sat back in his seat. "So. A German speaker, a trained marksman, and a beautiful woman…perfect qualifications for a spy."

It stopped her for a moment. Was he mocking her? But she kept to her purpose. "Good, then," she said. "Throw me into the trenches. Give me the chance to show you what I am made of."

Pieter was still for nearly a minute. The he leaned toward her. "You know Johan Steegen, *ja*? He has an auto repair shop on the Damstraat?"

"I do. My father trusts his beloved Daimler to him."

"Good. Steegen maintains for us a small arsenal among his stock of automobile parts. I will be at his shop in one hour. If you can meet us there – with the Daimler if you can, so that all seems legitimate – you may be able to help us to make the most of this evening's German meeting at the Cinema."

Mila was prepared when her father asked why she wanted the Daimler.

"I'm taking it to Amsterdam," she told him, "I will lunch there with my friend, Anna Nykerk. Never fear, Papa, I will be home in time for dinner – and I will send your regards to the Nykerks."

• • •

She drove the car into a bay at Steegen's auto shop minutes before noon. Johan and Pieter were deep in discussion when she swung through the shop's glass door.

"*Mevreow* Brouwer," Johan inclined his head.

"Mila, please. How are you, Johan?"

"As well as any," Steen said, as they moved off to a small office and closed the door. "Doing my best from day to day."

Pieter wasted no time. "As you may know, Mila," he said, "the Cinema here is open three days a week from noon until four, mostly showing short films and a lot of German propaganda. It is open today for the matinee before the Reich meeting this evening."

Mila nodded.

"The meeting presents a unique opportunity for us to rid the Reich of an untold number of officers. But it is dangerous, Mila. This is something Daan Mulder and I might have carried out ourselves but the timing is wrong. He and I are heading up another risky operation elsewhere tonight."

He paused. In any case, a lovely German speaker out for an entertainment might be the better option."

Mila listened.

"If you think you are up to it, you will attend today's matinee," Pieter said, looking over at Steegen.

Johan held out his hand, palm open, and Pieter held up one of two small devices.

"You would need to manage, sometime during the afternoon, to plant this small incendiary device someplace inside the Cinema where it will not be noticed."

He slipped the small, bullet-like object into her hand. "It is a flammable apparatus that can be activated from outside the building. You understand?"

"I think so."

"Step one is to place it discreetly this afternoon."

"And then?"

"Step two," he said, handing her the second device, "is to circle back to the Cinema this evening while the meeting of the Germans is in progress – sometime between eight and ten. You will carry this detonator in your pocket. It is an electronic connector, Mila. When you depress it, it will set off the device you planted earlier and the Cinema will go up in flames."

She nodded slowly, but her heartbeat quickened.

Pieter put a hand on her shoulder. "In any case, a beautiful young woman walking past the Cinema is less likely to be questioned, I think, than a man. But again, it is risky, Mila. We will understand if you are not ready for it…because if you are caught – "

He did not need to say anymore.

Mila closed her eyes her eyes for a moment. *What if she were recognized – accosted by someone who had sat at her father's table?*

Pieter seemed to read her mind. "It is reasonable to expect, I think, that once the meeting has begun, there will be few, if any, Germans outside the building. Still, I reemphasize the risk."

Mila took a moment. "I would not be honest if I said it does not frighten me, Pieter." She took a breath. "But I want to do it. I want to be the one to blast those Nazi pigs into oblivion."

EVI

It was warm under the heavy patchwork quilt, and there seemed no reason for her to hurry. Evi rolled over on her side and reflected once again on her encounter with the American airman.

He had been in hiding with a Dutch farm family for nearly six months, he had told Evi and the Resistance guards as they retreated from the German's hastily dug gravesite – since shortly after the Normandy invasion.

"I was damned lucky when I was shot down," he told them. "My parachute drifted in the wind and I landed in a wooded area less than a mile from here. I didn't know it then, but it was somewhere on the Beekhof farmland. Do you know them?"

Evi did not. Her companions exchanged glances.

"You are correct," one of them said in a mix of Dutch and English. "You were damned lucky you were not shot down by the Germans."

"I realize that," the American told them. "The Beekhofs took me in. They're fine people – hard-working farmers. Their young son found me while he was scouting the field for dry firewood. I had a displaced knee and a slight concussion. Somehow, they got me back on my feet, and I've been there ever since. I owe them."

"Why are you out here after dark, Officer Reese – I assume without proper papers?"

"*Behagen. Ik* Jake." The American had picked up some Dutch.

"Jake, then. Even here, outside the city, you put yourself at risk as well as the Beekhofs."

"No," he had said. "I have papers." He reached into his jacket pocket and produced them.

The men had squinted at the identification. "A German identification?'

The American had sighed. "A German who was living here in the Netherlands. The Beekhofs have a friend in the civic bureau. He was able to secure these for me."

"You know some Dutch."

"I'm learning. But it's hard to be shut up here, away from my unit. Sometimes I feel like I'm jumping out of my skin. I need to stretch my legs now and then…with any luck, maybe figure out some kind of way to get back to my unit."

He paused, glancing at Evi. "Anyway, as it turned out, it was a good thing for this young lady that I happened to be passing by."

It had occurred to Evi then that the American might think she was a prostitute – or a Nazi sympathizer – or both. She felt the color rising in her cheeks. But before she could respond, her bodyguards had circled around her.

"We were seconds behind you," the taller of her bodyguards broke through her mortification. "You are lucky we did not shoot you first…"

"We need to get this girl home," his companion said. "If you have any sense, Jake Reese, you will return straightaway to the Beekhof farm. In these dangerous times, it takes more than luck to survive."

• • •

Mam had been wide-eyed with fright by the time Evi slipped through the door of the barge – the more so when she saw the dirty smudges on her skirt.

"Evi, *lieve god*, are you alright?"

Evi had taken her mother's hands. "I'm fine, Mam."

"I was frantic, Evi. What happened?

"Everything was good," she said, skirting the truth. "We buried another German."

Mam examined the folds of her skirt.

"I took a little fall, that is all. It is dark out there in the woods."

Mam had looked deep into her eyes. When Evi said nothing, she sighed. "Evi, this is not a good idea. I think you should reconsider."

"I will not reconsider. The Germans are starving us, beating us in the streets. If this is the way I can make them pay, I will do that."

She wanted to say more – to tell Mam she had decided she would learn to shoot, not only for her own protection, but to kill Germans whenever she had the chance.

But this was not the time, she knew. Instead, she had smiled at her mother.

"Trust me, Mam, please. I do not do this alone. I have two big bodyguards who will not hesitate to shoot if I am ever in danger – and that is more than you can say when you are in danger of being caught every time you transport a Jewish refugee in the barge or go off to pick up a load of beets or – or tulip bulbs."

Mam stood straighter. "The beets and the tulip bulbs I bring home are keeping us, and many others, from starvation."

"Yes, but what if you are stopped by the Gestapo?"

"I am a Dutch citizen, Evi. I have my papers. I live on this barge. I have the right to be on the river."

Now Evi sighed. "On the river, perhaps. But not when you are moving refugees and contraband under the noses of the Germans."

Now there was nothing more for Mam to go.

Evi reached out to hug her mother. "Is there tea?"

"Yes."

Would you like some?"

"I would."

Evi moved into the kitchen and put the pot on to boil. She waited until the tea was poured.

"Mam," she asked, as though it were an afterthought, "Do you know a family called the Beekhofs? I think they have a farm outside the city."

Mam had knit her brows together. "Beekhof. I do not think so. Why?"

Evi had shrugged. "No reason. Someone mentioned them…that is all."

ZOE

Zoe was among the first to hear the bad news – largely because Daan Mulder, like the other Resistance leaders in Haarlem, had been advised of it almost as quickly as it began in the bitter days of mid-December. The German army was launching a major offensive against the Allied forces, striking once again, as they had done unsuccessfully nearly five years earlier, in the dense woods of the Ardennes Forest.

Because of the sheer number of troops bulking up, and the number of tanks lining up to support them, *Radio Oranje* and news outlets all over the free world were calling it the Battle of the Bulge.

"But this time, unfortunately," Daan paused. "There were only a few battle-worn American divisions stationed there – mostly troops who were there to rest and recover. It appears the Germans are having an easy time breaking through."

Zoe shook her head. "But we were so sure the Normandy invasion was a turning point – that the Allies were breaking through – "

Daan's mouth twisted. "We were wrong, Zoe. Hitler was not so easily deterred. His objective now, we think, is to drive through to the coast of the English Channel and split the strength of the Allied armies."

"Can the Allies rally, do you think?"

"We can only hope so."

Zoe sighed. "Will there never be an end to this war?"

There was a long moment of silence before Daan rose. "Well. There is work to be done tonight, as you well know, and if all goes well, we will at least have food on our tables. I am on my way now with Pieter to the target area."

Zoe, who had watched Pieter loading explosives into Daan's old British built Austin, was prepared and anxious. She looked at her watch. "I'm right behind you," she said. "God be with us."

• • •

It was dusk by the time she parked her bicycle against an oak tree in a clearing near the railroad tracks, some twelve kilometers out of Haarlem. She bent to inspect her bicycle's wheels, which had behaved a bit oddly, and cursed silently, noting the wear and tear on the tires. *Where in this world of shortage and want was she to find new rubber tires to replace them?*

A sudden wind howled, and she looked up to realize there were patches of snow here in the deep woods. She buttoned her hooded jacket to the neck and wound a woolen scarf around her head.

In the dim light, she saw Leela Bakker and her husband stamping their feet to keep warm. Behind then were bicycles fitted with high-sided wooden carts. She waved, and Leela ran toward her, pulling her wool cap down over her ears.

"There are fifteen others here with carts like ours waiting to get into that train," she said. "Is it on time, do you know?"

"I do not, Leela." She could see her breath. "But we will all know soon, I hope. Once the train blows up, there is a good chance there will be more of us than of German survivors. But we will have to be quick to grab up the cargo and be out of here before the Germans are able to dispatch more troops."

She paused. "Our people have studied the map, yes? They know to spread out on the way back to Heemstede, to look out for possible roadblocks?"

Leela hugged herself for warmth. "These are smart people, Zoe – and they are angry and hungry. We will do what needs to be done."

• • •

It was just after dark, sitting on the cold ground in the silence of the woods that Zoe felt, rather than heard, the train approaching – a low thrumming deep in the earth that slowly gave way to sound. She prayed Daan's calculations were correct.

In moments, she heard the train drawing near, could almost see it rushing forward beyond the clearing in a rush of wind that rustled the treetops. The sound was nearly past her before she heard the blast, a great, thunderous splitting of the air that lit up the sky and turned the world red and hot.

She brought a hand up over her nose and mouth, ducking down as far as she could, bringing one arm up to protect her head, and listened as the ear-splitting sound and the eerie light gave way to intermittent rumblings and occasional small bursts of flame.

Finally, as the smoke and the acrid smell began to clear, Zoe pulled her scarf up over her nose and mouth and ventured toward the tracks.

Nearing the scorched earth nearest to the mangled train, she took in the mass of torn and twisted metal, felt the hot breath of the still-smoking wreck spread-eagled over the rails.

She thought briefly of the lives lost in the blast, the Germans who had been beating and starving and killing her countrymen for years, and stealing crops from their farmers. She marveled at the sheer power of the explosives that had produced the twisted wreckage and blessed the precision of the crew who had placed them.

Slowly, as the smoke began to clear, she saw men and women cautiously approach the track, leaving their carts and wagons to inspect the ruins and assess the best ways to manage their assignment.

One by one, they clambered aboard the rubble of smoking box cars, and there were low-throated shouts and frenzied gesturing, and the carts and wagons began to fill. Zoe moved close enough to see cartons of powdered eggs and dried beef, and crates of winter cabbage and beets.

She cheered silently. The bounty would feed hundreds, including the displaced Haarlem families and the children in hiding at the hospital.

From the corner of her eye, she caught sight of a slithering form coming toward her in the darkness. Her blood quickened. She did not have a pistol, and would not know how to use it if she did. *But lieve god, was that the barrel of a rifle?*

"Shooter!" she screamed, praying to be heard above the chaos. "Shooter! Look to my left!"

She looked around, searched for a boulder, something large enough to stop the advancing form.

Then she heard it – a shot that pierced the air, so close that it echoed in her ears, and she fell to her knees.

A split second of silence.

"Got him! Nazi bastard!"

It was a voice Zoe did not know. She looked up to see a barrel-chested farmer inspecting the now-still German.

"He's dead," the man shouted. "But if one survived the blast, there could be others. Best to have a good look around!"

The chaos increased, people milling about, more pistols at the ready. Zoe watched, wondering again if she could ever bring herself to shoot.

Finally, the uproar faded. "I don't see any movement," someone shouted. "Quickly, now!"

"*Ja*, please!" Zoe cupped her hands and yelled. "We need to be quickly out of here."

• • •

She waved at Leela, who hurried past, hauling a wagon full of food. Her husband followed, and others came up behind them, cycling off in different directions and disappearing beyond the tree line. Zoe prayed. She wished she had had a cart to hitch to her own bicycle, though she wasn't sure now that her tires could have borne the extra weight.

She blew a stream of air into the night sky, wondering how long it would be before the train wreck was detected, before firefighters and railroad men and Nazi personnel arrived at the grizzly scene.

In the quiet darkness, she hopped on her bicycle. She would not stay long enough to find out.

MILA

Mila left the Daimler at home and walked to the Cinema, arriving at three in the afternoon. She paid her admission, then loitered in the rococo lobby with a half-hearted crowd of ticket holders looking, she supposed, for any means to escape the struggle of daily life.

Anxious, she did her best to blend in, avoiding eye contact, pretending to smoke a cigarette in the lobby and studying her surroundings as she waited for the show to begin.

Three potted plants badly in need of care stood against a window near the entrance. When she was finished with the cigarette, she approached one of the pots and tamped it out in the dry earth. As she did so, she dropped in the small device she had secreted in her hand and half-buried it in the soil. Glancing around her, she retrieved the used cigarette, dropped it into a trash can, and joined the twenty or thirty people making their way into the theater.

She sat through a thirty-minute travelogue touting the finest beer gardens in Berlin, Munich, and Hamburg, then an old Greta Garbo film about a wayward young woman being punished in a harsh reform school.

It was nearly intolerable, and by the time she got home at well after five, she was filled with a nervous energy. She took a bath to help steady her nerves, then dressed in a plain black skirt and sweater and moved quietly down the stairs.

She had picked up her coat and was nearly at the front door when her father's voice stopped her.

"Mila? Where are you off to?"

She turned to face him, her expression neutral. "Out to have dinner with friends, Father. I will not be late."

"A friend for lunch in Amsterdam and now friends for dinner." His expression was clearly skeptical. "No, Mila, I do not think so. In any case, it could be dangerous out there tonight. The Reich officers have called a meeting, as you are aware. You know how much they drink, my dear, and they tend to get unruly when they do."

"But I promised, Father," she felt her heart sink. "And we will not be out on the streets in any case."

Her father was adamant. "No, Mila. Please indulge me and cancel. We have no dinner guests scheduled this evening. Just your mother and me. The three of us. Won't that be nice?"

Mila thought frantically. "But father, I am to be the fourth at bridge. They will not be able to play without me."

"Then they will have each other for company. No, Mila. Dinner will be served at seven. Your mother and I will be delighted to have you to ourselves."

• • •

At seven precisely, she took her place at the table, dressed, as expected, in a proper dinner dress set off with her father's birthday pearls. She had alternately raged and fretted and agonized, even considered alerting Pieter that the mission was in peril. But in the end, she decided that if she could manage to sit through dinner, there should time enough for her to get back to the Cinema before the German gathering was over.

To her surprise, her mother was already seated. More and more frequently these evenings, she begged off with a headache and took dinner in her room. But tonight, she sat tall and elegant in navy blue silk, her steel gray hair in a fashionable chignon.

"You look lovely, Mila," she said, her expression rueful. "As well you should. Your dressmaking bills have been enormous."

Mila opened her mouth, but her mother shushed her. "It is not that we mind, for heaven's sake, Mila. You have an admirable fashion sense. Are you still wearing your own designs?"

Mila swallowed. "For the most part, yes. Mother – and I do have a wonderful seamstress."

"So you do…and in these trying times, the world is need of beauty.'

She leaned toward Mila as Reit filled her wine glass. "So, my dear, when this war is over, do you plan to go back to design school?"

Her father strode in. "Sorry to be late. I had to take a phone call." He seated himself, signaled for the wine. "Do I hear something about going back to school?"

Mila held a hand over her glass. "None for me, thank you." She looked at her father. "Possibly – perhaps some advanced classes in fashion design."

To her vast relief, her mother signaled for dinner to be served before the wine glasses were refilled. "Pity," she said, "for the universities to be closed just when we need them most."

As if, Mila thought, they had closed on their own simply to inconvenience the wealthy.

There was a roast of beef with potatoes and broccoli. Mila pushed the food around her plate, glancing at her watch under the table.

As dessert was served, she asked to be excused. "I can still make that bridge game, Father."

He looked at her for a long moment. "All right then, Mila, go ahead. Take the car, if you wish."

"I'll walk, I think, but thank you."

She said quick good nights, kissed her mother on the cheek, and hurried out of the room.

EVI

Mam's ear was glued to the *Radio Oranje* broadcast, her face inches from the contraband radio that sat on the table between them.

Evi listened with dread. The Germans had broken through the American front in almost the same spot where they had broken through years ago. But this time, apparently, the American troops had been depleted and unprepared, giving the Germans an opportunity to seize key crossroads on their march to the Meuse River.

So fierce and determined was the onslaught, the British commentor said, that some Belgian townspeople were already taking down their Allied flags and displaying swastikas.

Mam began to cry. "How could this happen?" she sobbed. "Only six months ago, after Normandy, we were so certain liberation was near!"

Evi took her hand. "God knows," she murmured, close to tears herself.

• • •

When she could listen no more, she picked up her mug of tea, went to her sleeping quarters and sat heavily on her bed. Then she set the mug on her nightstand, pushed open the curtain at the front of her closet, and fingered the silk scarves and taffeta dresses Mila had given her to wear for her rendezvous with German officers.

She recalled every moment of each encounter, the first one that went exactly as planned, the second less so, but successful in the end, even if it had taken an American airman appearing out of nowhere coming to her rescue.

She fumed for a moment. She *would* learn to shoot. She might not yet be seventeen, but she had proven herself to be capable under pressure – and picking off Nazis one at a time was not enough in the scheme of things. She wanted to kill dozens – maybe even hundreds, until there was food enough and freedom in the Netherlands.

It was clear from the *Radio Oranje* broadcast that the Americans needed help. They needed the French, the British, the Americans, the Dutch, all of them, to step up their efforts in whatever ways they could. How fast could they respond – and would they?

She sat on her bed and sipped the cooling tea. She would try to reach Mila tomorrow – or perhaps she could talk to Zoe Visser, who was near enough to Daan Mulder to plead Evi's case for learning to shoot.

ZOE

She was halfway to Heemstede, just past the Franz Hals Museum, when she came suddenly upon a makeshift German check point. She felt her heart begin to hammer. Had news of the train wreck spread so quickly?

She was too near, even in the murky darkness, not to have been spotted by the guards. But l*ieve god,* what of the others, carrying all that food?

"Approach and halt!" The guard spoke in rapid German, but there was no mistaking his intent. His rifle was pointed in her direction and her blood froze.

She managed to slow the bicycle to a stop and put both her hands in the air.

A younger guard, who looked barely old enough to shave, joined them. "Papers, *bitte.*"

She reached inside her jacket for her identification papers, keeping one hand in the air.

The younger guard examined them, looking up more than once to check her face against the photo.

"What is your purpose?" he said in passable Dutch.

Zoe tried a smile. "I was out for some exercise," she said. "I fell asleep, though, when I stopped to rest. I am horrified to be out after curfew – and look, my bicycle tires are damaged. I am afraid to pedal too fast."

The older guard looked at her sternly. "Your bag, *bitte*."

Evi could not remember all that was in her shoulder bag, but she handed it over and held her breath.

"I am a veterinarian – an animal doctor, in Haarlem," she said, with as much friendliness as she could manage. "I take care of pups and kittens who are sick."

The guard was not impressed. He pored through her bag, trained a flashlight inside, examined everything in the inner and outer pockets.

"Where are you coming from?"

She paused. "No place, really. A little clearing a kilometer or two up the road When I woke up and realized how late it was, I turned around to go home."

He regarded her through narrowed eyes.

"Please," she said. "*Bitte*, you must believe me. I fell asleep. I meant no harm."

"Sit." He motioned her to a bench.

Zoe sat, huddled into her coat, anxiety gnawing at her belly.

The pair of guards conversed in German, glancing back at her from time to time. They kept her sitting there for nearly an hour. It was all she could do to sit still.

Finally, the older guard beckoned her.

"*Gehen*," he barked. "Go!"

She moved to her bicycle, her mind working.

"My bag, *bitte*," she began.

But the stern-faced guard motioned her through, whacking his stick against the back of her bicycle as she passed.

Her breathing slowed, but her thoughts were frantic. Was there anything in her bag that could feed information to the Germans – a business card, a scribbled note, anything that could mark her as a Resistance fighter – or implicate someone else?

Were the Germans yet aware of the wrecked train? Where were the farmers and their carts? She prayed they were more vigilant than she about watching for, and dodging, German road blocks.

Pedaling hard, worried about her tires, she headed in the direction of the hospital. She sensed, rather than saw, a second check point on the approach to the city limits, and managed to circumvent it, certain now that the Germans were already hunting for connections to the demolished train.

• • •

At the hospital's loading dock, to her great relief, she saw half a dozen carts and wagons being offloaded – nourishment enough for weeks, perhaps longer. She looked for Leela or her husband, did not see either, but she recognized Lukas Jensen's mother.

"*Mevreow* Jensen," she said, approaching. "The German check points. *Godjjzdank, y*ou were able to avoid them."

The woman did not stop unloading goods. "We were careful," she said heavily. "We left our wagons behind, passed through the check point, then circled back and took another route. My husband stayed behind to warn the others."

"*Lieve god -*"

"Do not think of it, Dr. Visser. He will be fine. We would do it again in a moment."

It was dark, but Zoe scanned the horizon and saw another bicycle and wagon approaching. Other volunteers were leaving as their carts were unloaded, so it was not possible for her to know for certain how many were accounted for.

She decided to circle the property to be sure they were not being observed. The parking lot was sparsely filled, little movement this late in the evening, and the only uniform she saw belonged to the guard posted at the door, who waved at her as she approached.

By nine, the approach of volunteers had slowed to a trickle. Zoe shivered in the cold night air.

MILA

If she walked quickly, she would reach the Cinema by nine, she thought, counting her steps, looking for stars in the dark night sky, anything to keep her from thinking about what she was about to do.

In her mind's eye, the street would be deserted, all those Reich bastards packed like sardines in the cramped seats of the Cinema. She would walk past casually, across the street from the building, depress the detonator she held deep in her coat pocket and walk away quickly, undetected, as the theater burst into flame.

She gingerly fingered the small device, just to be sure it was still there, careful to avoid the lever. She was going to be fine…absolutely fine…assuming the connection worked. Assuming there was no one around to see her… Assuming her father did not find out and murder her if the Nazis did not…

The little she had eaten threatened to come up in her throat. She closed her eyes and swallowed. What had she been thinking, volunteering for this mission, what made her think she truly had the nerve to do this?

She reminded herself these were ruthless Nazis, the same leering pigs she had toyed with and loathed during her father's endless dinners, their polished boots firmly planted on the necks of the innocent, the Reich slowly smothering them to death.

She wished Herr Hitler himself were in that Cinema. How satisfying would it be to annihilate him…?

That was the thought on which she would focus. She could do it. Of course, she could…

• • •

To her distress, as she neared the Cinema, she saw three SS men in heavy black coats standing outside, smoking cigars. In the dark, she could not see their faces. It was not likely they could not see hers.

Head down, a scarf obscuring her face, Mila crossed, head down, to the other side of the street. She wished she had thought to take Hondje with her. Just a woman out walking her dog…

But she had not. *Lieve God*, she had not thought to do so. And now…now it was time.

EVI

Evi haunted *Radio Oranje* for news of the fighting in the Ardennes, but no amount of hoping or praying changed the disheartening fact; the Germans' surprise attack had overwhelmed the depleted American forces. Hitler's army was advancing, more or less unimpeded. On top of that, bad weather was prohibiting aerial reconnaissance, and American forces were suffering high casualties.

On the verge of tears, she stashed the radio in its hiding place and paced the barge's cramped spaces. The day was gray under an overcast sky, and from the window, she could see the river waters rippling under the might of a persistent wind.

Mam was at the Dans Hal, boxing up a supply of food that had appeared there out of the blue, and there was no one presently in the hold.

Unable to contain her own restless energy, she wrapped a woolen scarf around her head, put on gloves and her warmest winter coat, and let herself out the barge. She hopped on her bicycle and headed to the main road, pedaling fiercely against the wind with no destination in mind.

Perhaps Mam would bring home something besides root vegetables and tulip bulbs. She sometimes woke herself in the night dreaming of beef, or sausages, her tastebuds salivating, and cried soundlessly into her pillow, pressing her hands against her stomach to ease the near-constant hunger pangs...

• • •

She could turn off at the old school road and visit Sophie, she thought. She had not seen her since that last day of school. It seemed so long ago. Had Sophie seen or heard from Lukas Jensen since he joined the Resistance?

She could head to the pet *kliniek* and look for Zoe, or try to find out where Mila lived and plead her case for shooting lessons.

But she kept pedaling along the main road, eyes stinging in the unforgiving wind.

All at once, she found herself at the tavern where she had nearly been raped. She stared at the squat brick building now, drab and deserted in the daylight, and it came to her in a rush that she had never had the chance to properly thank the American who saved her.

She narrowed her eyes against the wind and looked around. She had no idea where the Beekhof farm was, but it must not be too far, she though, from the tavern where the American had come upon them.

Squinting, she saw perhaps half a kilometer ahead a road sign indicating a crossroad. She pedaled until she reached it, then hesitated. Left, or right?

She tossed a mental coin and turned right, pedaled a full kilometer before she saw the first sign of life – an empty pen, perhaps for sheep, far back from the road, and beyond it a farmhouse badly in need of paint, surrounded by fir trees, and seemingly deserted.

She pedaled closer, read the name on the mailbox – Van de Berg, with a slash of black paint crossed through it. Evi's shoulders slumped. *What had become of the Van de Bergs?*

These were large tracts, she discovered as she moved on, separated by lengths of rundown fencing, mostly withered acreage, and no sign of a working farm.

Pulling up short, she turned around and pedaled in the other direction, crossing over the main road with fading expectation. She had not gone more than two kilometers when a silo loomed into view, set far back from the road.

She pedaled faster until she came upon a break in the roadside foliage, a narrow dirt road that could be a driveway. Had she not noticed the battered mail box nearly hidden in a bank of overgrown ivy, she would have missed it altogether. She pushed the brush aside. *Beekhof.*

Hesitating, she sat there for a moment, then made her way up the dirt road, her tires spitting dirt. Eventually, the dirt road turned to gravel. She heard a dog barking as she came upon a pen with a few squealing pigs, a single horse grazing beyond a picket fence. A big German Shepherd loomed in front of her, barking furiously, racing at her side to the weathered porch.

She took in the two-story white frame farmhouse, its black trim peeling in places, and rang the doorbell. There was no answer. The dog danced around her, barking. She glanced at the windows, covered by curtains, and rang the doorbell again.

"Nice dog," she said, shading her eyes against the bleak winter sun. "I don't mean anyone any harm." She pedaled backward, looking for movement behind the upstairs windows.

She was about to give up, when the door was opened little more than a crack. A boy of perhaps fourteen or fifteen peered out. He wore denim overalls, a worn plaid shirt, and a decidedly wary expression. The Shepherd barked.

"Hush, Otto."

"Hallo," she said quickly. "My name is Evi Strobel. I hope I have come to the right place. I am looking for Jacob Reese."

The boy retreated, began to close the door. "There is nobody here by that name."

"Please!" Evi held a hand against the door. "Please, wait! The American airman saved my life."

The boy peered out again, eyes narrowed. "There is no American here."

He started to shut the door, but Evi was faster. "Wait! I am telling the truth. Jacob Reese saved my life! I want to thank him."

The boy stared through the narrow opening. "Why did your life need saving?"

"I was – I was in a very dangerous situation," she blurted, a hand still on the door. "Someone was trying to – hurt me, and the American came from out of nowhere and shot him."

A pause. "Where did this happen?"

She blinked. "At the tavern, just down the road."

The boy took a long moment. "Wait here."

Evi peered at the Shepherd. "Otto, is it? Hallo, Otto. My name is Evi."

The dog peered back, his tail wagging. "Good boy, Otto." She rubbed her hands together, swaying in the cold.

Finally, the boy reappeared in the doorway. "It is cold," he opened the door a bit wider. "Come in. Jacob is out in the field with my father. You can wait inside."

ZOE

Piercing sirens for most of the night made sleep impossible. Zoe tossed and turned, reliving the flash and fury of the exploding train, haunted by the fear that not all of the volunteers had made it safely home.

She was up and pacing before first light, and from the moment she emerged from her small apartment, she felt the tension in the air.

Word of the train explosion was likely everywhere by now, and if the liberated food was an unexpected windfall, there was little doubt the Germans would find a way to unleash new furies in revenge.

Daan was waiting for her at the *kliniek*. He motioned her into his office and closed the door.

"If I close my eyes," she said, "I can still feel the force of the blast."

Daan nodded. "Mission accomplished."

She did not wait for him to ask. "Wagons full of food were unloaded at the hospital, Daan, but German checkpoints popped up quickly. I ran into one myself, and *Godjizdank* I was not transporting food, or I might not even be here this morning."

She shivered at the memory of the cold-eyed German guards and prayed, once again, that there was nothing in her purloined shoulder bag that could be of any value to the Reich.

Daan's voice was soft. "We have managed two huge offensives in as many days, Zoe – the train explosion and a great blast at the Cinema building. The Germans are beyond furious. They are on high alert, and no doubt we will feel the repercussions."

He sighed. "But years of oppression have toughened us, Zoe. We all know the risks we take."

"*Ja,*" said Zoe, still anxious to know if all the volunteer farmers were safely home. "But some of us bear the burden of putting others in harm's way."

"And so it must be, Zoe," Dan leaned toward her. "If we did not, there would be no resistance at all and Hitler would long ago have had his way."

That much it true, Zoe realized. But it did little to calm her fear.

She sighed. "I need to go to the Dans Hal to see if everyone is accounted for – but the tires on my bicycle are wearing thin."

"Go, "he said. "Take my bicycle. It is just behind the building – and let me have a look at yours. Some have been repairing their worn tires with sections cut from garden hose. Let me see what I can do."

MILA

She must have blacked out when the force of the blast sent her flying, because the last thing she remembered clearly was depressing the device in her coat pocket.

Curled up in bed in her spacious bedroom, blinds closed, Hondje's warm body pressed against her left hip, Mila tried to bring it into focus. She felt – exhausted, triumphant, humiliated, and lucky to be alive. How was it possible to feel all those things at once?

She had been unprepared for the force of the blast, the noise, the smell, the rush of flames leaping in burning fingers from the Cinema building into the night sky. So sudden and powerful was the red-hot conflagration that it had tossed her into the air, and the next thing she knew, a pair of beefy hands had scooped her up and carried her away.

She had hardly heard the voice at her ear, so intent was she on the blaze, the screams, the stampeding feet, the brilliance of the night sky.

Then she had looked toward the source of the voice, and recognized the face of one of her father's more frequent German dinner guests, though she could not bring his name to mind.

"Mila?" His florid face was inches from hers. "Mila Brouwer, *ja? Geht es dir gut*? Are you alright?"

Fear snaked down her spine, and she did not recall answering, but he scooped her up, lifting her as though she were weightless, and carried her to an SS van. Ignoring her pleas, he had lowered her into the back seat, slammed the doors, and sped off into the night.

She could only think he was taking her to German headquarters, and she wavered between terror and resolve.

Slowly, the chaos and the unholy light receded, and the next thing she knew, the man was steadying her gently on the front porch of her home and reaching out to ring the door chime.

She remembered the confusion in her father's face, the narrowed eyes, the creased forehead, the question not yet formed on his lips.

"Herr Brouwer," the German was the first to speak. "There was an accident – a great explosion at the Cinema. Your daughter was nearby, but mostly unhurt, I think. It was fortunate that it was I who came upon her."

EVI

The room was worn but homey – chintz-covered furniture, a bookcase full of books and a slow fire burning in the hearth. Evi loosened her coat and took off her woolen scarf.

She was warming her hands, bent over the fire, when she heard the voice behind her. "Well, hey, so it *is* you! Hello there."

She turned to face the tall American, slim and broad shouldered in blue jeans and a too-tight flannel shirt, and younger than he had seemed to be in the dark of night. Suddenly, she found herself speechless.

He smiled. "You must have a name."

"Evi," she forced the syllables out. "My name is Evi Strobel. I – came here to thank you. I must thank you. If not for you, I do not know what might have happened to me that night…"

"I don't know about that. You had two big bodyguards there, ready to shoot the bastard. I just happened to get there first."

She nodded dumbly. In the light of day, he seemed perhaps no more than in his early twenties, with hair the color of wheat falling over his forehead, earnest hazel eyes, and a strong jaw line evident above his neatly trimmed beard.

"Well, my name, as you know, is Jacob Reese. Jake to my friends…"

"I wanted you to know that am not a collaborator, Jacob Reese," Evi blurted. "Nor am I accustomed to being with drunken Nazis in a beer bar…"

A hint of a smile. "I think I may have figured that out. I don't know what you were up to, but it's none of my beeswax, I guess."

She looked at him, '*Beeswacks?*"

"Business," he laughed. "I mean it was none of my *business*."

"Ah," she murmured, still staring.

After an awkward moment, he motioned her to a seat on the well-worn chintz-covered sofa. He sat cross-legged in a chair across from her. "How old are you, Evi Strobel? Fifteen? Sixteen?"

She looked down at her short plaid skirt. "Seventeen," she lied. "Eighteen next February. And I do what I do for the Resistance."

"Yep, I kind of figured that out, too, or you wouldn't have had those big guys watching out for you."

She stuck out her chin. "It is a dangerous job, but I will do it again, if they ask me to. It is my way to help rid the world of even one Nazi at a time."

She paused. "But next time I will carry my own pistol."

"Ah." The American seemed to take her measure. "And are you trained to handle a pistol?"

She shrugged. "Not yet. But I can learn. And I will."

"How?"

"I am not yet sure. Target practice. I plan to arrange it through the Resistance Council."

The boy who had answered the door – the farmer's son, Evi assumed, poked his head into the room. "My Mam asks if you want some tea."

Evi rose, Jacob Reese following. "Oh, no, please. Tell your mother thank you, but I do not wish to overstay my welcome." She grabbed her scarf from the arm of the sofa.

Jacob Reese followed her to the door. "So, how did you find me?"

She shrugged. "It is not far to look from the tavern where you found me."

"You live nearby?"

"Not too far."

He held the door open, peered out. "You bicycled here."

"I did."

"Well, Evi Strobel," he said, smiling, "I wish you good luck with your target practice. To tell you the truth, it felt damned good to me to take out that Nazi at the tavern."

She hesitated at the door, reluctant to leave, and not just because of the cold. "I um...I just want to thank you once again for coming to my rescue, Jacob Reese."

He loomed over her in the open doorway. "It's Jake. Jake will do."

She hopped on her bike and pedaled down the drive. "I like Jacob better," she murmured to herself, facing into the wind.

ZOE

The Dans Hal was abuzz with rumor and speculation. Zoe moved through the crowd, hearing bits and pieces. F*armer missing...Resistance offensives...A crisis for the Allies...what next?*

"Zoe, over here" Leela Bakker called to her over the din.

Zoe moved quickly, avoiding an ambush, followed her to the hidden office. "Leela, I can hear the chatter. Has someone gone missing?" she asked.

Leela bit her lip. "Jozef Haan," she whispered. "His wife is frantic. He did not return home last night."

Zoe closed her eyes. "The roadblocks. I do not know how the Germans reacted so quickly."

Leela shrugged. "My husband and I saw Jozef pedal off, carrying crates of food from the train. He was just ahead of us when we left. It was dark, Zoe. We were all on edge. Sad to say, we have not seen him since."

"I was detained at a check point myself last night – for more than an hour. I was terrified. *Godjizdan*k, I was not transporting food."

She paced the small office, worried again about the contents of the bag she had been forced to leave behind with the German guards.

"Is someone with Jozef's wife?"

"Yes," Leela nodded. "Several of the other wives. But that is little comfort, I am afraid. She is already fearing the worst."

Zoe threw her head back, frustrated. "I do not know what to say, Leela. I feel it is my fault for asking…"

Leela spoke through tears. "There is nothing to say, Zoe. You are not to blame. We knew the risk when we agreed to empty that train."

She laid a hand on Zoe's arm. "We understand the risk we face just trying to live through this horror, every minute of every day."

Zoe felt her own tears spring.

A moment of silence, then Leela's ragged sigh. "But there is reason to be proud, Zoe. Our mission was accomplished. There will be food on Dutch tables this Christmas."

MILA

In a fit of restlessness at four in the morning, leaning against the skirts in her bedroom closet as the shrill of air raid sirens blared in the background, she learned from Pieter that more than sixty highly placed officers of the German Reich had been killed in the Cinema explosion.

She searched her conscience for a shred of remorse, but she was unable to find one – only pride in what she had accomplished, and thankfulness that the German officer had been out for a smoke, and that he knew her, as a Brouwer, to be a friend of the Reich. She was begrudgingly thankful for the endless dinners she had sat through.

She still did not remember much of the aftermath of the blast, but she knew without doubt she would do it again if she had the chance.

Still, it was time, she knew, as she lay there hours later, curled around Hondje's warm body, for her to get out of her bedroom and face her father.

Sighing, she threw off the covers and sat on the edge of the bed. She had skirted the truth more than once of late. But she could not recall outright lying to her father since the summer day when she was nine, when she denied demolishing the raspberry kuchen Reit had left cooling on the kitchen sill.

She remembered praying, her blue eyes wide, that there was no jam on her chin as she told the outrageous fib – and her father had decided to accept her denial. Perhaps, he had said, some hungry itinerant had found it.

To this day, Mila could not fathom which had been the worst of her punishment; the stomach ache she had endured for more than a day, or the guilt she felt over the shameless lie she had told.

In any case, she had not lied to him again…obscured the truth, she admitted, moving to open the heavy satin draperies to the sunny day outside. Worse, she would continue to do so if that was it took to thwart his alliance with the Reich.

She blinked in brilliance and turned toward her dressing room. It was time to face her father's questions. She shuddered to think of the outcome.

EVI

The yuletide holidays had been difficult at best since the war took over their lives, but this Christmas Eve was the saddest Evi could remember. There was no tree, no gaily be-ribboned garlands, only a single, scrawny wreath Mam had fashioned from greenery at the edge of the woods.

They had both been glued to *Radio Oranje* of late, fearful of new tortures the Germans would rain down upon the Dutch in punishment for their dual humiliation – two successful Resistance offensives that not only took the lives of Reich officers but that embarrassed Herr Hitler who, it was said, was even now planning retaliation.

Worse, there was little encouraging news on the Allied front. This morning there had been reports that improved weather conditions helped the Allies launch air attacks on German supply lines. But what that meant for those who waited and prayed for liberation was still impossible to know.

To boot, Evi had heard from Sophie yesterday that the father of little Annemarie Haan, the freckled little redhead who had followed her to school one day, was missing – presumably detained, perhaps even murdered by the Nazis after his part in looting food from the demolished train.

Evi had never met the little girl's father, but she knew the heartbreak of losing her own papa, and she said a little prayer, useless as it likely was, for the poor man's safe deliverance.

She sat up, aware of a curious aroma wafting from the kitchen – a tantalizing smell not unlike the aroma of fresh-baked bread, as Mam used the last of Mila's flour and jam to prepare some version of Christmas kuchen.

"There," Mam said into the evening gloom, setting the still-warm pastry on the table.

Evi breathed in the yeasty aroma and rounded the table, inspecting it from every angle. There was no hint of cinnamon, no dusting of sugar, and surely no raisins or pecans. But the cake rested on Mam's favorite Christmas platter, a reasonable cousin of the original.

She smiled. "Mam, that is the best of all possible Christmas gifts. I will forever remember it. *Danke je.*"

Mam blinked away tears. "That is not all, Evi." She hurried off into her sleeping berth, returning moments later with a small package wrapped in re-salvaged tissue.

Evi opened it carefully to preserve the tissue, and shrieked as she unfolded the woolen cap inside. It had been handknit from the bright blue yarn Mam had rescued from the old crocheted afghan and it was embroidered on one side with what looked like a bright yellow butterfly.

Evi pulled it over her fine blonde hair. "Oh, I love it, Mam, *danke je*. I will wear it every day!"

She smiled. "Now, sit. I have something for you."

She slipped into her quarters and brought out the homemade candle fashioned from the scraps of candles past, and watched Mam carefully unwrap it and pretend, at least, to love and admire it.

"I wish it could have been more," Evi murmured, pushing back at tears. "How I wish it were a real Christmas…"

"It *is* a real Christmas," Mam jumped up to hug her. "We have each other, Evi. We have our good health – and there is Christmas kuchen!"

ZOE

Zoe tried to get through to her parents, to share some semblance of a happy yuletide, but the phone lines, even more unreliable since the dual explosions, were jammed.

Rations had been cut once again, and there were reports that SS officers were going from door to door looking for suspects, shooting people on the street for the flimsiest of reasons to avenge the German lives lost in the dual Resistance offensives.

Still, she felt suffocated, stranded in the confines of her flat, doomed to a lonely Christmas and anxious about the fate of the missing farmer. She was helpless, saddened, and silenced, and it made her jumpy

She drank tea, tried to read a paper on canine influenza, took in the seams of two woolen skirts to fit her shrinking frame.

At two in the afternoon, unable to sit any longer, she put down her sewing needle, donned a heavy sweater and one of the newly altered skirts, grabbed her coat and scarf and ran out into the cold.

There were few people on the street. Most families, she imagined, were spending the day at home, doing their best to make the most of a cheerless Christmas. Even the watchful Germans were less in evidence than she had feared as she navigated the windswept streets.

Withered brown leaves found refuge at every curb, leaving the barren trees to stand watch against a threatening, battleship grey sky.

Zoe pulled her scarf up around her face.

She imagined the lot of arrogant Germans, warm and beer-soaked in their *stadsplein* headquarters, feasting on roasted Christmas goose and strudel while Hollanders survived on hardtack and tulip bulbs.

Jamming her hands into her coat pockets, she walked and walked, and it was not until she rounded a corner and saw it straight ahead of her that she realized where she had been heading.

There were few cars in the hospital parking lot, what with petrol increasingly scarce, but there were bicycles parked near the entrance. The same guard she had seen the other night stood at the revolving door entrance, stamping his feet against the cold. He looked up and nodded to her as she slipped inside.

It was marginally warmer inside. She took the elevator up to Gerritt's office, but he was not in evidence, and the desks outside were mostly deserted. One young woman put down her book to say that several administrators had the day off, and that she did not know the whereabouts of Dr. Visser.

Zoe stood in the hallway and considered. She doubted her cousin had taken had taken time off for the holidays. Finally, she pushed the elevator button for the top floor and exited into an eerie silence. She made her way in semi-darkness past canvas-shrouded windows and construction clutter, and slipped behind the faux wall.

Even then, there was only muted sound. Zoe knocked gently, the pre-arranged knock they had agreed upon to signal that the visitor was friendly. Still, heads swiveled in her direction when she entered.

Gerritt was seated at a 'patient's' bedside. He rose instantly when he saw her, crossed the room and air-kissed her on both cheeks. "*Prettige Kerst*, cousin" he whispered. Happy Christmas.

"Happy Christmas," she said, returning his smile. But her eyes looked past his shoulder, searching the crowded room for the storyteller.

MILA

Her mother was resting with a headache, Reit told her in the kitchen. But her father was waiting to see her.

No doubt, thought Mila, allowing herself a slab of the cook's brown bread with a dollop of orange marmalade. She chewed slowly, holding off the moment, but in the end, there was no putting it off.

She passed through the great room, taking no pleasure from the enormous Christmas tree, or the fireplace festooned with greenery.

"Come in," her father responded to her knock on the study door. She slipped into the room.

Blue velvet draperies fronted the windows, tied back with heavy gold cord. The walls were lined with books and trophies, and a small, carved table held an enormous world globe. Mila waited in silence until father put down his pen and looked up. "Mila. You are feeling well?"

"Yes, thank you."

Another silence. "Then explain to me what in the name of God you were doing near the Cinema when Klaus so propitiously found you."

Her father rarely invoked a Creator. Mila raised her chin. "I was – merely passing by, Father. I was walking home. I was on my way."

"On your way home. What about your alleged bridge game?"

"My friends had given up and gone by the time I arrived." She hoped the heat in her face did not show. "I was late, as you know, as I had stayed home for dinner, and so I left and was walking home alone."

Her father looked at her through narrowed eyes. "Are you telling me you know nothing about the blast that took so many German lives?"

Mila stood her ground. "I was near the Cinema, and everything went black, and all I remember is the aftermath," she said, grateful for the shred of truth. "The blast must have knocked me off my feet."

She jumped nearly out of her chair as his fist smacked the top of his desk.

"Mila, do you have any idea how fortunate you were that it was the *Obersturmfurher* who found you? Do you have any awareness of what might have happened had you been found by a less friendly Reich officer?"

Mila blinked.

He pounded the desk again. "Do you?"

"I think so, Father. *Ja,* it was fortunate that it was he who found me and that he understood my innocence."

He took a moment. But his voice, when he spoke, held menace. "Swear to me, Mila," her father said slowly, "that you were in no way involved with what occurred last night at the Cinema…"

"Why would you ask that?" She skirted the question.

"I did not hear an answer."

She tamped down her dread, raised her chin. "Why do you ask such a question?"

"Because, Mila," his voice was steely. "I suspect that your actions not only betray me, but that your sympathies lie with the Resistance."

It took every ounce of calm she could muster. She met her father's gaze.

"No more so, Father, then you betray our country when you collaborate with the Nazis who are strangling us."

EVI

There was a flurry of snow on the day before the New Year. Evi let herself out of the barge and let a few flakes melt on her tongue, then shivered, pulled her sweater close around her and let herself back in.

She paced the small cabin, filled with nervous energy. The news from the front was not encouraging. School was closed for the holiday recess, and who knew if it would open again?

She had heard nothing from Mila, and she was eager to know if there would be another rendezvous at a beer tavern. Another German dead would suit her just fine, especially if she could shoot him herself.

She closed her eyes and pictured the scene – the drunken Nazi, reaching for his zipper, then panic on his miserable face at the sight of Evi's drawn pistol.

"I could do it. I know I could," she whispered to herself. All she needed was some proper training – and a firearm.

She sat for a moment at the kitchen table, looked out over grey river meeting grey sky at a barely discernible horizon.

She knew where Zoe lived, the little flat she had been to with Mam to deliver an armchair one day. Zoe worked with Daan Mulder, and Daan was one of the Resistance leaders. *He surely can arrange for shooting lessons.*

The snow had stopped. There were hours of daylight before curfew. Mam was working a shift at the pharmacy. Evi had no way to know if Zoe was at home, but the timing was perfect if she was.

• • •

Her nose was frozen and her fingers tingled in her woolen gloves by the time she rapped on Zoe's door.

A long moment. "Who is there?"

Evi thought she heard a tremor in the voice. "It is Evi. Evi Strobel."

Another moment, then the door opened. "Evi?"

Evi smiled.

Zoe opened the door wider. "Evi, is everything all right?"

"Yes, yes," she said., the door closing behind her. "I just – I needed to see you. I do not know where Mila Brouwer lives, so I came here with a request of the Resistance."

Zoe helped her out of her coat. "A request?"

"Yes," she pulled off her gloves and rubbed her cold hands together. "Daan Mulder is a leader in the council, yes?"

It occurred to her that Zoe might not know that Evi was fighting for the cause.

She pulled off the bright blue her cap Mam had made her for Christmas, shook her blonde hair into place, and assumed what she hoped was an earnest adult pose.

"Sit, please., Evi" Zoe said. "I have tea. Would you like some?"

She turned to put the kettle on before Evi could respond, then busied herself finding cups and saucers from a high shelf. "I don't often have visitors," she murmured.

The walls of the tiny flat were painted a pale green, and two braided green and white area rugs brightened the worn wood floor. Evi saw the upholstered chair that she and Mam had delivered in Leela Baakker's truck. She sat across from it in an ancient wingback, the only other chair in the room.

In minutes, Zoe laid a tea tray on the table between them. Evi took the steaming cup.

"Now," Zoe said, sitting. "Daan is one of the Resistance leaders, *Ja*. I am not sure I can help you, Evi, but tell me what it is you want."

Evi leaned forward. "I am not sure if you know this, Zoe, but twice now, under Mila's guidance, I have – I have helped to kill Nazi officers. I flirt with them in a tavern until they are drunk, then lure them into the woods, where Resistance shooters are waiting to kill them, take their uniforms and identification paper, and leave their bodies in a ditch."

Zoe's eyes widened. "I had no idea...how old are you, Evi?"

She was tired of the question, but she told the truth. "Sixteen. Seventeen in February."

Zoe took a deep breath. "Well. You are a very brave girl."

"Mila says that as well." Evi sat up straighter. "Do you know Mila Brouwer? She was the one who recruited me."

"I know of Mila, yes. I know that she is involved with the Resistance."

"Well, the last time I – the last time I grappled with a drunken German, I was very nearly..." she could feel her face redden. "The revolting pig was squirming on top of me before he was stopped by a bullet"

"*Lieve god*, Evi..."

"I was saved that night by an American airman. His name is Jacob Reese. His plane was downed in a Dutch field and he is in hiding with a Haarlem farm family. It was fortunate for me that he was walking about that night. His bullet saved my life."

Zoe's mouth dropped open.

"I should have been able to shoot the bastard, Zoe – and I would have if I owned a pistol. That is what I want from the Resistance leaders – a pistol and the training to use it."

There was a moment of silence as Zoe leaned back in her chair. "I think I understand," she said. "I understand the danger you face. You really are a brave girl, Evi. But you surely know that owning a weapon requires a permit – and that these days, they are harder to get except for a specific purpose – like training to become a police officer."

"Some of our Dutch police are Nazi collaborators - "

"Yes, but many others work on our side – and in any case, they were almost certainly issued their weapons after they joined the force."

"But –"

"Evi, even if you applied for a permit, you are not of legal age. I cannot think of a circumstance under which you could legally own a firearm."

Evi paused. "Illegally, then. Surely the Resistance leaders have their own stash of firearms."

Zoe's eyebrows shot up.

"I know they do, because I help to procure them. I think it is only fair to see that I am able to protect myself."

Zoe looked at her. She poured more tea. "Drink this while it is hot, Evi…I will take your request to Daan."

PART THREE

Haarlem, the Netherlands
January 1945

ZOE

There were no patients scheduled at the *kliniek* on this third day of January, and Zoe expected there would be few in the wake of the German crackdown.

She sat at her desk updating files, wondering how long the pet *kliniek* could survive without a steady, if diminishing, stream of income.

Already, they had had to let Lise go, and only days before Christmas. Daan had been heartbroken given the season, but Zoe had agreed to a cut in pay, and she knew that Daan had not had taken a salary for weeks.

She looked at the clock. It was after ten. Unusual for Daan to be this late. She busied herself reviewing professional dissertations that had been piling up for months – the first one dull enough to have her on the edge of nodding off.

She was sitting at the desk in a half-wakeful state, lulled by the rhythmic ticking of the clock, when the outer door crashed open.

"They've taken him!"

Zoe jumped up, her stupor shattered, recognizing the voice of Daan's wife. She ran to the outer office.

Ilke's face was white with fright, her blonde hair askew, her coat opened over a blue flannel nightgown.

"They beat down the door, Zoe. They dragged him away!" She clutched at Zoe's white coat.

Zoe blinked, grabbed for Ilke's hands, tried to lead her to a seat. But Ilke was too distraught to follow.

"They dragged him out of the door, Zoe, two big Gestapo bruisers. They never even told us why, just hauled him off without saying a word – hauled him down the stairs like a sack of laundry..."

"*Lieve god*," Zoe murmured, heartbeat thrumming. "Please, Ilke, sit."

Ilke burst into tears and folded into herself. Zoe led her to a chair.

"Daan tried to reason with them," Ilke wailed. "He tried, but the beasts would not listen."

Zoe sat in the chair next to Ilke, holding her shaking hands. "When did this happen, Ilke?"

"I cannot be certain...half an hour ago, perhaps..." Ilke drew a shuddering breath, her lovely blue eyes red-rimmed. "We were sitting at the breakfast table, drinking tea. Daan was preparing to go to work..."

She closed her eyes, sat back in her seat. "*Lieve god*, will I see him again...?"

Zoe wanted to assure her that she would, but the thought rang hollow, even to her. In her heart, she feared Dan's involvement in the train blast had put him in the line of fire. She panicked once again about what might have been in the shoulder bag the Nazis had wrested from her at the checkpoint.

"Ilke, let me talk to Pieter. Perhaps he can learn where they are holding him...perhaps there is something we can do..."

"What, Zoe?"

"I do not know...a trade, perhaps...something the Germans may want in exchange for Daan's return..."

Ilke's eyes filled with tears. "Oh, Zoe, do you think so?"

Zoe took a breath, squeezed Ilke's hands. "We can try."

Something occurred to her.

"The Germans must know you do not work for the Resistance, Ilke – else, they would have taken you, too. But you cannot be alone, and I must talk to Pieter. Is there someone I can call who can stay with you?"

Ilke sniffled, her face chalk-white. She looked wilted, like a sail with the wind knocked out of it.

"I do not know," Ilke murmured. "My sister, perhaps…I do not know…"

Daan Mulder's wife leaned back in her chair, silent tears running down her cheeks.

Zoe's mind was racing.

MILA

"I have been desperate to hear from you," Pieter said when Mila finally reached him from her wireless. "Are you alright?"

She had half-thought her father might order her from the house after their bitter confrontation. But he had only flushed and waved her away, as though she were a failed employee – and she had been happy to flee.

"Yes, Pieter. I am unhurt."

A short pause. "My office – this afternoon, if you are able."

She concealed the wireless, and returned to the bedroom, scooping Hondje up from the rug and depositing him on the unmade bed. "Poor baby," she murmured into his softness. "Your mam has been fretfully neglectful. I promise when I return this evening, we will go for a long walk."

Ruffling his topknot, she strode back to the closet and chose a pair of black wool trousers, one of two pair sent to her by her dressmaker for approval, and a loose-fitting, pale blue sweater.

There seemed to her to be a wariness in the streets, an almost palpable sense of doom. People walked quickly, wrapped in their scarves and woolen coats, looking down at the sidewalk as though to make themselves invisible.

SS officers and Gestapo were everywhere, standing in doorways, observing at crosswalks, looming seemingly out of nowhere.

Mila kept her head down and her face obscured lest she be recognized by one of her father's Nazi thugs, and traversed the few kilometers to Pieter's office as quickly as she dared.

• • •

Pieter's expression, when he looked up and saw her, changed from studied concentration to relief. He rose, his green eyes examining her from head to toe. He seemed to wrestle with himself as he came toward her. In the end, he only smiled. "Mila, please sit."

She did, and he sat back in his chair and regarded her. "You are truly fine, Mila. You were not hurt?"

She shook her head. "The blast knocked me off my feet. I think I must have blacked out for a moment, because the next thing I knew, a German officer was shaking me awake."

Pieter's eyes narrowed.

"Fortunately, he recognized me as Frederik Brouwer's daughter. He spirited me away from all the chaos and delivered me to my father's front door."

Pieter nodded slowly. "No suspicion of your involvement?"

"Apparently not."

"And then?"

Mila sighed. "When I was quite recovered, my father confronted me. We had some unpleasant words. He did not disown me, but neither does he believe me. He knows full well, I fear, that I am working on the side of the Resistance."

"That will make it difficult. My sincerest apologies for putting you in so much danger."

Mila closed her eyes for a moment, then leaned across the desk. "I hope the Allies come soon, Pieter, because I cannot do this kind of thing again – not here in Haarlem, anyway – and not just because of my father's watchfulness. Too many German officers here have sat at our table. If I am to continue doing the work of the Resistance, it must be where I cannot be recognized."

He smiled sadly. "For what it is worth, Mila, your work was flawless. But your comment is duly noted."

"I have no wish to abandon the work, Pieter. But I –"

She was interrupted by a pounding at the door. Before they could react, a young woman burst into the office, coat askew, and fright in her eyes.

"Pieter," the woman paused, paying no mind to Mila.

"Zoe." He stood. "What is it?"

"I dared not tell you by telephone," she panted. "It is Daan. He was grabbed by the Germans and dragged bodily from his home."

"When?"

"This morning. Ilke is frantic."

"*Lieve god*," Mila whispered.

Pieter drummed a fist on his desk. "We cannot assume anything yet. It may be a play for information. Did they search his home, his office?"

"Ilke said only that they barged in and took him…she said nothing of a search. And the Germans have not turned up at the *kliniek*, at least not before I left."

Pieter sighed. "Dr. Zoe Visser, this is Mila Brouwer. I do not know if the two of you have met, but you are both vital to the Resistance."

He paused, but only briefly

"Go back to the *kliniek* at once, Zoe. Do not enter until you are certain you are alone. Then search Daan's office for anything that might tie him to the Resistance – anything that could implicate anyone else or divulge any sensitive information."

"Yes, of course." Zoe ran a hand through her hair. "But Daan knows better than that. He keeps things in his head. He writes nothing down – no names, telephone numbers, nothing."

Pieter nodded. "I hope you are correct. But we cannot afford to take the chance."

Zoe's burden poured out of her. "Pieter, the night of the train explosion. My bag was grabbed at a check point. I do not – I would die if something in it might have led the Germans to Daan."

"Do not beat yourself up, Zoe. Things happen. We all take chances." He paused. "The farmer, Jozef Haan. He is still missing, yes?"

Zoe looked at him. "Yes."

Pieter's face was grave. "It is a common tactic in warfare. Most people can only withstand so much torture before they break down and tell what they know. There is no way to know where the leak came from. We will do our best to find them both."

Mila saw the tears pool in Zoe's eyes. She rose and put her arms around her.

"One thing is certain," Peiter said. "Daan is stronger than most. I know in my heart he will reveal nothing. Not even…"

He did not have to finish the thought. *Not even under pain of death…*

EVI

Evi drank a cup of weak tea. She felt jumpy, stifled, irritated. With Mam called to work a shift at the pharmacy, it was Evi who had stood in the ration line this morning, snaking slowly forward for more than an hour only to come away with a loaf of stale bread, a bunch of wilted carrots, and a small sack of oats.

The Germans were cracking down harder than ever since the two Resistance offensives, cutting power, disrupting phone lines, holding hunger over their heads with impossibly meager rations – and shooting people in the streets for the flimsiest of reasons, *Radio Oranje* reported.

Mam refused to discuss the increased danger. She continued her runs to bring back tulip bulbs and root vegetables with little regard for her safety. But all the while Evi worried for her, she found her own resolve strengthened. The Allies would prevail, she told herself, and until then, she would stay in the fight.

She had not heard from Mila since her last aborted tryst. Nor had she heard from Zoe about shooting lessons.

But the possibility that she might be called upon made her think of Jacob Reese. She rinsed her tea cup and dried it. With a rush of resolve that took her by surprise, she put on her coat, pulled on the blue knit cap with the yellow butterfly, and launched herself out of the barge.

In moments, she was on her bicycle, pedaling with decided purpose.

• • •

She was stopped, along with a young man who held two young children in tow, at a German check point that had suddenly appeared near the intersection near the now-shuttered schoolhouse. She held her breath, assuring herself the guards had no way of knowing about her encounters with German officers – and to her relief, the guard who checked her identification papers looked her up and down quickly and waved her off without comment.

She pedaled off, wondering with a mix of hopelessness and relief if she would ever begin to look her age.

But the stop made her cautious, and more than once, she looked over her shoulder to be sure she was not being followed. But she stayed on course until she came in sight of the well- hidden Beekhof driveway.

The shepherd, Otto, met her halfway up the driveway and flanked her, barking until she got off the bicycle and reached to scratch him behind the ears. Then he followed her, tail wagging, to the door.

She knocked vigorously, but no one answered. Evi stood back, surveying the house and grounds. A patch of garden to one side of the house had recently been plowed over, perhaps, she thought, in anticipation of a spring planting once the frost lifted. The very prospect of spring vegetables made her stomach growl.

To the other side of the house, a couple of empty wheelbarrows and a small plow stood in front of a few mostly bare trees, small patches of blue-grey sky peeking through their scraggly branches.

In the stillness, Evi thought she detected the low thrum of voices. She moved closer to the sound, Otto trotting beside her, and turned an ear to the side of the yellow plow to listen. It was quiet for a moment, and then she heard the sounds again. Perhaps they were out in the field.

She squeezed behind the plow and discovered to her surprise that the scrawny trees were not trees at all, but hefty boughs bound together, obscuring a gate that was nearly hidden behind a screen of ivy.

She hesitated, listening again. Now it was almost eerily quiet. When she pushed at the gate, it swung open and she found herself looking into the barrel of a rifle.

She jumped back, trying to find her voice.

"Wait!" Her voice was a squeak.

The rifle was lowered and a pair of angry, amber eyes bored into her. "Are you kidding me, girl? You could have been killed!"

Evi blinked, backing away. "I am sorry, Jacob, I was -"

"What?"

"I was just looking to find you."

Jacob lowered the rifle to his side. "A word of advice, Evi Strobel. Don't poke around in strange places. We live in a dangerous world."

She worked to attune her ear to his American accent, glad for all the hours she had spent studying English in school. "Yes, it is dangerous," she began, raising her chin, "and that is exactly why I wanted to find you."

Jacob's eyes narrowed.

"I want you to teach me to shoot."

Now the American seemed to swallow a smile. "You want me to teach you to shoot."

Evi nodded. "Yes. I want to be able to protect myself."

"From drunken Nazis who want to bed you."

She felt her face redden. "Yes, if it comes to that. But also, at other times. I want to do more to defeat the Germans than dispose of one Nazi at a time."

The American looked distinctly amused.

Evi flushed and straightened. "I have made a request from Resistance leaders for my own weapon and for shooting lessons. But there could be an issue because of my age, and so I am coming to you."

Jacob Reese seemed to take her measure. "You're serious," he said at last.

"I am."

"You are seventeen."

Evi sighed. "I will be seventeen in February."

"But you said –"

"I know. But I am not a child, Jacob – and as you very well know, I have reason to fear for my safety."

She saw the indecision in his face. "I would have to clear it with the Beekhofs," he said finally. "This is their land, after all."

"But you will try…"

Jacob sighed, his handsome face a mix of indecision and amusement. "I will do my best, Evi Strobel. Come back tomorrow at noon – and this time…"

He slowly began to raise the rifle. "Try ringing the doorbell."

ZOE

Zoe cycled once around the *kliniek* building on Daan's borrowed bicycle. She saw no SS vehicles in the street nor any hint that the office had been breached. She parked the bicycle next to hers and entered through the back door

The place felt eerily quiet. Ilke had allowed herself to be led home by her sister, but it was as though the poor woman's fear and dread had sucked the air out of the room.

A lone calico cat was housed in the kennel, an elderly male content to wear off his fever by sleeping much of the time. He was curled into himself and breathing easily when Zoe peered in. She closed the door, checked to be sure the front door was firmly locked, then made her way into Daan's office.

It was tidy as always, the desktop cleared of everything but a daily calendar, a business card file, an adding machine, a pen and ink stand and the telephone.

She picked up the calendar and rifled through the pages, but it contained only *kliniek* appointments, nothing personal in nature.

She combed through his card file, but found not a single business card that was not connected to *kliniek* business – not even a card with Zoe's home address, or his sister-in-law's, or anyone connected with Resistance business. She had expected nothing less.

Daan's desk drawers, too, provided little to reveal the personal business of its owner – only the usual assortment of pens and pencils, paper clips, a business checkbook, and assorted stationery supplies – and an extra pair of scuffed brown shoes in the bottom drawer.

She looked carefully through the metal file cabinet for anything outside of *kliniek* business, and examined every volume in the wooden bookcase. But her assertion to Pieter had been correct. Daan Mulder was too smart, and too careful, to have anything in his office that might tie him or anyone else to Resistance business.

Eyes closed, Zoe sank into his desk chair, touched a hand to the telephone, and felt around her the kindly aura of her determined employer and friend. She lost track of how long she had been sitting there when she heard the insistent pounding.

Her blood ran cold as she rose to investigate, but the front door crashed open and by the time she reached the reception desk, two impossibly big and grim-faced Gestapo officers were halfway across the room.

MILA

Mila sat, crossing names off a list while Pieter made as many phone calls as he dared. He was business-like but persistent, doing everything he could to find why Daan Mulder had been grabbed and where he might have been taken.

Mila made a few calls herself, under the pretense of seeking goods and services from the few questionably aligned Dutch vendors who served a high-end clientele.

But they came up empty.

It was cold, even here in the small inner office of Pieter's 'plumbing' office. She got up to stretch, pulled her heavy wool cardigan close around her. Then the phone shrilled on Pieter's desk.

He snatched it up and listened. After a moment, his green eyes darkened, and a muscle twitched in his jaw.

Slowly, he put the phone back in its cradle.

"The Resistance cell in Amsterdam.... If their intelligence is correct, the leak came from Police Captain Reimar de Boer... I cannot say I am surprised."

Mila considered. "De Boer? A Dutchman?"

"*Ja* – and not for the first time." Pieter's mouth twisted. "The bastard is not even a Nazi sympathizer. But he has been known to sell out his countrymen to the Germans for a wad of guilders...."

Mila's eyebrows rose.

"We can't be certain he's the source," Pieter said. "But it would not be the first time – and the tip came from a highly placed infiltrator in Dutch police circles. De Boer learned somehow of Daan's involvement in the train explosion, and was able to cash in on it."

By implication, Mila knew, it could mean there was a price on Pieter's head as well. He knew it too, she was sure.

Not for the first time, Mila wondered where he slept at night.

She wondered, too, at the deep roots of the Resistance, how extensive their reach, how much they knew or could guess from their network of informants all over the continent.

She looked at Pieter with new respect. "If money will help...a ransom..."

Pieter shook his head. "We have banker friends who quietly subsidize our mission," he said. "And funds come, too, from a couple of Dutch brewing companies making piles of money from all these beer-soaked Germans."

He drummed his fingers on the desk. "Unfortunately, we do not yet know where they are holding Daan." His voice was bitter. "But it is well past time to do something about de Boer."

EVI

It was precisely noon when she rang the doorbell at the Beekhof farmhouse. Otto, tail wagging, trotted alongside her, uttering a few half-hearted woofs.

Evi felt an odd sense of satisfaction that he no longer barked wildly at her approach. Instead, he nudged against her until she scratched behind his ears, his pink tongue conveying his pleasure.

The door was answered by a wiry, gray-haired woman wrapped in a bulky brown sweater – *Mevrouw* Beekhof, Evi surmised – who peered at her through the half-open door. "You are looking for Jacob?"

Evi nodded. "*Ja*, I am Evi Strobel."

The door opened wider, and Evi entered the now-familiar room.

"Klara Beekhof," she said. "Jacob has talked of you...Follow me, *behagen*. The men are in the back acres."

In the cold, clear afternoon, the Beekhof acreage seemed to stretch on forever, much of it already plowed over. A swath of a pathway had been carved through what might once have been a cornfield, but she could see no further than that.

An iron triangle hung from a rope just outside the back door. *Mevrouw* Beekhof struck it firmly with a short length of pipe, and before long, Jacob Reese emerged from the choppy brush. His beard was gone. Evi stared.

"*Dank u*, Mam Beekhof.. I am here," he said.

The woman nodded and slipped back inside. Jacob turned his attention to Evi.

"Hallo," she murmured, suddenly shy.

He looked at her, a bemused expression on his handsome face. "You really want to do this, eh?"

She nodded firmly, and watched his smile widen.

"Well, then," he said. "Let's get to it."

He led her to a clearing out of sight of the house. It had been prepared for target practice, she saw, a flat board placed on top of a felled tree trunk with an assortment of old tins and bric-a-brac neatly stacked on the ground beneath it.

From the jacket of his coat, Jacob brought out a pistol, which looked larger and blacker and far more menacing close-up than it had when she had seen one from a distance. Evi studied it.

"This is a forty-five caliber Colt M-1911," Jacob said, holding the pistol out in front of her. "It's standard issue in the U.S. military."

Evi leaned in for a closer look.

"It isn't loaded, because you will not be doing any shooting today. Today, you will learn every part of this device. You will take it apart and put it back together, again and again, until you know it by heart, and then you will hold it, handle it, and work with it until it feels like an extension of your hand."

Evi took the pistol, startled at how heavy it was, and studied it from every angle.

Jacob watched her. "This is the grip," he said, pointing.

Magazine... Rear sight...Trigger guard... Trigger... Muzzle... Slide stop... Front sight. In her wildest dreams, Evi would not have believed the weapon could have so many parts. *Take down lever...Take-down notch...Barrel...Chamber...Hammer...*

Again and again, Jacob quizzed her, making her recite the name of each part and describe its function.

"Next time, you'll disassemble this thing and put it back together," he told her. "It's more information than you'll ever need, but I want you to know this pistol like the back of your hand before you go out there intending to use it."

Evi nodded, though her patience was wearing thin. "If that's what you think I need to do, Jacob."

He nodded firmly. "All my friends call me Jake."

She looked down, turned over a stone with her foot. "I like Jacob better."

He looked at her for a long moment. "Okay. Jacob it is."

He led her to the back door. "Evi's back, *Mevrouw* Beckhof," he called.

In the doorway, he receded slowly. Evi took in the amber eyes, the even-featured, clean-shaven face. He did look younger without the beard – perhaps no more than twenty or twenty-two.

Mevrouw Beekhof appeared in the doorway. "Can you stop for tea, Jake?" she asked.

"No, Ma'am, but thank you. We're making progress out back, but we need every hand."

The farmer's wife nodded. "*Gaan*, then," she said. "And you, Evi Strobel…your nose is red with the cold. Come in and have a cup of tea before you get back on your bicycle."

Evi waved at Jacob's receding form. "Wednesday at noon," he called over his shoulder.

She followed *Mevrouw* Beekhof into a neatly scrubbed kitchen. "*Dank u*, but I -"

"Sit."

Evi sat, taking in the faded yellow walls of the kitchen, the array of well-used pots and pans that hung over the stove, the Delft dinnerware neatly stacked on shelves.

Mevrouw Beekhof put a steaming cup in front of her, retrieved her own cup and sat across from her.

"So, why does a pretty, young girl like you need to learn how to shoot?" she asked.

Evi did not hesitate. "I work for the Resistance. I need to be prepared to meet the enemy."

The older woman nodded, blue eyes narrowing in a thin, surprisingly unlined face. "Ah," she said. "I see....but so young…"

Evi's chin went up the slightest bit. "I will be seventeen next month."

Mevrouw Beekhof smiled, making her unlined face look even younger. "I see. You know, Evi, you need to be careful when you talk about Resistance activities to people you do not know very well – even to me."

"But you are hiding Jacob - "

"*Ja*. Still, for your own safety."

The farmer's wife paused for a moment, then rose and brought down a blue flowered tin from a shelf over the kitchen table. "On the other hand," she held out the tin. "A young woman who fights against the Germans needs to keep her strength up."

Evi could smell the sugary contents before she saw them. Her mouth watered and her stomach began to growl.

"Please, take all you like."

Evi took a ginger-studded pastry from the tin. "*Gemberbolus*," she murmured. "Ginger cookies."

"*Ja*."

Evi's eyes filled with tears. "My Mam used to make them, before the war."

"I have used my rations only sparingly."

The near-forgotten sweetness exploded in Evi's mouth. She closed her eyes let the tears flow.

ZOE

The German's face was inches from hers, ruddy, angry, insistent. "Papers!" He backed her toward the wall.

Zoe found her voice, tearing her gaze from the rifle at his side. "In there," she pointed. "In my office."

"*Geh mit irh*," he shouted, turning on his heel to his companion. "Follow her."

Easing out from behind the German's bulk, Zoe left the room, aware of heavy footsteps right behind her. Fumbling, her heartbeat loud in her ears, she searched the office for her bag and reached for it.

"*Halt!*" her pursuer raised his pistol.

Zoe backed off, watched as the younger Nazi rummaged through the bag. He tossed it back to her. "Papers!"

She withdrew her identification papers from a zippered section in the bag, silently handed them over. She could hear a commotion coming from Daan's office, the thump of objects being tossed about, what sounded like desk drawers crashing to the floor.

There was nothing there to connect Daan to Pieter or the Resistance, she was certain, but these German brutes would not give up until they had combed through every inch of his possessions.

Poor Ilke. Zoe guessed the Mulder home had by now been thoroughly scavenged.

The square-jawed officer, his mouth a thin line, inspected Zoe's ID papers, looked up twice, comparing her photo to her face.

She recalled instantly the night of the train explosion, the bag she had been forced to leave behind. Once again, her stomach roiled. She prayed silently there had been nothing revealing in its contents.

The German's harsh voice cut through her reverie. "What is your business here?" he barked in surprisingly good Dutch.

"I work here," she kept her voice even. "I am a licensed veterinarian."

"You know this man, Daan Mulder."

"He is my employer."

"He is an enemy of the Reich," the German spat. "You work with him for the Resistance."

It was a statement, not a question. Zoe stiffened. "I am a veterinarian…an animal doctor. I work here at the *kliniek*. That is all."

The older Nazi strode into her office, exchanged words in German with his companion.

The younger man brushed Zoe aside, began pulling drawers from her desk.

"You," the older German directed her to the reception desk. "Sit."

Zoe sat, working to keep her anxiety under control as the two Gestapo officers rampaged through her office, ripping files from the cabinet, scanning reports on her desk, rifling through every book in her bookcase and roughly tossing them aside.

When they finished in her office, they attacked the reception area, flinging aside supplies and equipment yanked from the desk, from the rows of neatly marked small storage bins.

By the time they were finished, the place was a shambles, but finding nothing of import seemed only to make the Germans angrier.

"You work for the Resistance!" the older one insisted.

"I work in the *kliniek*," she said again, working to keep control of her voice. "I am a veterinarian. I treat dogs and cats when they are sick."

The man narrowed steel blue eyes. "Do you know you are working for an enemy of the Reich?"

Zoe fought against the trembling inside. "Daan Mulder is my employer at the *kliniek*. That is all that I know of him."

• • •

In the end, they left with the same swiftness with which they had smashed their way in. To her relief, they had asked her nothing about her family, nothing about the train explosion, nothing about the food and supplies pilfered from the mangled train wreck. They only warned her to stay within their sights, to be a visibly compliant Dutch citizen.

They never asked her where Daan was. But of course, they already knew. She closed her eyes, as close to prayer as she could muster, willing him, with every fiber of her being, to be alive, to stay strong.

MILA

She was still in Pieter's office when the call came from Zoe.

"You are not hurt?" she heard him ask.

He listened quietly, gave a quick instruction, then hung up and turned to Mila.

"The Gestapo has been and gone from the pet *kliniek*. They tore the place apart, found nothing, and left Zoe with an unholy mess and a warning."

"How can I help?"

Pieter's fingers tapped a rhythm on his desk. "I need to talk with the rest of the council. I cannot go forward without support, and it will take every contact we have to determine where they are holding Daan."

He paused.

"This much I know," he said finally. "If we can be sure that de Boer sold him out, that traitor is our next priority."

Briefly, he drummed his fingers on the desk. "But Zoe needs help – now – and reassurance that she is not alone. Can you go the *kliniek*, Mila? Perhaps call on a few more hands to help clean up the chaos the bastards left her with?"

"Of course." Mila rose and gathered her things.

She knew whose help she would enlist.

EVI

The young woman had been delivered to the barge in the wee hours before dawn – a small, dark-haired woman, a research scientist called Rachel, who had been spirited out of Germany by friends in the dead of night and who, with the grace of God, and help from the network of Resistance volunteers, might one day find refuge in Belgium.

Mam had taken the girl in, fed her soup and tea, and persuaded her to sleep for a while, huddled under blankets in the hold. Now, at close to eleven in the morning, she was explaining to Rachel her plan to move her downriver when a knock sounded at the door.

Evi froze at the sound of the knock, and the young woman, Rachel, jumped nearly out of her skin, her dark eyes as big as saucers.

"Who is there?" Mam asked.

"Hallo, Lotte, it is I – Mila."

Evi exchanged a glance of relief with Mam. She touched Rachel's arm. "Not to worry,," she assured her, opening the door. "Mila is with the Resistance."

Mila glanced at the three of them, quick to understand "I am so sorry," she said. "I did not mean to frighten you. I just – we need your help, Evi, if you can."

Mam, who was pulling an extra sweater over the young woman's head, watched warily.

Mila wasted no time. "Zoe Visser needs help at the pet *kliniek*. The Germans have seized Daan Mulder. They broke into the *klineik* this morning and left it in ruins. I am on my way there now, and I hoped you might come along to help."

It was not what Evi expected.

"Of course," she said finally. She turned to Mam, whose hands covered her face. "I expect I will be back here, Mam, by the time you return. If not, please do your best not to worry."

She touched the shoulder of the young scientist. "Rachel," she murmured. "God speed."

"Mila, take my bicycle if you like," Lotte called. "Be careful – and please tell Zoe my prayers are with her – and with Daan."

Evi grabbed her coat and the blue knit cap with the yellow butterfly. She followed Mila out onto the wharf and opened the shed to retrieve the bicycles.

• • •

They were halfway to the *kliniek*, pedaling in tandem, when they were stopped at a makeshift checkpoint. Two young German guards, faces inscrutable under their combat helmets, looked them over slowly. One muttered something in rapid German.

The other snickered, then raised his rifle. "Papers!"

Evi put a foot on the ground to steady her bicycle and held one hand up as she reached under her coat for her papers. She saw Mila's mouth tighten as she reached into her bag.

The soldiers took their time examining their identification papers, looking up, looking down, peering from one to the other, a running commentary between them in rapid German. Something in their tone put Evi in mind of the German who had tried to rape her.

One of the men stepped forward. "Where are you going?" he asked in passable Dutch.

"To the Dans Hal," Mila said calmly. "It is time for us to begin the new decor. Dutch Carnival begins soon."

Another exchange between the soldiers, both looking faintly amused as they circled slowly, examining the two of them from every angle.

Evi held her tongue, her anxiety rising, but Mila's expression turned from annoyance to amusement. To Evi's surprise, Mila inclined her head in the flirtatious manner she had worked so hard to teach Evi. She said a few words in German that Evi could not decipher, and the young soldiers looked up in unison.

Muttering something, they handed back their papers and retreated.

"*Danke,*" said Mila grandly, tucking her papers into her shoulder bag, already beginning to pedal off.

Evi followed, pedaling fast to catch up.

"What did you tell them?" She asked when she reached her.

"Nothing of consequence," Mila said, looking straight ahead. "I suggested I could report them to a high-ranking officer who is a personal friend, and they suddenly lost interest in the pair of us."

ZOE

Zoe sat cross-legged on the floor, willing her breath to slow. The silence in the room was palpable. She was angry, bitter, alarmed, and tearful, surveying the ruins the Germans had left behind.

Were they apt to return? *Lieve god*, where was Daan? What had put him in the Nazis' crosshairs?

She thought of Jozef Haan, the farmer who had not surfaced since the night of the train blast. Could he have betrayed Daan to save himself? Was it something in the bag that was lost to her at the road block?

Hot tears sprang to her eyes. She brushed them away and looked at the mess around her.

She was getting to her feet, slowly, cautiously, when the ring of the telephone pierced the silence. She stepped over a pile of books, reluctant at first to answer, then struggled to muster her most professional voice. "Mulder pet *kliniek*. May I help you?"

The tears spilled over when she heard Pieter's voice. *Help was on the way,* he told her. *The Resistance, the entire nation, owed her a debt of gratitude....*

Zoe mopped tears with the hem of her skirt.

A moment later, she took a shuddering breath and tried to focus on the task at hand. She was gathering papers, sorting themt into piles that made sense, when she heard women's voices at the back door.

"Zoe, *lieve god*," Evi rushed into the room the moment it was unlocked. "They did not hurt you?"

Mila Brouwer, right behind her, opening her arms and folded Zoe into them.

Zoe let herself go weak. She allowed herself a moment to be rocked and sheltered. She was too spent to protest.

Evi joined them in a three-way hug, and they swayed, the three of them, in silence.

MILA

It was past four when they stopped to rest and survey the what they had managed to accomplish. There were still piles of paperwork for Zoe to sort and return to the files, but the reception area was cleared, the furniture righted, the books mostly back on their shelves.

Mila stretched, arching her back. *"Een fluitje van een cent!"* she announced grandly. *A piece of cake!*

Zoe and Evi, sprawled, exhausted, on waiting room chairs, smiling wanly at her attempt at humor.

"If you have a piece of cake," she implored, "please pass it over! I am starving!"

Zoe sighed, "I do not know how to thank you both. Imagine if Daan were to come back to such a shambles…"

Mila and Evi exchanged glances.

Mila sat on the rug in front of them. "Did you know, Zoe, that Evi, too, has been working for the Resistance?"

"I did," said Zoe. "She came to me not long ago asking for shooting lessons and a weapon. I have not yet had the opportunity to ask, but I promised to take the request to Daan or Pieter."

Mila's eyebrows rose. "A weapon and shooting lessons! Why, Evi?"

Evi's chin rose. "I owe my life to the American airman who happened to pass by that night when I was fighting off that Nazi rapist at the tavern. If I am to do this sort of thing again, Mila, or anything like it, I want to be able to protect myself."

Mila was aghast. "This is the first I have heard of your being rescued that night by anyone – much less an American soldier. Where were the Resistance shooters?"

"In the woods, waiting, I suppose. But my attacker moved – more quickly than we expected, and the bodyguards were a few hairs too late."

It was something Mila had not foreseen. "I will talk to Pieter," she said finally. "But, Evi, you are young for firearms…"

Evi raised her chin. "If I am old enough to lure Nazi officers to their death," she muttered, "I am old enough to learn to handle a pistol."

Zoe heaved a sigh. "And I as well, I suppose, although the very idea of it makes me shudder. But I have found myself more than once facing into a German firearm." She paused. "I am willing to do anything to help end the suffering…and Evi is right. We need to have the means and be well prepared to defend ourselves."

Mila considered. "How old are you, Zoe?"

"I was twenty-four last August."

"Then I will take you to a shooting range myself – and Evi, I will take this up with Pieter."

Evi said nothing.

Mila took it as approval. "It is getting late," she said, looking out of the *kliniek* window at the gathering dusk. She scrambled to her feet. "And it seems there are more check points now than ever. We had best be on our way if we are all to be home before curfew."

The front door was splintered where the Germans had pounded on it. Zoe checked the lock to be sure it held. Then she led the way to the back door.

"Evi, may I take your mam's bicycle home," Mila asked, "I will return it tomorrow."

"Of course."

Mila looked for a moment at their strained faces. "Hope," she whispered.

"Hope," they echoed.

Another three-way hug, long and heartfelt.

They hopped up on their bicycles and pedaled into the settling twilight.

EVI

"I have business to attend to this morning," Evi told her mother. "I will not be long."

Lotte looked at her strangely. "Business?"

Mam had been edgy since her last trip downriver. She had been able to pass Rachel, the young research scientist, to her next handler without incident, but she had felt, she told Evi, an eerie sense that it had not been entirely without notice.

Evi had pressed for more, but Mam had shrugged it off, saying only that she had no wish to stop aiding Resistance efforts, any more than did her daughter.

"Well, then," she said now, "this is something I have to do, Mam. "I will be home soon."

• • •

It had sleeted the night before, and it was rudely cold. Snowflakes melted on her tongue as she mounted her bicycle. Watching for Nazi checkpoints, Evi pedaled to the Beekhof farm. She looked once, then again, in all directions before pedaling up the narrow driveway.

She had no idea why she had not revealed to Mila that Jacob was teaching her to shoot. But she did not in the least feel guilt-ridden. She was doing what she needed to do to for her own protection... and anyway...she felt her mouth curve into a smile - being with Jacob made her forget she was hungry, forget she was frightened, forget everything but his face and his voice and what she was there to accomplish.

Otto ran beside her on the way to the door, then sat still, tail wagging and panting for her attention. "Good boy, Otto," she murmured, scratching behind his ear. "Yes, you know who I am, don't you?"

Mevrouw Beekhof greeted her, led her out back and struck the triangle with a pipe. Within moments, Jacob emerged, jogging through the brush from the back acreage.

"Hi there," he said, making a funny face at her, and something in Evi's heart began to dance. But he was all business, leading her to the makeshift practice range, bringing the Colt from under his jacket.

"Today," he said, "we review the components, and you take the pistol apart. Then, if you put it back together correctly, we can start shooting at targets."

She had the pieces memorized, had reviewed them in her head in the last few evenings, sometimes barely hearing when Mam spoke to her. She was glad the young scientist had been successfully handed off, grateful for the mostly edible potatoes Mam had found at the marketplace in Middleburg. But pleasing Jacob, proving her courage, seemed infinitely more essential.

He watched her take the pistol apart. She read his face as he watched her. Deftly, she put the pieces together, and looked up at Jacob, beaming.

He started to reach out, as though to hug her, then stopped and put his hands on her shoulders. "Good job," he said, grinning. He was close enough for her to see the green flecks in his amber eyes, the tiny nick above his left cheek where he might have cut himself shaving.

They stood like that for a moment, Evi's heart beating fast. Then Jacob blinked and backed away.

"So, Evi Strobel," he said. "Are you ready to fire this thing?"

She swallowed hard, stepped back, and nodded.

Jacob stood behind her, lifted her arm, adjusted her hand in the grip. The Colt felt heavy, awkward.

"Look through the sight," he instructed, leaning down, his chin nearly resting on her shoulder. "Look straight ahead. Do you see that empty feed bucket sitting there?"

She nodded."

"Look for the letter A in the middle of the label."

Evi peered through the sight.

"Do you see it? The letter A?"

"*Ja.*"

"Okay, good. Now squeeze the trigger. But slowly…slowly, Evi, never taking your eye from that letter A."

Evi squeezed. She heard the loud report – and felt herself jolted backward, landing flat against Jacob's broad chest.

"Whoa," he said, reaching to steady her. "I should have warned you about the blowback."

An acrid smell hung in the air. The sound echoed in her ear drums. Worse, when she wriggled around to look at the target, the feed bucket sat there, untouched, the big letter A mocking her.

Eyes wide, she turned to face Jacob.

"It's okay." He smiled ruefully, as though to a child, adding anger to her fierce humiliation.

She wrenched herself away. "Again," she said, raising the Colt.

"Sure. Only this time, plant your feet a little further apart. You're such an itty-bitty thing, you need to steady yourself against the recoil."

She did not know the meaning of 'itty-bitty.' She thought she liked the sound of it on his tongue, but she was not certain it was complimentary.

Gripping the weapon, she planted her feet apart, pressed her lips together, and stared through the sight at her target.

ZOE

Air raid sirens had kept her awake for much of the night again, and Zoe faced the wintry day filled with a restless energy. There had been no further word of Daan – nor did she expect it, really, in her heart of hearts.

She had spent the evening helping Ilke and her sister put the Mulder's ransacked apartment back in order, and made her way home, exhausted, half-expecting to find her own apartment similarly ransacked.

To her relief, it was intact, although she knew full well the Gestapo could turn up at any moment – not that they would find anything in her small living space that would be of any value to them.

From her window, she saw a dusting of snow sweep the cobblestones. Resolute, she dressed warmly, buttoned her old grey coat, and wrapped a red wool scarf around her chin and nose.

She was turning the sign on the front door of the *kliniek* from 'closed' to 'open' when a young girl and her mother came around the corner, a mixed breed, short-haired puppy wrapped in a blanket in the woman's arms.

The poor pup was constipated, they told her, and her little nose was warm with fever.

Zoe found a clean, white coat, took the pup into an examining room, and took his temperature. She put a few drops of peppermint oil into some cool water to help bring down the fever and applied it to the dog's paw pads. She inserted a laxative and advised the pair to walk her more frequently – and take longer walks in spite of the cold.

"Food is scarce, I know" she told them, handing over the pup. "But if you can feed her some fruit peelings or potato skins now and then, the fiber will help her, too."

Her patients gone and room quiet, Zoe faced the pile of paperwork that still needed to be re-filed. But she could not find the drive to begin, or the patience to sit at her desk.

Sighing, she turned the 'open' sign back to 'closed,' locked the front door, and went out the back, where she unfastened Daan's bicycle from its mooring and set out for the hospital in Heemstede.

• • •

Kurt Schneider smiled and waved as she made her way across the makeshift ward.

"Your timing is wonderful," he said in Dutch, his accent distinctly German. "I was just about to begin a story time."

He peered at her, seeming to examine her face. "Are you alright?"

"I have had better days," she sighed. "My employer at the pet *kliniek* – and my very dear friend – was grabbed up by the Gestapo. We have no idea where, or even if…" she could not bring herself to finish the thought.

Kurt sighed. "He works with the Resistance, no doubt…"

Zoe nodded. "Two big Nazi henchmen crashed their way into the pet *kliniek*," she said. "They tore it apart, but Daan was a careful man. I am certain they found no trace of Resistance activity among his things…but still…"

Kurt's face was a mask. "Zoe, these Germans will not rest in their search. Please believe me. I know that." His eyes searched her face. "Are you safe where you live?"

"Who knows? I told them I knew nothing. I do not know if they believed me. They have not invaded my apartment – at least, not yet."

She saw Gerritt coming toward them. "Zoe, I have been trying to reach you."

She peered into his anxious face. "What is it?"

Gerrit glanced at Kurt.

"It is fine," she said. "You know as well as I that he can be trusted."

Gerritt kept his voice at a whisper. "I had a visitor this morning in my office…a high-ranking German official. He was very polite. Not at all threatening. But he asked for a roster of all our patients – and a complete list of staff."

Zoe blinked.

"I told him it would take us a day or two to get up-to-date lists together. He told me he would return for them on Friday."

Could this have something to do with Daan? The explosions…the transfer of food…?

Gerritt looked around the crowded ward. "Every Jewish patient and medical worker we have here is hidden away on this floor, along with the hiding families and children."

"*Ja…*"

"I will, of course, provide the officer with accurate lists of the patients and staff on the first four floors of the hospital," Gerritt said. "There is no one there the Germans want. And let us hope to God this floor is never searched."

Zoe nodded, keenly aware of the anguish on the face of the storyteller.

MILA

Mila sipped her wine. The dining room table was laden with food, a roasted pork loin with apples, potatoes and currants, but she could barely abide the rich aroma, never mind the taste of it.

Her mother, sick with one of her convenient headaches and despite her father's clear misgivings, had left the job of hostess to her. She arranged the folds of her grey silk skirt, then slowly twirled the stem of her glass.

The conversation had been less than useful. But her pulse quickened as the hawk-nosed *Obershtumfuhrer* seated across from her began talking about the explosion at the Haarlem Cinema.

"Dozens of loyal German officers dead," he growled. "Almost as many injured, many gravely. I was very nearly caught in the flames myself."

Her father listened, a stern expression on his face. He did not look at Mila.

"The source of the blast is still being traced," the German said. "But we know the Dutch Resistance was behind it. Herr Hitler himself is enraged."

"I do not doubt it," her father said."

"We have already begun to exact revenge, beginning with another cut in Dutch rations. We feel certain that somewhere, someone with a starving family will come forward with information about the perpetrators."

"And if not?" her father asked.

The German cut into the slab of meat on his plate and shrugged. "Then Herr Hitler has given us our marching orders. We will begin to eliminate two Dutch citizens for every German murdered until the debt is paid."

Mila blinked. To her knowledge, there were only three people who knew the origin of the Cinema blast – Johan Steegen, Pieter, and herself. Nobody else had information to share…but her heart sunk to realize how many innocent Dutch would pay the price.

She cleared her throat, and leaned forward, exposing the cleavage in the deep neckline of her dress.

"How tiresome, all this talk of death and destruction," she purred, ignoring her father's searing look. "What I long to know, my dear

Obersturmfuhrer, is what is happening on the German stage these days!"

She raised a glass. "Nobody, after all, does music like the Germans. I would give anything to own a recording of Marlene Deitrich's *"Lili Marleen!"*

"Ach," the German beamed, clearly pleased to find common ground. "I heard the song played just yesterday on OSS Radio. Glorious, is it not? It is said even the Americans are making much of it, though I cannot for an instant think why!"

He leaned across the table." Did you know, Fraulein Brouwer, that the words to that song were written some thirty years ago by a German school teacher from Hamburg?"

Mila smiled and shrugged deeply, again baring her cleavage. "I did not know that, *Obershtumfuhrer*!! How very clever you are!"

The German leaned forward, looking pleased with himself, she thought, and openly admiring the view. He mopped his brow with a linen cloth. "I will personally see that a copy of *zis* recording is delivered to the lovely *fraulein*."

Mila sat back as Riet brought in a sugared apple tart.

"*Wonderbaarlijk!*" She smiled at their guest. "May I serve?"

• • •

"When you play with fire, Mila" her father told her when his Nazi dinner guest had gone, "you will almost certainly be burned."

Mila did not respond and her father did not persist. She went to the kitchen, instructed Riet to pack up the dinner's considerable leftovers and deliver them to the Dans Hal in the morning. They would feed more than one hungry family, she thought with satisfaction.

In her bedroom, she settled Hondje with a few bits of the pork, then closed the door of her clothes closet behind her.

"It appears, *Godjizdank*," she reported to Pieter, "that the enemy still has no idea who originated the Cinema blast – except, of course, that it was a Resistance operation."

She could envision Pieter, drumming his fingers on his desk as he listened.

"If right is on our side, they never will know," he said. "But they are inflamed, and more alert than ever, especially since it came on the heels of the train explosion and the loss of all that cargo."

"Hitler, himself, is enraged, we were told. In addition to cutting rations again, the rank and file has direct orders to retaliate at their discretion – eliminating two Dutchmen for every German lost, if starvation doesn't kill us first."

She could hear Pieter's sigh. "No doubt they will exact their pound of flesh in any way that suits their purpose."

Mila hesitated. "Is there any word of Daan?"

"Only confirmation of de Boer's betrayal – this time by his personal driver who, it turns out, is supportive of Resistance efforts. Stand by, Mila. We are formulating a plan. Not another Dutch hero must be sacrificed to the bastard's greed."

EVI

In all her life, she had never hidden anything of consequence from Mam. But the Colt pistol that Jacob had entrusted to Evi – a duplicate of the one he kept for himself – felt like a hot potato in her hands.

She hid it first in a rain boot. She put it under her mattress, concealed it under a pile of sweaters on her shelf. Finally, she stowed it in the bottom of her book bag, where Mam would have no reason to look.

If she felt awkward as they ate their watery cabbage soup, her mother did not seem to notice. In fact, she was unusually quiet.

Finally, Mam dropped her spoon in the empty bowl. Evi jumped at the sound.

"*Lieveling*," she said, leaning back in her chair. "I talked today with Leela Bakker. It seems that some German Jewish escapees have been hiding out for months in one of the old limestone caves near Limburg.

But the farmers who have been aiding them, Leela said, are crying out now for food and medical supplies – and even clothing."

Evi frowned.

"God knows we do not have much to spare, Evi, but those people are desperate." She paused. "Leela is gathering together what she can…and she asked me to –"

Evi's head snapped up. "Mam…"

"Evi, you know as well as I do that whatever we can provide will be more safely delivered over water."

"Mam, you told me yourself that you think you might have been observed when you transported Rachel…"

"One trip, Evi. That is all I agreed to. Who can navigate the inlets and canals better than I can?"

"But Mam, the Germans are more watchful than ever. Checkpoints are springing up all over…"

But her mother's face was set. "That is precisely why the waterways are better, Evi. There are Resistance volunteers all along the Meuse who can help me get these life-saving supplies to their destination."

Evi spooned up the last of her soup.

"I will be careful, Evi, I promise. I can do the turnaround in the daylight hours, when many boats are on the water…."

She put her hand over Evi's. "And it is no more dangerous than what you have been doing, trolling for German officers to be murdered."

Evi looked into her mother's earnest face, thinner and more lined as the months passed. She had not been asked to repeat her tavern performance since the last near-debacle. But neither was she afraid to do so if she were summoned – and once she perfected her proficiency with the Colt, she would be ready for more critical assignments. She fully expected such missions would be forthcoming once she proved she could take care of herself.

She saw the Colt in her mind's eye, hidden in the depths of her schoolbag.

"Mam, are you certain…?"

"I am, Evi. I must help these poor people trapped in a cave. You know I must."

Evi raised her water glass high. "Then may God keep us both from harm."

ZOE

Zoe had had enough. She pored over the *kliniek* appointment book. With fewer and fewer appointments scheduled, and Daan only God knew where, she thought it only sensible to close the doors for a while – at least until she could figure out where supplies could be replenished and how to keep the business going in Daan's absence. Or perhaps, by the grace of God, until the Allies managed to push their way through.

Food supplies were scarcer than ever, even for those who stood in long ration lines. She had heard from Pieter that two Swedish aid ships loaded with food and medical supplies had arrived at the port in Delfzjjl. The Germans had offloaded the bounty to their channel barges – but none of it had thus far been distributed to the starving Dutch.

Queen Wilhelmina, according to *Radio Oranje*, had personally appealed to both President Roosevelt and England's King George for food assistance. But if it arrived, the *verdomd* Germans would likely appropriate that as well…and since the self-exiled Queen was not yet ready to return, it would be foolish to think the war would end any time soon.

Zoe found herself becoming more despairing by the day – not least because of Daan's abduction. The food they had managed to get to the hospital after the train explosion would not last much longer, not with dozens of mouths to feed, and with the Germans continuing to demand patient and medical staff rosters, the state of affairs in Heemstede was becoming dire.

In the past, she would have taken her concerns to Daan. Now, she knew, she must go to Pieter. She was about to pick up the receiver and dial when she heard a pounding at the front door. Not the Gestapo, surely, she told herself, fearing the worst as she grappled with the locks on her door.

But the man in the Dutch police uniform who slipped quickly inside was the young *marechaussee*, Lukas Jensen, who had helped transport some of the uprooted families to the hospital.

"Lukas?"

He nodded. "Dr. Visser, the Dans Hal," he breathed heavily, as though he had been moving quickly. "The NSB – they are preparing to raid the Dans Hal. You must alert them."

The NSB, Zoe knew, were a group pf Dutch fascists and German sympathizers who regularly betrayed their own people. An image of Daan passed through her brain.

"When, Lukas, when?"

"I do not know for certain. Perhaps tomorrow or the next day. I just – I happened to overhear, but it is not safe for me in this uniform…"

Zoe understood. Hers mind raced. The underground newspaper…Resistance supplies…falsified identification papers…half the tools the Council relied upon lay behind the outwardly innocent walls of the Dans Hal.

"*Danke*, Lukas." She led him out the back door, and locked it firmly behind them.

MILA

Pieter looked tired, his expression as grave as Mila had ever seen it. She longed to reach out, to offer some comfort, at the very least to take his hand in hers. But his manner toward her remained friendly but reserved. It was a bridge that had yet to be crossed.

"A penny for your thoughts," he smiled wanly.

A little white lie. "I was thinking of Daan."

Pieter sighed. "Unless he is being held in captivity, I fear we may never see him again…Worse yet, our sources tell us that a young couple hiding two Jewish children in their attic are the latest to be sacrificed to the Germans for cash by Police Captain Reimar de Boer."

He reached for a communique on the edge of his desk, lit a match to it and watched it burn.

He tossed into a metal wastebasket. Mila watched it turn to ash.

"However," he said, leaning back in his chair," we have eyes in Amsterdam observing de Boer's daily routine – and his driver has promised assistance if we should need it.

He drummed his fingers on the desk in the way, Mila knew by now, meant he was deliberating. "But whatever we do to stop the man's treachery, we will have to be quick and precise. Our first chance will be our best chance – perhaps our only chance…we had best get it right."

"And how will we do that?"

"I was hoping you would ask, Mila," Pieter's eyes sought hers. "It is well known in de Boer's circle," he said, "that the man has an eye for pretty women."

She waited.

"Perhaps…and this is a lot to ask, Mila, this is something we can accomplish together."

EVI

Evi planted her feet apart, took careful aim, and fired. In successive shots, all five of her targets fell from their resting places.

Jumping excitedly, she grinned and turned to Jacob, who pumped a fist in the air.

"Good job, Itty Bitty," he said.

But Evi thought he seemed oddly distant, as he had for most of the afternoon.

She hefted the Colt and waited for his instruction. When it did not come, she turned to face him.

"I think maybe that's all for today," he said, looking at his watch. "It'll be getting dark soon, and there are things I need to do."

She frowned.

"I know. I'm sorry to cut your session short."

"I understand," she said, although she did not. She stashed the pistol in the bottom of her book bag. "Um…When shall I be here again?"

Jacob hesitated. "I'm – not exactly sure," he told her. "Anyway, I'm not sure you need me anymore. You're already a pretty damned good shot."

Her mouth dropped open. Alarm flooded through her. "But Jacob…" She could not find the words.

He sighed, finally, placing his hands on her shoulders. "Look, Evi…"

His amber eyes begged for understanding. "We figured out there may be…a way for me to get home."

She felt her breath catch. "Home?"

"To America. To my unit. Do you understand?"

She nodded, although she had no idea what he was thinking. *Would she ever see him again?*

"This is something I need to do," he said, lightly touching her cheek. "And I need to do it now - tonight."

She nodded dumbly, not wanting to move, not wanting his hand to leave her face.

But he pulled away. "I'm sorry," he breathed, turning away.

She watched his receding back for a moment, then ran to the Beekhof's back door.

Inside, Mevreow Beekhof was peering into a pot at the stove. Evi moved past her, closed the front door behind her, and did not stop until she reached her bicycle.

• • •

She had no idea what made her back the bicycle into the shrubbery and wait for Jacob to appear. But she did, and after a while, as the early winter dusk began to fall, Jacob strode out of the Beekhof's front door.

An olive-colored backpack was strapped to his back, a cap pulled low over his forehead.

She watched him walk down the long, curved driveway on foot, and when she lost sight of him, she walked her bicycle quietly down the drive behind him.

When he reached the roadway, he stopped for a moment and peered in both directions. Adjusting the backpack with a shrug of his shoulders, he struck out quickly to his left.

ZOE

Zoe made her way through the cobblestoned streets, maintaining as normal a pace as she could manage so as not to attract attention, and thankful, when she reached the back door of the Dans Hal, that the alleyway was deserted.

She pounded on the door with a full fist, knowing the sound would be lost if there was no one in the hidden back office, or if the mimeographs were cranking out papers. When there was no answer after she tried a second time, she went around to the front door, knocked once, and quietly slipped in.

She saw the usual hum of Dans Hal activity, women at large tables drawing, cutting, pasting, chatting, while children milled about at their feet. It was precisely the image Resistance personnel wished them to project – an average, apolitical group whose only goal was maintaining Dutch culture.

But there was certain danger if, as Lukas had warned, German authorities or their Dutch collaborators were to look beneath the surface – past and present issues of the underground newspaper, foodstuffs hidden away for the desperate, evidence of the Dans Hal as a beehive of activity by and for the Resistance.

She scanned the faces for Leela Bakker, spotted her at a back table and hurried to her side.

"Leela, we need to talk."

Leela dropped her scissors, led Zoe past the false wall, into the hidden office.

Zoe spoke quickly, reluctant even with Leela, to reveal Lukas Jensen's dual role as Dutch police officer and informer.

"I have been warned by a reliable source," she told her, "that the Dans Hal could be raided by the NSB – perhaps as soon as tomorrow. I know you do what you can to keep this office hidden, but if it is breached – "

"I understand." Leela looked around her. "All the papers – everything needs to be removed…We can take most of it to our homes, I think, carried out in book bags. I will get the women started and put out the call for volunteers."

Zoe nodded.

"What about the mimeograph machines?"

Zoe thought for a minute. "There is no way to move them discreetly – and maybe no need. Have one of the women draw up dance party notices – and Dutch Carnival. Crank out a few copies, leave them lying about as evidence of what the machines are used for."

"Business as usual…" Leela nodded, already in motion, gathering materials for removal.

"Our best hope if the Germans enter the hall," Zoe said, "is that we give them no reason to look beyond the outer room. Be charming, be busy, perhaps a dance class for the little ones. Show them photographs, Carnival brochures, dance invitations, handmade decorations…."

"We will do our best," Leela said. "*Leive god* for the warning…"

Zoe felt the tightness in her chest begin to easde. Leela could be relied upon to take charge.

"Leela, " she began.

"No need, Zoe. Go! Take a stack of these with you in your handbag."

MILA

Mila packed a small overnight bag – a black jersey dress with a deep vee-neckline, black high-heeled pumps she'd buffed to a shine, a change of under garments, some make-up. Checking the contents one last time, she closed the lid, snapped the bag shut, set it near the doorway of her bedroom.

Pieter had secured an automobile and enough petrol for the short trip to Amsterdam, no more than a twenty-minute drive. The plan they had conceived was deceptively simple…the best kind of plan, Mila knew, a small variation of the operation she had mapped out for Evi Strobel.

De Boer, according to his driver, lunched each weekday at the same Amsterdam restaurant – an elegant brasserie near the *Rembrandtsplein* underwritten by the Germans, primarily for their own enjoyment and for friends of the Reich.

Mila was to charm her way in, catch de Boer's eye, and hopefully arrange an evening date, subtly suggesting the promise of sex if he would agree to meet her first at the famous fountain on the *Leidersplein* so she could see it at its glorious lighted best

She powdered her nose and made a last turn before the mirror. If all went well, Pieter would be waiting to deliver a bullet and melt away into the night. It was a clean, straightforward plan, and if the traitor's driver could be counted upon to keep his word, as foolproof as any plan could be.

She looked at her watch. It was time. Straightening, she took a deep breath, picked up her overnight bag and quietly headed downstairs. She had arranged with Reit to be sure Hondje was fed and walked in her absence. Now, all she needed to do was avoid a confrontation with her father.

At the bottom of the stairs, she peered around the corner into the hallway. It was quiet. Her father was either working in his study or had gone to his office near St. Bavo Church. Either way, she was able to avoid him. She slipped quietly out the front door.

• • •

As arranged, Pieter was waiting for her in the next street behind the wheel of a pre-war gray Renault sedan. He got out when he saw her, and went around to open her door.

Mila bent to get in, brushing lightly against his coat, aware of the tweedy scent of him.

"You are well?" he asked.

She smiled in response.

"Ready?"

"Yes."

"*Guod.*"

He closed her door, moved back to the driver's side, slipped into the vehicle. "We will first check in to the hotel."

EVI

Jacob walked quickly, clearing brush out of his way as he moved, staying close to the inner edge of the road.

Evi followed a distance behind, far enough behind that she had to pedal fast around the curves just to keep him in sight in the dimming light.

What am I doing? she scolded herself. *I will be mortified if Jacob sees me.* But curiosity pulled at her in much the same way as Mam pulled the yarn to unravel her afghan blankets. *Where on earth could he be going?*

She fell once, tangled in the wheels of her bicycle, scrambling to duck out of sight when he looked behind him, as he frequently did. She clambered up again and righted the bicycle. Now she recognized the terrain.

To her astonishment, Jacob was nearing the tavern where he had shot her would-be rapist. He passed by the precise spot where it happened, in fact, then began to make his way into the pines behind it.

Too puzzled now to stay well back, Evi hopped off the bicycle, left it lying in the brush, and threaded her way into the pines, just far enough back to keep Jacob in sight.

She saw him stop in the midst of a clearing – perhaps, she thought, the very clearing where the Resistance shooters had waited for Evi to show up with the drunken Nazi. In the dim light of a sliver of moon, she saw him check his watch, look up at the sky, pull out a flashlight, and send a beam of light up into the darkness.

In the dead quiet, she heard a low thrum. Jacob again flashed a beam of light into the sky, and the thrumming sound came closer…an aircraft.

Behind her, in the same instant, she heard the back door of the tavern thrown open. She heard the hearty laughter of drunken soldiers bantering in their native German. She held still as the raucous laughter receded. She hoped the Germans were moving toward the roadway.

The noise above her deepened, and in the semi-darkness she saw a helicopter over Jacob's head, rotors turning.

Looking up at the hovering aircraft, she saw the U.S. Air Force logo on its side.

Where were the German officers? Surely, they had heard the racket, too. Evi peered behind her, drawing back into the shadows.

"*Amerikaner!*" someone shouted as two of the Germans looked up at the whirling rotors and drew their pistols.

Evi could not see Jacob from where she stood, but she knew he was out there in the clearing, and as the helicopter hung overhead, and a rope ladder began to descend, she began to understand what was happening. *Lieve god, how could she warn him?*

Panicked, she threw her bookbag to the ground, rummaged inside for the Colt.

The Germans shot first, the sound exploding in her ears. *Could they see Jacob in the clearing?*

Hands shaking, she raised the pistol, held it with both hands to steady herself. Grateful for even the bit of moonlight, she peered through the sight, took aim at one of the Germans, and slowly squeezed the trigger.

Before the man could fall, his companion whipped around, trained his gun in her direction.

Sight. Aim. Trigger. *Squeeze!* This time, she watched the man fall.

Shaken, hardly daring to breathe, she heard the back door of the tavern slam open again. No doubt they had heard the commotion.

Scurrying backward on trembling legs, she huddled at the side of the tavern, then sank to the ground, hands still gripping the pistol. She could not see Jacob, but three or four men were rushing to the side of the fallen Germans.

The helicopter lifted, and began to retreat, the rope ladder swinging in the night sky, one of its rotors at an odd angle.

In the next instant, Jacob appeared seemingly out of nowhere, his own weapon raised.

"Jacob…" she managed, crouched low on the sodden earth.

Jacob squinted, strode toward her, disbelief on his face.

"Evi?"

He grabbed her by the arm and propelled her through the brush, back in the direction of the farmhouse.

"Evi," he said again. "Where in the hell did you come from…?"

Now the tears came, fear and relief…

Godzijdank. He is alive…

ZOE

Zoe scraped the last of the yellow flesh from a small wedge of Gouda, a prize recovered from the train they had pillaged. She ate the cheese slowly, savoring every bite. Who knew when she would find such a treat again?

Tying her hair back with a length of old ribbon, she threw a dark scarf over it, tucked the scarf into her coat, and headed out into the cold.

Outside, she wavered briefly. If Lukas's warning had been correct, the Dans Hal was in safe hands with Leela. She was less sure how Gerritt was faring with the Germans' inquiries at the hospital.

It began to sleet, and she found herself slipping through the dirty slush that pooled at her feet. She ducked into the depot, hoping perhaps to catch a bus to the hospital, and counted herself lucky to find one bound for *Heemstede*. She climbed aboard, paid the fare, and settled into a seat near the back, the less to be noticed or engaged.

. . .

The ride was uneventful. Shaking off cold inside the hospital, she took the elevator to the second floor and peered into Gerritt's office. It was empty – and as usual, though most of his office staff knew her by now, she was told only that he was out.

She made sure the elevator was empty and took it to the fifth floor.

Sher picked her way around the familiar jumble of mattresses, sawhorses, ladders, and paint buckets and made her way down the hall, peering behind her as she slipped behind the false wall and rapped out the designated code.

The door opened. It never ceased to amaze her how quiet the room was, given its dozens of occupants.

Gerritt came forward, airbrushing her cheek. "Cousin…"

"Hello, Gerritt. How are you managing? I worry every day."

"With good reason," Gerritt sighed.

A toddler crawled between their feet, a mischievous little towhead quicky retrieved by his mother – or his hiding mother – and shushed him silently before he could cry out. All around them, people read, slept, spoke in low tones.

Zoe's gaze swept the room, found Kurt in his storyteller's spot, and waved. He looked up, smiled, and waved back.

Gerritt led her to a pair of wooden stools, seated himself across from her. "So! As promised, I presented a list of patients and staff to the German commander – edited of course. He surveyed it rather thoroughly, I thought, almost as though he was looking for specific names. He did not question the list…just asked for my word that they were current and accurate."

Zoe waited.

"He tucked it into his briefcase with a caveat – a caution, really, more than a threat. He said he would be back, expecting updates every week as the roster changed…"

Gerritt ran a hand over his face. "He asked for my assurance that I would be truthful and forthcoming, so that '*no further action need to be taken.*' I must tell you, Zoe, it was a chilling moment. There was no mistaking the warning behind the words."

"But he gave no indication of what he was looking for – or whom?"

"No. But I pray with everything in me that we can end this charade, and soon. I cannot afford to put myself or this hospital in jeopardy for very much longer."

Zoe sighed. "I understand, Gerritt. I do. No amount of gratitude can minimize the risk you are taking. If liberation does not come soon, I do not know what any of us will do."

"Am I interrupting?" Kurt appeared at their side.

"No," Zoe managed a wan smile. "We were weighing the safety of maintaining this charade in the face of escalating scrutiny."

Kurt came close enough that she could count the hairs on his upper lip. "I heard on the BBC last night that the Soviets are nearing the Auschwitz death camp," he whispered. "It seems the SS is beginning to evacuate the surviving Jewish prisoners."

His mouth tightened. "They clearly want the camps emptied before the Allies arrive, but the poor souls are out on foot, forced to march in the freezing weather," he said. "The BBC is calling it a death march."

Zoe grimaced, then looked up. "You have a radio?"

"In my knapsack. I listen when I can, mostly late at night when I am able to press it to my ear while most of the others are sleeping."

"A death march. *Lieve god,*" Gerritt said. "There is no end to what we will suffer if the war does not end soon."

Kurt looked from one to the other. "As one who may be actively hunted," he said, "I join you in a prayer that it does."

MILA

The dimly lit bistro was small but elegant, crystal chandeliers over white linen tables, a pleasing cacophony of muted conversation. She heard the pleasing clink of silver and glassware, the occasional pop of a champagne cork. Mila could not recall the last time she had encountered such gentility outside of her father's dining room.

She had little difficulty gaining entrance to the German stronghold. She had only to smile at the young maître and drop the name of the German officer who had suggested she lunch there while in Amsterdam.

The young man took in every aspect of her bearing and attire, and promptly bowed from the waist.

"Will someone be joining you, Mademoiselle?"

"Alas, no," she said. "I am in Amsterdam only for the day. But I was told not to miss the opportunity to dine here."

"Of course." He led her to a table in a quiet corner, with a good view of the room. "Shall I order some champagne for you to start?"

"I think a glass of white wine – a good French chardonnay, if you have it."

"Of course."

Mila raised the hem of her dress above her knees and crossed her legs so that the shapely calf and slim ankle above her black spike-heeled shoe protruded just a bit into the aisle. She checked her watch and peered at the menu, more than a little surprised at the depth and breadth of the selections. But then, she reminded herself, the whole establishment was run by and for the Nazis.

A waiter brought the wine. "Mademoiselle."

He offered it to her for approval.

Mila sniffed and sipped. "Perfect."

Bowing, he set the glass before her. "I shall give mademoiselle a moment with the menu, *ja*?"

"*Bitte*." She said, replying in German.

She picked up the menu, pretended to peruse it, checked her watch again. At precisely one o'clock, as she had been told to expect, a portly man with a full handlebar moustache entered the restaurant and tapped his fingers on the reception kiosk.

The maître d hurried to his side.

She could not hear their brief exchange, but there was no mistaking the face she had studied in the photograph or the storied air of arrogance. He was police captain Reimar de Boer.

She moved slightly, so that her foot extended into the aisle just the tiniest bit more. The maître de moved past without the slightest notice, but the portly de Boer, following in his wake, slowed for a moment to examine the extended ankle and follow the line of sight to Mila's face.

"So sorry, *Meneer*," she flashed a brilliant smile, pulling in her foot just a fraction.

De Boer paused for a milli-second, bowed slightly, and moved on. Mila picked up her menu.

She had given up hope that the ruse would work when de Boer suddenly appeared at her side, his cashmere coat draped over one arm, felt derby hat in his hand.

"*Pardon, Mademoiselle,*" he said in poor French, his ruddy face no more than a foot from hers. "Have we met?"

Mila nearly choked at the oldest pick-up attempt in the world, but she managed to look up and smile. "I do not think so, *Meneer*," she replied in formal Dutch. "I live in Maastricht, not far from the Belgian border. I am in Amsterdam only overnight."

"Ah," de Boer seemed to drink in her presence. "A visitor to our city. The maître' d tells me you are dining alone, *ja*?"

"Alas, yes" she simpered. "I have a bit of business to complete this afternoon. But then I am at odds, I suppose. I am afraid I know no one in Amsterdam."

A click of his heels, a nod of his head. "Allow me to introduce myself if I may. I am Reimar de Boer, a police captain in this fair city. The maître d' can vouch for my authenticity."

"Anna de Groot," she held out a manicured hand. It was all she could manage not to draw back in as his fleshy lips descended upon it.

"If I am not being too forward, *Mademoiselle*, may I perhaps join you for lunch?"

She gestured amiably to the seat across from her. "I would be pleased for the company. I was just enjoying a glass of Chardonnay. Is there anyone who prefers drinking alone?"

De Boer heaved his bulk into the red banquette, folding his coat beside him and placing his hat precisely on top of it.

"And if you have the time after you complete your business, I would be happy to show you the sights of Amsterdam."

He picked up the white linen napkin and spread it across his lap. "I realize we have only just met," his gaze caught sight of her neckline. "But who could be a safer companion than the city's police chief?"

Mila smile and inclined her head. *Who indeed?*

EVI

Bicycle forgotten, book bag over her shoulder, Evi followed in Jacob's wake as he forged a path for them through the brush between thickets of trees.

"We need to move faster, Evi," he called over his shoulder. "Those bastards may well be on our tail, trying to figure out where those shots came from."

Evi struggled in the darkness to keep up with his stride. "I'm right behind you, Jacob," she huffed.

He clearly knew the terrain, she realized, knew where he was going and how to get there. He must have walked these woods, inch by inch, more than once in the months he had been secreted with the Beekhofs – and *godjizdank*, for both of them that he had.

Branches fell away at her feet. Leaves crunched underfoot. She followed blindly, trusting Jacob's lead as night deepened and the air around them grew colder. Soon, she began to recognize the land nearing the driveway to the Beekhof farm.

Struggling for breath, she slowed her pace. "Please, Jacob, I need to rest."

"Okay, here," he told her, jogging up the secluded drive and slowing under a towering elm. He collapsed under it, Evi falling beside him. She listened to their breathing slow.

"Damn…" he muttered. "Snafu…"

Evi frowned. "Sna-fu?

"Old army term." He muttered. "Situation Normal…All Fu…" Never mind. It's done. It's over…"

She could think of nothing to say.

"Well," he said finally, into the silence. "It seems we are even Steven…"

Now she looked at him. "Even steven?"

She was close enough to see his crooked smile. "An American expression…It means…well, it means what it says. We're even."

Still, she struggled to understand.

Finally, he looked directly into her eyes, expression sober "You saved my life tonight, Evi. I don't why or how you followed me, but you did. So, now we're even."

She swallowed hard. What was there to say? She would have ripped out the woods, tree by tree, to ensure that Jacob was safe.

"The helicopter," she managed finally. "It was coming for you…?"

He drew a breath. "Yeah… I thought we could pull it off though… The Air Force did, too. We never figured on a bunch of drunken Germans."

Evi listened, searching his face.

"I managed to contact my CO – my commanding officer – on an old wireless the Beekhofs had in their basement. I was ecstatic. My CO thought it was worth a try. So, we made the plan for my exfiltration – "

"Exfil…"

"For the Army to retrieve me, send a rescue 'copter to a precise location at a specified time and pluck me into the air. I thought maybe that clearing in the woods could be an ideal place to try it." He screwed up his mouth. "...I guess it wasn't..."

A cold wind riffled through the elm.

"Lousy timing. Lousy luck," he said. "And I think one of the rotors was hit. I pray to God that ace makes it back to safety."

Evi shivered.

Jacob put an arm around her. "You're cold."

"Yes."

He drew her to his chest. She turned her face up.

Slowly, so slowly she was not sure it was happening, he began to close the distance between them. Close...so close...

Then she felt him pull away.

Evi blinked, aching in a way she had never felt before to feel his lips on hers.

Jacob shook his head. "You are sixteen years old, Evi. Sixteen. Jailbait, we call that in America."

"What does that mean?"

"It means...never mind what it means. Just thanks, Itty Bitty. That's all. 1 don't know what possessed you to follow me. But my Jewish mother would thank you, that's for sure."

Evi's eyes widened. "You are Jewish...?"

Even in the darkness, she saw his lopsided grin. "A Jew *and* an American pilot. No wonder the Huns are after me, eh?"

ZOE

Two Gestapo officials had, as Lukas warned, paid a visit to the Dans Hal, Leela told Zoe. Unlike their ransacking of the pet *kliniek*, however, their manner had appeared to be less threatening than information-seeking.

"I offered them the grand tour," Leela reported coolly. "I showed off the posters we have been making to promote our Carnival Week dance. Even though festivities must be curtailed, I told them, we are doing everything we can to maintain Dutch tradition. It is helpful in keeping up morale during these uncertain times."

Zoe raised her brows, listening.

"I invited the gentlemen to sit in and watch a toddler ballet class – I even told them we would be glad to accommodate if they or their comrades had youngsters here who might like join our dance class…"

Zoe gaped. "Leela, you are amazing."

As if on cue, a teen-aged girl Zoe did not know led five little girls in frilly skirts onto a makeshift stage. The cheerful strains of Tchaikowsky's *Nutcracker* wafted in from somewhere.

Leela stopped to applaud the little girls, then turned back to Zoe.

"Then I showed those Nazi bastards all around the hall," she said. "Including the office space, which had been thoroughly cleared. It all looked innocent enough."

"But what if they come back?" Zoe asked. "What about *Het Parool*?"

"We must be quick to get copies out of here as they are printed – to keep the shelves and counters clear at all times," Leela paused. "And everything else we carried out is stored in our cellar at home."

"But what if –"

Leela sighed and shrugged. "If they come for us, they come," she murmured. "For nearly four years, we have lived or died at their whim. It is a chance we must take until we are free. *Lieve god* it will not be much longer before the Allies prevail."

Zoe stared, amazed and thankful for the moment of sober levelheadedness.

"Leela, you are the calm in the eye of a storm."

"No more than the rest of us, Zoe. We do what we must."

She moved closer. "Is there any word of Daan?"

Zoe shook her head.

"Nor of our missing farmer…:" Leela sighed. "But," she lifted her head in the air. "There is some good news."

She led Zoe into the office space, cleared of everything but some dance posters on the wall and the two ancient mimeograph machines.

Leela reached into her bag and held up a handful of what looked like ration books. "My sister, Miep, has worked for more than two years in the government office here in Haarlem. She now has charge of the distribution of ration books. And she is very well trusted."

Zoe nodded.

"Two days ago, she reported a break-in." Leela's dark-eyed gaze was hard to read. "It seems a thief broke into the office and stole more than a hundred ration books."

Zoe began to understand.

"The police are still searching for the' perpetrator,'" Leela said. "But the 'stolen' ration books are in our cellar at home, along with the other things we stowed there. We can parcel them out to those who need them."

"What if the Germans –"

Leela held up her hands. "So be it."

Tears sprang before Zoe could stop them.

A look of understanding passed between them. *It was risk that was keeping them alive.*

MILA

It was dark in the alleyway in Amsterdam, and cold. Mila pulled her woolen scarf close and peered at the bubbling fountain in the *Leidseplein*. She had seen it many times, but never with such nervous trepidation.

What was it about men like Reimar de Boer, she mused – men with power but no principles – who thought they were exempt from payback?

The police captain had squired her around the city as though he had built it brick by brick for her pleasure – the Rijksmuseum, and the Prinzengracht Canal, miraculously spared from the bombing

And all the while, he told her of the evening he planned for them – an evening, thanks to her insinuation, ripe with the promise of sex.

It had not been easy, when she insisted on a change of clothes, to dissuade him from collecting her at her hotel. But she had been adamant and charmingly insistent that they meet at the celebrated fountain.

"I will enjoy it more seeing it with you," she had coaxed – and he, in his eagerness to get under her clothing, acquiesced.

"I will meet you at the fountain at eight o'clock," she had told him, her hand stroking his thickset wrist. "I have been told it is extraordinary at night. Tell your driver to pick us up at the entrance to the square at eight-fifteen promptly. Then I shall be yours for the night."

Mila looked up, glad for the nearly starless sky and the slowly gathering mist. She checked her watch again. By seven-forty-five, if all went well, Pieter would be positioned in a dark alleyway across from the entrance to the square.

It was risky to choose a spot where people might gather. But Pieter was a good marksman – and on such a cold night, they chanced it would be relatively deserted. As she looked out now toward the appointed meeting spot, she was relieved to see they had been correct.

Stamping her leather boots in the cold, she squinted into the square. Traffic was light, but the minutes were passing, and there was no sign of de Boer's black BMW.

What if it all went wrong? What if de Boer had grown suspicious? What if Pieter was not in place, or if de Boer's driver, whose assistance they counted on, was less trustworthy than they hoped?

Minutes went by. Mila worked hard to tamp down anxiety.

At seven-fifty-nine precisely, an automobile emerged out of the gloom, black and sleek, she thought..

A BMW? *Ja!*

The driver parked on the far side of the entrance, as planned, away from the nearest street lamp. A door opened facing the curb, and de Boer's bulky figure emerged. He leaned back into the car, perhaps to say something to his driver, then shut the door and straightened up.

Mila could do nothing but hold her breath.

It was over almost before she knew it – one…two…three seconds before de Boer's foot stepped onto the curb. She did not hear the report of the pistol, but she thought she saw the flash, and she watched as the big man lurched, swayed, and in the second it took her to blink, fell, as if in slow motion, face forward into the street.

EVI

Willem, the Beekhof's boy, pedaled alongside Evi on the trek back to the river's edge, the consensus being that if anyone were to be stopped so near to curfew, best that they were underage children.

Evi's bicycle had been forgotten near the tavern, and the one she borrowed from Mevreow Beekhof required more strength to maneuver. She struggled to keep up, and it was just after curfew when she bade Willem goodnight, urged him to stay safe, and made her way into the barge.

Mam was waiting, her graying hair askew, her eyes wild with fright. "Where in God's name, Evi? I was mad with worry! Where on earth have you been?"

Her heart and soul still under the elm tree with Jacob, Evi fought to find an answer. In the end, she thought it best to stay close to the truth. "I was out – learning to shoot."

Mam stared. "Learning to shoot…a firearm?"

Evi reached into the bottom of her knapsack, laid the Colt on the kitchen table.

Mam could not have appeared more dumbstruck if she had laid a suckling pig at her feet.

Evi swallowed. "This was given to me by a friend. He has been teaching me to use it. I thought – in the event we need protection."

"Protection? *Lieve god*, Evi, from what?"

"Oh, I don't know…" Evi found herself suddenly outraged. "Gestapo thugs behind you when you insist on navigating narrow canals to deliver supplies to a cave…"

Mam fell into the nearest chair. "You are prepared to shoot them? The Germans?"

"*Ja,* if I need to." She held her tongue about the German officers she had shot hours earlier for Jacob. "You can trust me, Mam. I know quite well how to handle this pistol and I will never use it unless I need to."

She tried to interpret the look on her mother's face. It was as though she were looking at a stranger.

"Mam," she began.

"Put it away."

Evi did not hesitate. She placed the Colt back in the bookbag, stashed the bag under her bed. It was at that moment that she could have sworn she heard a baby cry.

She walked back into the kitchen. Mam was on her feet. The sound came again, louder this time, distinctly the bleat of an infant.

Mam straightened. "I would have told you right off," she said. "But I was out of my mind with fright, Evi, not knowing if you were alive or dead."

Without another word, she moved to her sleeping quarters and emerged a moment later, cradling a bundle wrapped in a pale green blanket.

The baby whimpered.

Evi fell into a chair.

"I could not leave him in that cave in Limburg, Evi. The poor baby had no one. His mother took him there to hide from the Germans shortly after he was born …and then she died, Evi…some sort of fever. He cannot be more than two or three weeks old."

Evi stared, unable to speak.

"They managed to keep him alive, the others in the cave…I do not know how without his mother's milk. But look…" She peeled away the woolen blanket. The infant was painfully thin.

"And look here…" Mam unfastened the scrap of diaper. "Something is wrong with his thin little legs…or maybe with his little left hip…"

The baby's left leg seemed oddly splayed. When he kicked, it came up at an angle.

"Do you see?" Mam insisted. "Something is wrong. The child needs help. Evi. How could I leave him in that cave?"

What began as a whimper began to escalate, and soon became a shuddering cry.

Mam moved to the kitchen, where Evi saw, for the first time, three glass baby bottles lined up next to the sink and a tin of powdered formula.

"Where on earth – ?" she began.

"It was providence, Evi. These things were among the donated supplies I picked up and took with me to Limburg – and that was before we had any idea there might be a newborn in hiding…"

Mam turned to her. "Here, Evi. Hold him while I prepare a bottle."

Startled, Evi settled the bundle on her lap, moved the green blanket aside and stared into a tiny face.

"His name is Jacob."

Evi's head swiveled. "What?"

"His name is Jacob Rood. It is the name his mother gave him. He is Jewish. Do you see? He is circumsised."

Evi was not sure she knew what that meant, but it clearly meant something to her mother. She stared into the tiny face. *Jacob…..?*

"You can see why I could not leave him in that cave, Evi. He needs to see a doctor. But a doctor here, how can we be sure he would not be reported to the Germans?"

Evi was speechless.

"There is nothing for it but to get him across the border into Belgium, where he can safely get the medical care he needs. He has an aunt there, I was told in Limburg, his mother's sister in Antwerp."

"Mam – "

"I know the route to Middleburg, you know that, Evi. How many refugees have I transported? From there, if he survives, there will be other volunteers who can help to get him across the border."

Mam bustled over with the bottle of warm milk. "Here."

She handed it to Evi, who held it for a moment as though it might sprout wings, then lowered it to the vicinity of the tiny mouth and gasped as the infant squirmed and wriggled and sucked until the rubber nipple was plugged firmly between his lips.

His little eyes were tightly closed, but it seemed to Evi that she could feel in her bones his utter bliss in that instant …the sheer will of this tiny being to survive.

Jacob, she whispered solely to herself…..*Jacob…baby Jacob…Lieve god…*

ZOE

Zoe placed twenty of the ration books that had been appropriated by Leela's sister on top of Gerritt's desk. He looked up, his drawn face questioning.

"They are perfectly legitimate, cousin – procured by someone in the rations office who took a great risk to keep us fed."

Gerritt stared at them, riffled the pages, then rose slowly and placed them in a locked file cabinet.

"Our cooks are becoming quite skilled at making something from nothing," he said. Whatever we can get with these will help. *Danke.*"

It seemed to Zoe there was more of a grey streak in Gerritt's dark blonde hair. "You look troubled, Cousin."

"I am…" Gerritt sat heavily in his chair. "For one thing, it is getting increasingly difficult to maintain quiet in our sanctuary. People are people after all, Zoe, and after so many weeks in close quarters – no exercise to speak of, no way to vent – squabbles break out, the children especially, but even adult tempers flare…"

Zoe bit her lip. "I can imagine…"

"I do not think you can, cousin. Men, women and children, virtual strangers, sequestered together day after day. There is always – always something, a crying child, a missing toothbrush…"

Gerritt leaned forward, his hands clenched on the desktop. "I feel as though I am forced to be a summer camp instructor these days rather than a hospital administrator. I am aware every moment of every day that the slightest noise, the smallest altercation, may be all that stands between safety and discovery…"

"I know, Gerritt. I don't know how you manage -"

"I don't know either, Zoe." He looked at her closely. "And there is more."

He reached into a desk drawer. "I hesitate to show this to you, Zoe, because I think I can see where your feelings lie. But yesterday I received a missive from Gestapo headquarters. It is a list of co-called 'enemies of the Reich,' people of interest to the Germans… people who are to be reported immediately should they turn up at the hospital for treatment."

He handed over the letter. "Would you care to read it?"

Zoe took the letter, unfolded it, began to read the alphabetized list of names. "I am afraid I do not know these people by name, Gerritt," she said after a moment.

"Then I can tell you that seven of the names on this list are Jewish physicians who have been in hiding with us for months," he said. "Since before you came to me, in fact. Four others, who are with us now in our 'renovating' top floor, are among the Dutch families suspected by the Reich to be hiding Jewish children…"

He paused. "And look toward the bottom of the list, Zoe, among the names beginning with S…"

Zoe read, and the name leapt out. *Schneider, Kurt…Lieve god…*the storyteller.

PART FOUR

Haarlem, the Netherlands
February 1945

MILA

The plan was for Mila to reunite with Pieter at the auto park within moments after de Boer went down. But from the time the big man hit the ground, nothing went as expected.

Sirens sounded almost at once. Whether a passerby had telephoned police headquarters or whether the two police vehicles that screeched to the curb simply happened by was irrelevant. Floodlights lit up the area almost at once, and uniformed officers began to cordon off the streets.

From behind her, the few hardy souls out walking in the cold began rushing toward the tumult at the fountain, making it risky for Mila to push the other way without drawing suspicion. On the other side of the square, she feared, Pieter could be trapped with a pistol in his possession, unable to flee.

More police vehicles, sirens wailing, rolled into the square. A pair of helicopters maneuvered into place and hovered above the scene at the fountain, and the loud, unnerving *WAH-wah-WAH-wah* of an ambulance echoed in the frigid night air.

Mila watched, frozen in place, as de Boer was loaded onto a stretcher and tethered by technicians to what looked like a jumble of tubes. *Could the traitor still be alive?*

Allowing the procession of bystanders to pass, she walked quickly in the direction of the auto park, praying Pieter had been able to flee.

She rounded a corner to find herself face to face with four advancing Gestapo.

"*Fraulein? Wohin gehst du so schnell?*" Where are you going so quickly?

"*Unteroffizieres,*" she began in fluent German. "I have been out enjoying this beautiful city. Even in winter, it is spectacular."

The officers looked from one to the other.

"*Sie sind Deutche?*" You are German? *Identifikation!*"

"*Deutche, nein,*" she smiled, producing the false papers that identified her as Swiss. "*Nur ein bewunderer.*" Only an admirer.

The taller of the two studied her papers, looked up at her with narrowed eyes. "Are you aware there has been a shooting?" he asked in German.

"*A shooting?*" she repeated, blue eyes wide, grateful for her fluency in the language. "*Vo?*" she asked innocently. Where?

More narrowed eyes. Whispered words between them.

She was about to invoke the name of her German benefactor when, finally, the tall one handed back her papers. "Go back to your hotel, Fraulein" he warned. "At once."

She inclined her head, a puzzled look on her face. "*Ja, sicher,*" she said. At once."

She could feel their eyes on her back as she traversed the street, turned left at the next corner. She walked faster as she neared the grey Renault. Her shoulders slumped. It was unoccupied.

Shivering, she retreated into the shadows of the car park. *Lieve god,* what now? What if Pieter had been unable to retreat? *What if de Boer's officers had grabbed him?*

EVI

Baby Jacob lay sound asleep in her arms, a dribble of formula trickling from tiny rosebud lips onto his rounded chin. Evi, lost in the infant's contentment, dabbed at the drip with a bit of cloth.

"Evi…" Mam stood over her shoulder. "For the baby's sake, I am glad for your help. But please…Do not get too attached."

"I know…"

"Arrangements are in place, and there is only so much formula. I must move him downstream today, while there is still enough to keep him fed him on his journey across the border."

"Please, Mam, be careful…"

"I am always careful."

"Yes, but…" Evi sighed. "There are Germans everywhere. They are more watchful than ever."

Mam stood with her hands on her hips. "Perhaps you would like to come with me, Evi, *ja*? You can look after the baby while I navigate."

Evi wavered. She had thought she might go back to the Beekhof farm. Jacob must surely still be upset at his failure to – *ex-fil-trate*.

But Mam needed her help today – and little Jacob, as well…

• • •

They were on the river before nine in the morning. Evi piled cushions and woolen blankets in the hold to make a bed for the baby. She fed him a bottle, still wondering at the sight of this tiny child struggling, as they all were, to survive.

He was asleep before the bottle was half empty. Evi climbed to the main cabin as Mam piloted the barge.

They were past The Hague and nearly to Rotterdam. Evi was near to nodding off herself when she heard the gears begin to grind.

"Evi!," Mam shouted. "There is a spit of land on the port side. Get ready to jump!"

"But – ?"

"Do not ask questions, Evi. Jump! Now! Find your way back to Haarlem!"

"But the baby – "

"You cannot carry him. Let me worry. Now, Evi, jump *now*!"

Evi glanced toward the hold. Glanced back at Mam. She had never heard such urgency in her voice. Grabbing her bookbag, she leapt from the port side, landed heavily on a gravel-filled slope, clawed her way to a grassy knoll, her left knee badly scraped. She swiped at the blood with the hem of her skirt and sat to catch her breath, scanning the horizon for the barge.

Just down the coastline, she caught sight of it, inching its way toward shore, followed, to her horror, by a German patrol boat, big and grey, pulling quickly alongside.

She watched, terrified, as two black-booted Germans leapt from the e-boat onto the barge before it was fully stopped against the pilings.

She tried to move, to do as Mam had told her, but she could not take her eyes from the barge. It seemed to take forever before Mam emerged, her red shawl around her shoulders, one of the Germans close behind, his rifle at her back.

Evi leaned forward, squinting into the wind, and watched, unbelieving, as the rifle sounded and Mam, like a rag doll tossed into the air, tumbled soundlessly into the sea.

ZOE

Kurt made a place for her on the wooden bench where he sat to tell his stories. His voice was barely above a whisper.

"I told you, Zoe, that I was able to smuggle Jews and German dissenters across the border. My routes took them from Cologne to Rotterdam where, if they were wily, and fortunate, they could make their way to safety."

Zoe studied the lines of Kurt's face, a prominent nose under warm brown eyes, dearer to her each time she saw him.

Kurt sighed. "I was part of a group called *Die Rote Kapelle* - the Red Orchestra – a network of Resistance workers united against the Nazi regime. Among those I helped to escape were some high-level military defectors and diplomats the Reich had been pursuing."

Zoe listened.

Kurt paused, leaning back. "Needless to say, when the Gestapo caught on, they began pursuing me, as well – especially in Rotterdam, once they realized I had slipped out of Germany. So, I took a new name and re-settled here, first in Amsterdam and then in that little house in Haarlem before the Germans starting grabbing up land."

"*Lieve god* you were able to dodge them…"

"Thus far, anyway. Apparently, at the time we were told to evacuate, they had not yet identified me…But now, one way or another, it appears they have made the connection."

Zoe wondered who might have betrayed him – and what the Reich had paid them for their loyalty.

She held up a hand. "But Kurt, they have no way of knowing, at this point, whether you are alive or dead…"

Kurt offered a wry smile. "And still my name appears on your cousin's list of 'most wanted…"

Zoe glanced across the room, where Gerritt was deep in conversation with two of the Jewish physicians who were still treating those who needed care, even here, in this secret sanctuary, with the barest of supplies.

"Kurt, you know that Gerritt will never give up anyone to the Germans – not as long as we –"

"Not as long as we are able to remain hidden."

She nodded.

Tentatively, he placed a hand over hers. It felt warm and protective. "I love your passion, Zoe," he said. "And your faith in goodness and right."

She placed her other hand gently over his.

"But the Reich is relentless," he whispered. "I fear you are far more confident than I that we can remain out of sight for very long."

MILA

Minutes passed, each longer than the last. From the shadows of the auto park, she saw flashing lights on the move, no doubt Dutch and German police prowling the streets for the assassin.

Assassin.

She trembled, as much from fear as from the cold. What on earth was she to do if Pieter did not find his way back…?

At long last, she saw a tall, slim figure in a dark overcoat moving slowly toward the auto park. She peered through the night, hardly daring to breathe, until she could be sure.

Pieter.

She moved forward until he saw her and signaled. Glancing around her in the near-empty space, she slipped into the grey Renault.

He looked solemn and spent in the glare of the klieg lights still emanating from the crime scene.

"*Godzijdank,*" she murmured, wanting to touch him, to embrace him in the joy of knowing he was alive. But she only looked at him and held her hands in her lap.

"So many police, so very fast," she murmured.

As if he read her mind, Pieter reached for her, an awkward hug hindered by the steering wheel. "I am here, Mila… I am here."

He touched her face, then straightened. "But I cannot be certain de Boer is dead."

Mila frowned. "I saw him being lifted into the ambulance…"

"A passerby got in the way of my shot. My aim was less than perfect."

She blinked. "You think de Boer is still alive?"

"I cannot be sure. But if he is, we may not have another go at him. The Gestapo and their Dutch police accomplices are already on high alert."

He turned the key in the ignition and the engine sprang to life.

"The pistol…" she asked.

"I have it. A German Mauser with a long and complex history. There is little chance it will ever be traced to the Resistance."

Pieter looked carefully in all directions before pulling out into the street. "I wanted this kill," he muttered. "For Daan…"

Mila looked straight ahead. "I know."

She knew, too, that if de Boer was still alive, neither Pieter nor she would be completely safe.

Flashing red and blue lights still pierced the night air, but Pieter drove cautiously, avoiding main arteries, constantly checking the mirrors.

"What if we stay in Amsterdam?" she ventured.

"No," he said. "There is nothing more to be done here now. We will know de Boer's condition by morning."

• • •

It was after eleven when the Renault drew up in front of the Brouwer estate. There were lights on in the imposing entryway, but the windows were mostly dark.

"Mila –" he said, turning toward her.

"You know I am glad to have done my part, Pieter. I would do it again in a heartbeat."

"You are brave and beautiful, Mila. The more I know of you, the more I want to know. If only –"

"What?"

"If only we lived in a time when life was…predictable."

She shrugged. "Life is not predictable ever, Peter. We can only plan…and hope."

He turned off the engine, opened his door. "Come. I will see you to your door."

He took her hand to help her out of the car, and held it as they walked up the driveway. At the door, he turned to her and without a word, drew her face toward his.

EVI

She had no idea how long she stood on that knoll, screaming, crying, stomping the ground beneath her feet as though a tantrum might somehow will Mam back into her sight.

But soon enough, the German e-boat sped off, and the barge began to drift, unmoored and unmanned, and it was not until she had cried until there were no more tears that Evi remembered the baby.

Baby Jacob. *Lieve god*, where was the baby? Had the Germans killed him, too?

Frantic, freezing in the thin sweater she wore, she wrapped her arms around herself and rocked, grappling with what to do next.

She could try to swim. It was not that far to the drifting barge. But the freezing water might kill her, too, and what could she do even if she reached it? She had never once taken the helm – and even if she could figure out how to do so, it would not bring Mam back…or baby Jacob.

In the end, with no more tears to shed, she remembered what Mam had screamed at her: *Find your way back to Haarlem.*

With a last piercing glance at the yellow barge, and the choppy water beneath, she clambered to the next knoll, then farther up the slope, gasping for breath between her tears, and fighting the wind until she reached what appeared to be a packed dirt roadway.

From this distance, looking back, the drifting barge was no more than a dot on the horizon. Finding, from somewhere deep inside, a new reserve of tears, she sat in the roadway, pulled her sweater around her, and cried until her face was wet with tears and mucus.

Then, spent, she wiped her face with her sleeve, rose to her feet, and began the trudge to look for civilization.

ZOE

Zoe used a warm, wet washcloth to wipe the discharge from the Schnauzer's left eye, then carefully flushed the eye with saline solution and took a closer look.

"I think you're going to be just fine, little Fritzi," she said, smoothing the dog's coarse, wiry coat. "A bit of an infection, that is all this is."

She filled a syringe with the last of the antibiotic solution and deftly, holding the animal still and its eyelid wide open, approached from behind and applied it directly into the eye.

"There," she steadied the pup on the table as it blinked and tried to squirm away. She smiled, looking directly into the questioning chocolate eyes. "As I told you, little one," she repeated softly, "you are going to be just fine."

Coaching the animal to rise to its feet, Zoe attached a lease to the collar and walked it out to the waiting room, dispatching its anxious young owner and her father with instructions for aftercare and a packet from the shrinking supply of oral antibiotics.

She sighed, watching the trio exit. It felt good to be doing what she was trained to do. She missed the busy days, the succession of animals needing her care. Mostly, she missed Daan…and she worried.

Just this morning, she had heard on a BBC broadcast that Canadian infantries had been successful in clearing German forces from the east side of the German/Dutch frontier – and that the assault, part of the American General Eisenhower's strategy, was helping the Allies to advance. At the same time, the Soviets had taken most of Poland and were advancing their own march into Germany.

It was cheering news. On the face of it, as a mostly clear February hinted at an end to the long winter, there was reason to hope for a German surrender.

Zoe sighed. *Would it come soon enough to keep the top floor of the hospital hidden? Soon enough to keep Kurt and the others safe, and Gerritt from an almost certain charge of treason?*

Zoe stripped the used protective paper from the examination table. There was only a single roll of it left in the supply room. What would she do when it ran out altogether? When no antibiotics remained? When hope, like the last of their dwindling supplies dissolved, like so much soapy water, down the drain?

MILA

The morning edition of the German language newspaper ran the story above the fold on page one, along with lurid headlines and photographs.

Mila devoured the details; Amsterdam police captain shot in the street in front of the *Leidsplein* fountain by an as-yet unknown assailant…attempted assassination…critical condition…held under guard in hospital…massive search for assailant…

Exasperated, she threw back her head. The traitor was alive. The painstaking scenario she and Pieter had planned was a failure.

She was finishing her tea, alone in the dining room, when Reit appeared with a package.

"This came for you, *Missen*, last evening."

"Thank you, Reit."

She took the flat package, used a silver knife to slit it open, and stared wordlessly at the contents; inside a colorful cardboard sleeve, with a sensual photograph of the artiste, a recording of Marlene Deitrich's '*Lili Marleen.*'

Mila sighed, recalling the dinner party when she had stopped the conversation about the Cinema blast with her wish for the popular recording.

She fished inside the package, and brought out a note, written in loopy German script. *'With kindest regards to a beautiful lady.'* It was signed, *Obersturmfuhrer* Franz Becker.

No doubt the leering wretch would expect something in return – likely her company away from under the eye of her father.

Unlikely that would happen! Not if she had any say in the matter...

Tossing the record and its wrappings over the newspaper on the table, she called to the housekeeper in the kitchen. "Thank you, Reit. You may clear these things. I will be out for a while."

Grabbing a cashmere coat and scarf from a hook by the door, she set off into the morning. The sky was a dull and sullen grey, and the last of winter's withered brown leaves swirled at her feet at the curbsides. It was not as cold as it had been of late, but she strode the few kilometers to Pieter's office against a persistent wind.

His response to the news of de Boer's survival, she knew, would be both practical and rational. He was far less emotional than she...

And yet.... she felt her face flush. His kiss last night had been anything but restrained. If she closed her eyes, she could taste his lips, urgent and wanting, and her body responding with a rush she dared not think about.

She walked faster, low heels tapping on cobblestones, looked over her shoulder by habit, and made her way to the brick building that had become her second home. Not for the first time, she wondered if a plumbing service had ever operated in the space, or if the prominent signage had been a ruse by Resistance planners from the outset.

It was not too far a leap to wonder if the SS had eyes on it....

• • •

Pieter kissed her on both cheeks, then to her surprise, pressed his lips lightly against hers. She liked the way her body fit against his, as though it had been made for that purpose.

"You are cold," he murmured into her hair. "And beautiful with your cheeks all rosy."

She leaned in again, but he pulled back. "Not here. Not now," he said softly.

She nodded agreement, seating herself as he crossed behind the desk. "So," she said. "You have read the news."

"Of course." He sat back in his chair, arms folded in front of him. "But we know little of his condition. Now we can only hope for the best – or the worst, as it were, if he is critical. Either way, we delivered a message. If de Boer survives, he will guess we are aware of his treachery."

Practical. Rational. As Mila had expected. "Pieter, my concern is pushback..."

"The bastard and his allies will have to find me first, and that will never happen."

"The driver..."

Pieter shook his head. "I spoke with the driver late last night. He was crestfallen. He abhors the man. Investigators will get nothing from him."

"And the bullet –"

"From an untraceable pistol now resting in the depths of the Spaarne." He leaned forward, meeting her gaze. "For now, we are patient. We wait."

EVI

Eventually, the road gave way to broken cobblestones, but by the time the first outbuildings came into view, her worn black shoes were dusty brown with dirt and she was numb, weary, and hungry.

She hung back, peering at her bleak surroundings with suspicion, trying to formulate how she might ask for help.

If she managed to find a police station, how could she know where their allegiance lay?

Anyone could be a Nazi sympathizer – or a friend to the Resistance. *Mevreow* Beekhof's words came back to her in a rush; *Be careful what you say to strangers, Evi, even to me…*

How was she to know who to trust?

Worse yet, she had leapt from the barge with nothing but her bookbag and the clothes she was wearing. She had no money bag, only her identification papers…and the weighty reassurance of the Colt.

Shivering, she passed a deserted farmhouse and forced herself to continue walking.

• • •

She must have looked as cold, bedraggled, and miserable as she felt, because the old woman who spied her loitering at the edge of the market square peered at her with narrowed eyes. But after a moment, she bustled over, threw a grey woolen shawl around Evi's shoulders, and led her wordlessly to a small wooden stool.

Evi sat, gazing vacantly at her steely gray-haired benefactor, piercing blue eyes in a lined face under a dark blue kerchief. Her expression was questioning, but Evi was too tired, too listless, too empty inside to make the attempt to speak.

The woman watched her for a moment, bustled off, and returned with a tin cup of water. When Evi nodded her thanks but said nothing, she ambled off toward rough-hewn wooden handcart that displayed a few potatoes and cabbages.

Evi gulped water until she began to choke, then sipped the rest slowly, feeling every drop begin to saturate the empty space inside her. She pulled the grey shawl close around her, watched the old woman tend to a customer, and glanced around at what appeared to be a small village marketplace.

No more than a clearing in a wooded area, it held a few worn wooden tables and handcarts, several rusting bicycles leaning against a shed, and four or five vendors selling produce, fresh and dried fish, and sewing goods from their carts to a small but steady stream of buyers.

The briny smell of the fresh fish roiled her empty stomach, threatening to bring up the water she had gulped. Evi swallowed hard, trembling under the woolen shawl, aware the old woman was watching her.

After a while, the woman came toward her again, bearing a small, green apple. "Eat it slowly," she warned.

Evi rolled the apple in her hands, sniffed it and took a cautious bite. It was at once sour and sweet, and she felt her mouth fill with liquid.

"*Dankuvel*," she managed when she had swallowed.

The woman nodded. "So, you can speak.".

Evi looked around. "Please, where is this place?"

The old woman squinted. "This is *Vlaardingen*," she said. "It is not far from Rotterdam. My name is Alettte."

Evi wailed, a small, thin sound, hardly recognizing the sound of her own voice.

The woman persisted. "How did you come here?"

Tears came. Evi swiped at them. "From the sea. I jumped from a barge."

"From a barge..." The woman's eyes narrowed.

Evi pointed vaguely toward the coast. "Somewhere down there. The Germans came. I jumped from a barge. My Mam told me to jump ashore..."

Tears from a place deeper than she knew escaped and blurred her vision. "They killed her...They murdered my Mam...The Nazi bastard raise his rifle and shot her. I saw her fall into the sea..."

"*Lieve god...*" the woman called Alette winced, sinking down on one knee to Evi's level. "What is your name, *kleintje*? Where do you come from?"

"My name is Evi...Evi Strobel," she sobbed. "We were coming from Haarlem. That is where we live...on the Spaarne..."

Alette nodded. "Do you have family here?'

Evi shook her head. "No."

"In Haarlem then. Friends, perhaps."

She hesitated. *Mila, perhaps? Zoe?*

"There is a train to Haarlem from Rotterdam," Alette said. "But better, I think, if someone could come for you and take you there."

Evi drew a shaky breath.

Alette rose to her feet, wiped her hands on her striped apron, buttoned her coat to the collar. "I will take you to my home, *kleintje* It is not far away. There, I have a telephone – if there is service."

ZOE

She was cleaning the holding cages when the telephone shrilled. She ran to answer it. "Mulder Pet *kliniek*. How can I –"

She stopped.

What she heard was an agonized sob.

She tried again. "This is Dr. Visser. Who is this?"

"Z- Zoe,- " She did not recognize the voice. "It is Evi…"

A pause. "Evi? Evi Strobel?"

"*Ja…*" Zoe heard the quiver in her voice. "Mam is gone, Zoe. Dead. The Germans murdered her. I jumped from the barge. I am in Vlaardingen…"

Zoe struggled to make sense of what she heard. *Vlaardingen…Lotte dead?* "Evi, when did this happen?"

"Early today. We were on our way to Middleburg with baby Jacob - Oh, lieve god…" The girl broke into anguished sobs.

Baby Jacob?

Zoe let Evi cry for a moment. Her voice, when she spoke, was gentle. "Evi, *alstublieft*. Please…You are going to be fine. Is there someone there with you in Vlaardingen?"

In a moment, a new voice came on the line. Evi sobbed in the background.

"Hallo?"

"*Ja*, I am here. My name is Zoe Visser - Doctor Zoe Visser. And you?"

"I am Alette Spierhoven. I am here with your young friend in Vlaardingen. She is very sad, and barely coping. She needs to get home. Can you help?"

Zoe struggled to make sense of what she heard. Then her brain sprang into action. "*Ja, ja, natuurlijk..* Can you tell me exactly where you are?"

• • •

She paced for a moment in the empty *kliniek*. A train, perhaps, to Rotterdam. She did not have access to an automobile – and even if she did, there was no petrol.

A thought surfaced. She picked up the phone, quickly dialed a number.

"Plumbing company."

"Pieter, it is Zoe. I am at the *kliniek*." Quickly, she told him what she knew, about Lotte's murder at the hands of the Germans, about Evi, impossibly stranded somehow, in a small village near Rotterdam.

Pieter cut her off. "I understand. I can drive. It is not so long a way." He paused. "Or perhaps, Mila would be a better choice. Evi knows Mila well. I will talk to her at once. One of us will collect you at the back door of the *kliniek* in one hour."

• • •

Zoe was standing in the alley behind the *kliniek*, tying a scarf around her head, when Mila drove up in a dark green Daimler.

MILA

"Whatever has happened?" Mila asked, as Zoe slipped in beside her in the front seat of the Daimler. "Pieter told me only that Evi needs help in Rotterdam…*Rotterdam?*"

Zoe took a breath. "In Vlaardingen, actually. Evi telephoned, totally distraught – and with reason. As I understand it, she and Lotte were on their way to Middleburg this morning when German officers boarded the barge. Evi was able to jump to safety onshore, but Lotte – Lotte was shot – murdered as Evi watched from the shore."

Mila slumped in her seat. "*Lieve god…*"

"Evi found her way to a marketplace in Vlaardingen, where a woman took her in. I spoke to her. Her name is Alette. She sounded trustworthy. For Evi's sake, I hope that is true. In any case, she told me precisely where to find them. *Bedankt* that you are able to drive."

"It is only an hour's journey, I think…I will make up some story for my father…*Schamel* Evi. Poor Evi…*Schamel* Lotte…"

She turned to Zoe. "Where is the barge?"

"Afloat somewhere, I suppose," Zoe told her. "I only know that Evi was frantic."

She paused. "She said something about a baby…Lotte was moving a baby to safety, I think…."

Mila's brows rose. "I know that Lotte has transported refugees many times…but where would this baby have come from?"

Zoe shook her head. "I do not know. But the poor child was likely murdered as well…These were German invaders, after all."

Mila stepped harder on the gas pedal.

Zoe turned to her. "First Daan Mulder. Now Lotte. Who will be next, Mila? The Germans are becoming more malicious than ever. There is no safety anywhere."

Mila remembered the *Obersturmfuhrer* – Franz Becker of the Deitrich recording – who had warned of Hitler's threat to murder two Dutch citizens for every German soldier lost in the dual explosions…

Zoe broke into her thoughts. "Mila, are you aware of the hiding families and the others we have sequestered at the hospital in *Heemstede*?"

"Pieter told me about them, yes," Mila said. "You set aside food for them that had been rescued from the Gertman train."

"Yes," Zoe said. "But I fear the German thirst for revenge is growing. They are now demanding the names of all patients and staff at the hospital where these families are sequestered. I live in fear that stormtroopers will one day storm the building."

Mila considered. "How many people are in hiding there?"

"Thirty, perhaps…a few Jewish physicians…the hiding families – at least one wanted German patriot…"

Mila stole a sidelong glance. "A German patriot?"

"*Ja,*" Zoe paused. "His name is Kurt Schneider. He fled Germany early in the war when the Gestapo came after him for helping refugees escape…"

Mila listened.

"Kurt is a kindly person, Mila – a gentle soul who tells stories to the children to keep them quiet and occupied in their shelter."

Mila smiled. "It sounds as if you know him well."

"Not well," Zoe said, looking out of the window. "But I would be lying if I said I do not feel drawn to him. A German, of all people…and yet I confess that in any other world, I would like to know him better…"

Mila nodded, the depth of Zoe's caring clear to her.

"Not every German is cut from the same cloth, Zoe," she said. I am sure there are many who abhor Herr Hitler."

And then there are Dutchmen like Reimar de Boer, she thought, who sell out their countrymen for a price…

She had heard no more of de Boer's condition, only that he was recovering under heavy guard at an unnamed Amsterdam hospital – and despite Pieter's confidence that his pistol could not be traced, she could not help fearing for his safety.

She drove the last few kilometers in silence.

"We are nearing the turn to Vlaardingen," she said at last. "Tell me the signposts we are to look for…"

EVI

Mevrouw Spierhoven – Alette, she insisted – fed her soup that was rich with vegetables, and homemade noodles made from wheat she said she had grown and ground herself. She insisted on making a bed for Evi on a sofa piled with colorful handknit blankets.

The colorful blankets reminded her of Mam, and Evi wept silently into their softness. She was wide awake, heavy with grief, when she heard the motorcar stop. She sat up, throwing off her covers.

An automobile door closed, and then another. Evi ran to the door of Alette's cottage.

"Evi?"

It was Mila. She would know her voice anywhere.

"*Ja, ja*, I am here!"

And there was Mila in the doorway, and Zoe, too, and Evi leaped into their arms, and tears from a seemingly endless wellspring wet her face again.

The two of them held her, uttering soothing words, until finally she was able to pull back, wipe her face with her sleeve, and take a shuddering breath.

"Mam is gone," she whispered, working to find her voice. "The Germans murdered her in cold blood. They shot her, while I watched from the shore…I saw her fall into the sea…"

Mevrouw Spierhoven – Alette – came from behind her. "The girl has been inconsolable, and with good reason. It is a blessing that she found her way here."

"And the baby," Evi cried. "Baby Jacob. He was cir-cum…he was Jewish. Likely they murdered him too…"

Mila sighed, stepped forward, took the old woman's hands, and thanked her profusely for her kindness.

From her place at the door, where Zoe still held her, Evi saw the older woman shake her head. "Three years ago," she said, "I stood here, helpless, while the Jews of Vlaardingen were rounded up and ripped away from us by the Germans…I am glad to be able to help in some small way today."

"Thank you," Mila said, "for keeping our Evi safe."

Alette nodded. "I will not forget her sadness – or her courage."

Evi moved forward, suddenly overwhelmed, and took the woman's hands in hers. "I will remember your kindness always, Alette. Thank you from the bottom of my heart."

Zoe joined them, placing her hand over theris. "*Mevrouw*, you are a brave and good woman. We are fortunate it was you who found our Evi."

Once again, tears pooled in Evi's eyes.

"Come, Evi," Mila said. "It is time to go.

• • •

"*Stop!*"

As they drove past a promontory high above the sea, Evi scanned the horizon.

"There," she pointed. "Can you see it?"

It had begun to rain, and the sky had darkened.

"Yes, I think so," Zoe said.

No more than a kilometer from the shore, Evi was certain she saw it – the yellow siding, the dark roof, the old barge bobbing in the restless sea.

Mila pulled to side of the road. "Yes, I see it…Oh, Evi, I am so deeply sorry."

Evi gazed out to sea.

"Evi, how did it happen?" Zoe's voice was gentle. "And where did the baby come from?"

Evi sighed. "Mam took supplies to some Jewish refugees who are in hiding in the caves near Limburg," she managed. "She brought back a baby…a tiny baby whose mother was dead. He needed to be seen by a doctor…"

She looked again out to sea. "We were on our way to Middleburg, where other volunteers could try to move him across the border to an aunt in Belgium, when the e-boat – when the Germans drew up alongside us…"

She paused, recalling her mother's frantic shout.

"I did not see the e-boat approach," she said. "I was in the hold, tending to the baby, but I could feel we were abruptly changing course. I came above to see what was happening, and as we scraped up against a rocky bit of coastline, Mam screamed at me to jump ashore.

The long silence was thick with grief.

Evi buried her face in her hands, in her mind's eye images of Mam and baby Jacob, forever lost at sea…

ZOE

They were nearly back to Haarlem before Zoe could bring herself to ask the question.

"Evi," she said softly. "With the barge lost at sea, you will need to decide where you would like to stay the night…"

Mila was quick to jump in. "I am certain our volunteers will make every effort to retrieve the barge and bring it back to its berth," she said. "Until then, I am quite sure my family would welcome you to stay with us."

"Or you can stay with me," said Zoe. "My apartment is small, but I would be glad for your company."

She felt, rather than saw, the hesitation in Evi's face. But when at last the girl spoke from the back seat, her voice was firm.

"Thank you…thank you both," she said. "You are dear and very good friends. But I have another idea. There is a farm on the outskirts of the city…it is not far, Mila, from the tavern where we planned my first mission…"

Evi paused. "The farm belongs to a family called Beekhof. That is where I would like to go."

Zoe glanced at Mila. "Beekhof…I do not know of them. Are they friends of your family?"

"Not exactly," Evi said.

Again, a sidelong glance at Mila. "Well, then, how do you know them?"

A long silence, as though Evi was deciding what to say next. At length, she leaned forward in her seat.

"They American airman who came to my rescue that night, Mila. Do you remember?"

"*Ja*, of course…"."

"The Beekhof family has been hiding him on their farm since his parachute landed in their field," Evi said. "They helped him to heal his injuries. They are fine people. They even found false identification papers for him…"

Zoe looked at her. "How do you know all this, Evi?"

Silence.

"Evi?"

Another hesitation. "I have – spent a few afternoons on their land," she blurted. "Jacob has been teaching me to shoot."

"Jacob?"

"The American."

Zoe turned in her seat. "The American airman is teaching you to shoot?"

"Yes. "I have become quite proficient…" Her voice trailed off…

"Proficient enough," she said, finally, "to save Jacob's life when the ex-fil-tra-shun failed…"

Zoe stared. "The exfiltration – ?"

Evi slid back in her seat. "Now, we are even Steven, Jacob said…We have each of us helped to save the life of the other…"

Zoe detected something more in Evi's voice. "I see," she murmured.

"But how can you be sure, Evi," Mila said, "that this Beekhof family will take you in? For them it means another mouth to feed, and who knows how long it may be until – even if the barge can be rescued…?"

Evi's voice was firm. "*Mevrouw* Beekhof is a kind woman. She likes me. She will understand."

A short silence.

Zoe placed a hand on Mila's wrist. "Evi has been through the gates of Hell today, Mila. I think we need to do as she asks."

Mila took a moment, then sighed softly. "Where, precisely, is this farm?"

• • •

It was dark, but Evi clearly knew the way. She guided Mila to a near-hidden driveway just off the main road. A long, graveled driveway them led them to a modest structure. Zoe could see a dim light inside, but the farmhouse was otherwise dark.

"Come," she said to Evi. "I will take you to the door. Mila?"

"There is no point in overwhelming the family, Zoe. You go. I will wait."

Evi did not wait. She hurried to the door, knocked urgently. Zoe heard a dog barking.

"Slowly, Evi," Zoe whispered. "We do not wish to alarm them…"

"Who is there?" she heard after a moment.

"It is Evi," the girl said, leaning into the door. "Evi Strobel."

Another moment.

The door slowly opened. A woman stood against the light, a wary-looking Shepherd huffing at her feet. She looked between the two women. "Evi…?"

Evi began to cry.

The Shepherd quieted, bounded through the doorway, and nudged his snout under Evi's hand.

The woman looked at Zoe, seemed to take her measure. Then she turned to Evi and opened her arms wide.

MILA

It was well past the dinner hour when Mila returned home. She parked the Daimler in its place in the garage, wondering what, if anything, could be done to rescue the ill-fated Strobel barge and bring it home. Everything Evi owned in the world was aboard it…

The front door was open when Mila tried it. She would just have soon gone straight to her room, but she was not surprised to hear her father call out.

"Mila, is that you?"

Sighing, she hung her coat on a peg and walked into the dining room, relieved to see that only her parents sat at the half-cleared table.

"Good evening, Mother...Father..."

"There are leftovers in the kitchen," her mother said mildly. "We missed you, Mila."

"Thank you. I am not very hungry. Father, I hope you do not mind that I took the Daimler. I had some errands..."

Her father peered at her, then nodded stiffly. "Urgent errands, I expect."

Mila shrugged.

"There was a telephone call for you from Franz Becker. You remember the *Obersturmfuhrer*? He wanted to know if you received the Deitrich recording he went to great lengths to procure for you."

Mila swallowed her distaste. "I did, father. Please thank him for me when you speak to him next."

"I will not," he said, holding a spoon over his ice cream. "You will be courteous enough to telephone him yourself and convey your thanks. You can reach him at his headquarters in the *Stadsplein*."

"All right, Father," she worked to keep her voice neutral. "But I am quite tired. If there is nothing else –"

"But there is."

Mila waited.

Her father cut a swath through the mound of ice cream. "It was reported to me that you have been seen more than once near a certain plumbing office near the Bloemendaal."

She worked to keep from looking startled. *Was she being followed?*

A protracted pause. "Is there water leaking somewhere in your wing of the house, Mila?"

"No, Father."

He reached for a bowl of chocolate sauce. "Then I can think of no reason for you to be conversing with a plumber," he said, pouring the sauce over his dessert in a thin but even stream. "Especially a plumber who is suspected of having ties to the Resistance."

• • •

She had escaped to her bedroom and kicked off her shoes when a knock sounded at her door.

"I have brought you a sandwich," Reit said. "And I took Hondje for a walk before supper."

Mila smiled at the woman of indeterminate age who had been with the family for as far back as she could remember. "You are so good to us, Reit.. *Heel erg bedankt.* I am grateful."

She watched the maid retreat, locked the bedroom door behind her, and settled in the confines of her closet. Once, twice, she keyed in the digits, but there was no response from Pieter.

It was late, she told herself. He could be anywhere…

She began undressing, slowly, deliberately. But her heart was racing nonetheless.

EVI

Despite the late hour, *Mevrouw* Beekhof insisted on preparing a light supper for Evi. She disappeared into the kitchen, and came back moments later, her arms full and her expression questioning,

At the wooden dining room table, she handed Evi a plate containing a slab of bread, a small chunk of Gouda cheese, and a dollop of canned tomatoes.

Evi looked around the table. A single lantern burned on the sideboard, casting odd shadows on their faces…*Meneer* Beekhof, with whom she had rarely exchanged a word, dark-haired, bearded, imposing…Willem, who seemed to be growing inches by the day, awkward, fidgeting in his seat…*Mevrouw*, patient and waiting…and

Jacob, dear Jacob, his brows knit together, leaning forward, searching her face.

Taking a breath, halting now and then to force back tears, Evi told her story – the baby Mam had rescued from a cave, her insistence on taking him to safety…the Germans boarding the barge, Mam falling into the sea…and finally Alette, at the marketplace in Vlaardingen, who had taken her in and helped her to contact her friends.

"Perhaps I should not have come here," she finished, looking down at her lap. But in the next moment, to her surprise, she felt *Meneer* Beekhof's big hand close over hers, saw *Mevrouw* rise and come around the table.

Willem sat, his blue eyes wide, as his mother reached to embrace her, and Jacob, a white-knuckled fist to his mouth, glared silently, fire in his eyes.

"You did right, Evi…"

"Bastard Nazis…"

"Eat, Evi, eat…."

She could not make out all of their jumbled words. But there was no mistaking the warmth behind them. She breathed deeply, for the first time, she realized, since Mam had screamed at her to jump.

"I have hot soup as well," *Mevrouw* said, bustling in the from the kitchen with a huge kettle, which she set in the middle of the table. "Willem! The bowls!"

The boy jumped up to set spoons, linen napkins, and blue Delft bowls at each place. He had barely settled back in his seat when Mevrouw clasped her hands in front of her and glanced meaningfully around the table.

One by one, they followed suit.

"Willem," she said. "You may say grace."

The boy fidgeted, looked around as if for help, seemed to realize that none was forthcoming. He glanced at the folded newspaper on the sideboard as though for inspiration, and bowed his head.

"Lord, we thank you on this sixteenth day of February," he began, "for food and family, for keeping Evi safe, and for keeping the Germans from our door."

Evi looked up, eyes wide. A sound escaped before she could stop it.

Mevrouw looked up. "What is it, Evi?"

She looked around the table in the flickering light.

"It is my birthday," she whispered, shaken to the core. "Today is my seventeenth birthday…"

ZOE

Zoe stopped short as she neared the hospital. A green German Kubelwagen jeep was parked at the entrance, the driver sitting tall and straight.

She hopped off Daan's bicycle, locked it to a stand to one side of the building, and considered.

It was not likely the driver's German passenger was there for medical attention. It could only mean her cousin was being hassled once again by the SS officer demanding lists of staff and patients.

She shuddered, wondering how long it might be before the he demanded a tour of the place. Could the troops he brought in see through the façade on the hospital's fifth floor?

The trappings of renovation remained in place – the jumble of furniture, ladders and paint, even the few live 'workmen' who could be called from the sanctuary on a moment's notice.

But why, a cunning German might ask, was the hospital spending precious guilders on renovation when bread and heating oil were scarce?

Zoe shuddered and pulled her scarf close, glancing again at the Kubelwagen. She was debating whether to push through the hospital doors when a tall figure in an immaculate German uniform stepped out and hopped into the back seat. He leaned forward to speak to the driver and the vehicle roared to life and sped off.

Zoe nodded once to the expressionless guard, and made her way into the lobby.

• • •

Gerritt was, as she expected, pacing in his second-floor office.

"It's no good, Zoe," he said. "We cannot keep up this charade for much longer. The Germans are intent on finding people who have eluded them, and they will not rest until they have exhausted every avenue to find them."

She nodded, touching her cousin's shoulder. "Sit, Gerritt. I know. We need to talk."

It was as though he never heard her. "They are looking now specifically for Aaron Bernheim, a Jewish physician from Berlin who has been with us for months," he said. "And for the escaped German called Kurt Schneider, who is high on their list of Reich deserters."

MILA

The headline in Amsterdam's *De Telegraaf* sent a shiver through her spine. '*Haarlem caregivers shot.*'

'Four elderly Dutch care givers,' Mila read, 'volunteers who routinely transport Haarlem patients for their doctor visits, were lined up and shot in an alley off the *Rembrandtsplein* on Tuesday by a squad of SS enforcers.

'The incident was the second in a string of random shootings carried out under direct orders from Hitler, sources say, in retaliation for Dutch Resistance sabotage efforts that took the lives of more than a hundred German soldiers…'

Sitting at the breakfast table, Mila crushed the paper to her lap. There was no mention on the front page of the attempted assassination of Dutch Police Captain Reimar de Boer.

Straightening the paper, she scanned the inside pages, looking for an update on de Boer's condition or on any progress by Amsterdam authorities to identify the attempted assassin…but there was nothing. Not a single word. *Why not?*

Het Parool, the underground paper, was rather more forthcoming, reporting that the assassination of eight Dutch nationals was almost certainly in retaliation for the blatant assault on de Boer – and that Amsterdam Police were attempting to tie local Resistance cell leaders to the failed assassination.

Mila crushed both papers beneath her elbows, worry churning in her gut. She had not been able to contact Pieter since her return from Vlaardingen with Evi and Zoe – not on the wireless concealed in her bedroom closet, nor by telephone to his desk in the plumber's office. She was shaken to realize she had no idea where he lived.

She heard the hall telephone ring, but ignored it, until Reit brought the instrument to her.

"For you, *Missen.*"

Mila took it. "This is Mila Brouwer," she said formally.

"Ah, *Vermissen* Brouwer – Mila, may I? This is *Obersturmfuhre*r Franz Becker! I am so sorry to have missed your call!"

At her father's insistence, she had dialed the German headquarters to thank the man for the Deitrich recording. She had been happy to find him out and leave a message. But she was not surprised that the portly Becker wanted more.

"You talked about the German stage, if I recall correctly," he said in his curious mix of German and Dutch. "While I cannot promise a rendition of *Lily Marleen*, it pleases me to say there is an entertainment by German performers planned on Saturday next at our headquarters here in Haarlem."

"I see," she said, already searching for a reasonable way out.

The German did not wait for an answer. "If you are willing, Mila – may I call you Mila? I will bring a car for you that evening at seven. There will, of course, be a dinner served afterward…"

It was days away, Mila thought with relief, glad for the time to look for an excuse. "That sounds *wunderbar, Obersturmfuher,*" she simpered at last. "I shall await the date with pleasure. *Danke schön.*"

"*Goed* - as will I," said Becker. She could almost see his heels click together. "*Unt* if I may…for you, it is Franz."

Mila ended the call and rose to dispose of the morning's *Het* Parool before it caught her father's eye. She called out to Hondje, who came running.

The dog's tail wagged furiously at the sight of the leash, and the poor thing waited less than patiently as Mila donned a coat in the hallway and tied a scarf around her head.

A walk might be the best thing for both of them, Mila thought, fastening the leash and following Hondje out the front door. It would give her time to think – first about how she might gracefully bow out of the unwanted rendezvous with Becker – and second, by far the more important, how she might determine if Pieter was safe.

EVI

Evi lay sleepless on the sofa in the darkness of the Beekhof's sitting room. Otto snored softly on the rug below, freckled snout resting on his front paws. She listened to the pop and crackle in the hearth and peered out the window into the starless night, feeling so much more than she could ever put words to.

She was mortified and wretched to have blurted out that the sixteenth of February was her birthday. Truly, given everything she had been through in the last few days, she had not given the date a thought until Willem mentioned it – and moments after the Beekhofs had saved her from homelessness.

She was embarrassed about dissolving into tears over it, but it was the first time in her life that she had had a birthday without Mam at the center of it – and the realization filled her with sorrow that birthdays would never be the same again.

Still, as they ate, there had been birthday songs and heartfelt wishes for Evi's health and happiness. She was still not sure, even after *Mevreouw* handed her a nightgown and robe and prepared a bed for her on the sofa, that she would ever be worthy of their graciousness.

She had turned seventeen, she understood now, with a heavier heart than she could ever have imagined.

Jacob, watching *Mervouw* bring the blankets, had rushed to volunteer his bedroom. "Evi should have it," he insisted. "She needs it far more than I do."

But Evi had asserted just as strongly that she could fit much more easily on the sofa than he, and when she held her ground, he retreated.

"If you change your mind," he had said, backing down the hallway. "One word and the bedroom is yours…"

"Thank you, Jacob, but I will not change my mind," she vowed, helping with the sheets and blankets. In moments they had all retreated down the hall, leaving her in the uneasy quiet.

She imagined Jacob in his bed, eyes wide open, hands behind his head, longing, she hoped, to be as near to her as she longed to be near him.

She imagined Willem, lost in the sort of adolescent dreams that she could barely remember.

She thought of the Beekhof elders, of their faith and generosity, curled, perhaps in each other's arms, sheltering one another from the frenzied world in ways she could only guess at.

And as the last of the moonlight drained from the sky, and she could no longer battle the insistence of sleep, she closed her eyes and saw the yellow barge bobbing somewhere in the cold North Sea – forever guarded, she wished with all her heart, by the ghosts of her mother and the poor, sick baby, Jacob Rood.

ZOE

Zoe met her cousin's gaze. "Gerritt, you've been kind and patient throughout this whole ordeal," she said, "and resourceful, hiding these fugitives behind the semblance of a faked renovation."

"*Ja*, but I am increasingly worried as my German friend becomes more demanding," he told her. "I am not all certain, should he send in troops to search, that they would not simply bully their way past our little subterfuge."

Zoe pressed her lips together. "I have been wondering the very same thing," she said.

Gerritt sighed. "The fifth floor seemed like the best option, Zoe, because it is light by day, which is at least a more normal way for people to live."

He paused. "But the prospect that a German search party might find it fills me with something very close to terror."

As it should, Zoe understood. Gerritt's own life would then be in jeopardy…

"Also," she said, "there is no escape route, Gerritt - nowhere for the fugitives to run. They would be sitting ducks should the Germans find them…"

When he spoke, Gerritt's voice was firm. "That is something that has nagged at me from the start," he resumed his pace.

Finally, he sat. "There is another option," he said. "The basement. It is where we housed our pathology lab until the power was cut, and we were forced to move it. It still houses the morgue. I rejected it as a hiding place because it is below street level. There is little natural light, to speak of, and space is limited. But there is a doorway there that leads to the ambulance bay outside."

"Zoe pondered it. "The morgue. I can see your reluctance, cousin. It would be a difficult space for anyone to inhabit…"

Gerritt nodded.

"Also," he said, "there is a small sub-basement. It was used for storage at one time, I think, but now it is mostly empty. There is a short staircase leading down to it from the morgue that also empties into the ambulance bay – and since the sub-basement is not a part of the elevator system, it might more easily escape notice."

"That's perfect," Zoe said. "A search party cannot find what is not there."

Gerritt was quiet, but Zoe plowed ahead.

"We would need to be careful about moving the refugees," she said. "On gurneys, perhaps, a few at a time, as though they are headed for the morgue...If we manage it right, with no undue sense of urgency, it should not alert staff on any of the other floors."

Gerritt's face registered his hesitance.

"It will not be an easy place for people to co-exist," he said. "It will be cramped at best, with little available light. Anxiety levels will soar, and it may be all but impossible to keep the little ones from acting out."

A vision of Kurt reading stories passed before Zoe's eyes.

"We can bring in some light – lanterns perhaps," she offered.

"But people will have to make do with pallets or blankets on the floor."

Zoe brought her hands to her face. "It is far from ideal, Gerritt. But little is these days – and in the worst case, with the ambulance bay outside, there's a chance, at least, that some of these people may be able to outrun German bullets..."

MILA

Without a conscious thought about where she was going, Mila found herself staring across the intersection at the closed and padlocked door of the plumber's office. There was no sign of Pieter or anyone else.

Heartsick, and wary of being seen in the area after her father's admonition, she tugged gently at Hondje's leash and turned the corner – and realized almost instantly that she was not far from the auto parts shop where she had met with Pieter and Johan Steegen.

She stood for a moment outside the shop, and watched as Steegen slid out from under a silver-colored Porsche. Hearing the tinkle of a bell over her head, she opened the door and ducked inside, Hondje close at her heels.

Steegen, seeing her, rose and looked around him, as though to be sure no one was watching. Then he nodded formally. "*Missen Brouwer.*"

He reached down to ruffle Hondje's topknot. "We have not seen you for a while. Is there a problem with your father's Daimler?"

Mila smiled. "Not that I am aware, *dank u*. I was – I thought perhaps you might know how to help with another matter."

His heavy brows knit together.

"Is there something else?"

Mila bit her lip. I have been trying without success to contact Pieter," she whispered. "Have you by any chance seen him of late?"

"I have not," Steegen said "But it is quite possible he is in Amsterdam."

Mila's brow furrowed. "In Amsterdam?"

Steegen inclined his head. "It appears there is – a mission he is intent on completing."

Surely not, Mila's mouth fell open. Surely, Pieter would not have gone back to mount a second attempt on de Boer's life….

Steegen's expression did nothing to dispute it.

"Is there something else?" he asked.

Oh, Pieter….

She cleared her throat. "As a matter of fact, there is," she murmured. She told him briefly about the assault on the barge, the Nazis' cold-blooded murder of Lotte Strobel.

"There is no way to know how far the barge might have floated," she told him, "Or if it can even be located. But if it can be found, is there a way, do you think, to bring it back here to Haarlem?"

The tall Dutchman met her gaze. "Off the coast of Rotterdam, you say?"

"*Ja.*"

Steegen passed a big hand over his face. "I cannot promise," he said at length. "But we can try. I will need help. Let me talk to Bakker and some of the others."

Mila bit her lip. With Daan gone, and Pieter who knew where, she understood their resources were dwindling.

Steegen lifted a tray full of nuts and bolts. "I must get back to work," he told her. "One never knows who may be watching…"

Mila nodded, backing toward the door, winding Hondje's leash around her wrist.

EVI

It seemed to Evi that the morning sun was warmer on her back. It made her feel less burdened, somehow, as though winter might after all come to an end – that soon there would be spring vegetables, and some of the grief that still consumed her might begin seep away in the sunlight.

She had followed Jacob out the back door of the farm house, her jacket open, the Colt tucked into the waistband of her skirt. A target practice, Jacob had suggested, might be just the thing to keep her focused.

"I have butchered a chicken," *Mevrouw* Beekhof had called from behind them. "*Behagen*, the two of you – remind Papa and Willem to be here in time for Evi's birthday dinner at noon."

Evi's eyes widened. It was a difficult choice, she knew, for *Mevrouw* to deal with the few chickens left in her yard – whether to keep them for the occasional egg, or surrender them one by one for food. That she had sacrificed one of them on Evi's behalf touched her to the core – and the very thought of roasted chicken for lunch was enough to lift her spirits.

"I will race you to the targets," she shouted to Jacob, running through the cleared brush. "The last one there is a *kaskop*!"

"What's a *kaskop*?" Jacob took up running beside her.

"I think in English, it means, cheese head," she called. "And that will be you! You are a cheese head!"

"So, you say," Jacob panted, picking up enough speed to pass her, but flagging at the end so that he nearly collided with her when she turned, hands triumphantly on her hips, at the target range.

"Whoa," he managed, grabbing her by the shoulders. "Damn, I am seriously out of shape!"

Breathing hard, Evi said nothing, just stared into his amber eyes. He was close enough that she could feel his breath, and she all but swayed at the memory of the single kiss they had shared that night under the oak tree.

She willed him, yearned for him to kiss her again. But he blinked after a moment and pulled away.

"Good job, Itty-Bitty," he said.

Embarrassed now, she backed away and reached for the Colt. "I'll bet I can out-shoot you, too."

"Hah!" he retorted, bringing out his pistol. "That will be the day You're on!"

• • •

After an hour, it was quite clear Jacob could absolutely out-shoot her, hitting the collection of makeshift targets very time. But Evi hit them often enough to take pride in her own skill.

He looked at his watch. "Time to round up the Beekhof men for your birthday lunch," he said. "Wait here. I'll go down and get them."

Evi cocked her head. It was not the first time she had observed Jacob and the Beekhof men going off to work in the lower field.

"It is too early to be planting," she said, "What are the three of you doing in the lower field?"

"Clearing," Jacob told her. "Just clearing the field. It's a long, tiring job."

She shaded her eyes, watched his broad back recede, shifted her weight from one foot to the other. After a moment, the earlier playfulness returned.

"Wait," she called. "I will race you!"

She could not be sure whether his silence was assent, or whether he simply had not heard her, but she began to lope after him, through tall grasses that seemed to go on forever. She thought she heard voices, stopped to listen, but saw no one.

"Jacob? Willem! Where are you?"

She moved closer to the source of the sound, made a full circle, bewildered – and to her surprise, as she shaded her eyes and surveyed the land, she caught the glint of sunlight on water.

She squinted. She had had no idea that the Beekhof farm was bound on one side by water…quite likely, she realized, now that she considered the arc of land, an inland arm of the Spaarne – the same river that had been her home for more than four long years.

She contemplated the course of the terrain, certain she heard voices.

"Jacob?" She called, more assertively. "I can hear you, but I cannot see you."

Then another curious thing happened. To her right, what appeared for all the world to be a grassy berm began to fall away before her eyes, and Willem's rangy form emerged as if from nowhere. Behind him came Jacob, and finally Papa Beekhof.

She looked from one to the other, but the silence was long and deep.

"There's a tunnel, Evi." Jacob said finally, looking over at the older Beekhof. "We've been clearing out the tunnel Papa Beekhof dug years ago as an escape route for Jewish refugees."

Evi's mouth dropped open.

"Klara and I were horrified when the Germans began rounding up the Jews," Papa Beekhof leaned on a hoe. "I think, in the first months of 1941, perhaps a hundred or more escapees made their way through this tunnel – down through the Spaarne, in small boats, to the North Sea and beyond."

They were more words than Evi had ever heard from the reticent, bearded farmer. She nodded, though she was truly dumbstruck.

"Hard to know how many actually made it to safety," Jacob shrugged. "The North Sea can be rough. But one thing for sure; the escape route is damned hard to detect."

Evi marveled, looking from one to other. *How fortunate was Jacob when he dropped from the sky to come to rest on Beekhof land…*

She nudged Willem. "Lunch is ready. I will race you back to the house."

ZOE

The elderly physician hopped onto the gurney with more agility than she expected. "God bless," he said.

Patting his shoulder, Zoe covered him with a sheet so that only his toes were exposed and pushed the gurney out from behind the makeshift ward toward the freight elevator. He was the fifth of the high-profile refugees she had transported that day – mostly the Jewish doctors in hiding who continued to treat their fellow refugees.

Moving smartly through the corridor in her starched nurse's uniform, she pushed the elevator button for the basement.

Gerritt met them in the morgue. "I think, for the moment, we have met the limit of the 'deceased' we are able to accommodate here," he said. "But perhaps it is safe to move ten or twelve people into the old pathology lab – and then, if we need to, we can put the hardiest among them into the sub-basement."

Zoe adjusted the nurse's cap she had pinned to her hair. "We can do that," she said, though her heart broke to think of the spartan conditions these people would be forced to endure.

She lifted the sheet from the face of the 'deceased' physician. "I am affixing a nametag to your big toe," she told him. "It is not your real name, of course."

She completed the task quickly, and eased the gurney nearer to his 'deceased' companions. "Will you be all right here?" she asked.

The older man offered a wan smile. "I have never been much addicted to daytime napping," he said. "But it is infinitely more attractive than the prospect of eternal sleep at the hands of Hitler's thugs..."

"Amen to that," his colleagues murmured.

Zoe smiled and pulled the sheet back over the old man's head.

Gerritt moved from one to other of the counterfeit corpses. "A little drill," he said. "The door to the morgue will be locked. Entry is restricted to Zoe and myself and the few trusted nurses who bring your food."

He paused. "This soft knock," he demonstrated, "will signal to you that one of us is about to enter. Anything but this distinct knock and you run and warn the others."

Zoe heard the murmured assents.

"You may sit up and walk around a bit for a while after meals," Gerritt continued. "Use the toilet or whatever. But as mealtimes approach – and you know the timing – please assume your prone position until you can confirm who has entered."

His voice grew increasingly sober. "Lastly," he said, "If you detect any sort of commotion outside these doors, take the stairs down to the sub-basement until, *als god*, the danger has passed or you exit through the ambulance bay..."

God help them if they are forced to run into the streets, Zoe put a hand over her heart. "*What would become of them then?*

• • •

The population of the makeshift ward had been reduced by more than half, Zoe guessed – including the youngest children, who were the first to be relocated with their parents or hiding parents.

Her gaze swept those remaining for the storyteller who tugged at her heart, and who had refused to leave, in spite of the danger, until the last of the refugees were safely moved.

She watched him talking with a pair of teenaged boys who, like him, had decided to stay until the others had been moved. Kurt threw his head back, as if laughing at something one of the teens had said.

Zoe shook her head slowly from side to side. *A hunted German refugee*, she reflected. *Who would have believed, in this time of bitter war, that she was losing her heart to a German?*

MILA

Mila pushed food around her plate. It was another of those rare evenings with just the three of them at the table. But more and more often, conversation between them was stilted.

Her mother, still opting for dinner in her room most evenings when her father's German guests were at the table, seemed to be shrinking into herself, neither strong enough to oppose what her husband was doing, nor meek enough to support it. Her apathy was awash in a sea of red wine, leaving Mila sad and helpless.

And what could she expect her father to share? She watched him out of the corner of her eye. That his shipping business was busier than ever? That he was helping the enemy transport food and supplies for enemy German troops? Moving another shipment of arms from Berlin with which to murder Dutch citizens?

She passed the scalloped potatoes when he asked for them.

Perhaps she could tell him about Lotte Strobel's death at the hands of his Nazi *'business partners'* – about the daughter they had left both motherless and homeless, dependent on the kindness of strangers.

Or remind him that, on just the other side of their handsome doorway, innocent Dutch were being starved and murdered by the disciples of an arrogant madman…

She gazed at the huge bouquet of pink and white orchids resplendent at the center of the table.

What would he say of her calculated 'tryst' with the traitor Reimar de Boer – of the part she played in his failed assassination, or her passion for the man who fired the shot?

"Will you want a new frock, Mila, for your evening with Franz Becker?" Her father broke the silence.

She jumped at the sound of her name. "No, Father, I have many lovely dresses," she replied. "And I doubt the *obersturmfuhrer* is a connoisseur of women's fashion."

"Nevertheless, my dear, he occupies a special place in the Reich hierarchy. He will expect you to look elegant on his arm."

And what else will the obersturmfuhrer expect, she wondered, suddenly on the verge of bringing up the few bites of food she had swallowed. Was her proud father willing to offer up his daughter as nonchalantly as he offered up his shipping routes?

Feeling ill, she tossed her napkin on the table. "Excuse me, Father. I am feeling tired."

"But you haven't had dessert," her father said blandly. "Reit has prepared a toffee pudding."

Mila forced a smile. "But we wouldn't want my dress to be too tight around my hips," now would we?"

EVI

The kitchen windows were so heavy with steam that she could see nothing beyond them. Inside, it felt warm and comfortably moist. She mopped her face with the hem of her apron.

"I am ready for those jars, Evi" *Mevreouw* Beekhof said.

Evi jumped to pick up a pair of metal tongs and fish the jars, one by one, out of the boiling water, setting them on towels on the kitchen counter.

She watched, fascinated, as *Mevrouw* filled the jars with a small crop of rhubarb that had somehow survived the cold, and which she had diced and stewed with the last of her stock of honey.

Mam had been a passable cook in the years before the war, but never in Evi's memory had she canned vegetables as *Mevrouw* was doing now.

"There," *Mevrouw* said, wiping down the jars with a clean cloth. "We will leave them to cool and eat some for supper, and the rest we will put aside in the cellar to be there for us on another hungry day."

She put the kettle on. "Sit, Evi. I will make us a cup of tea."

The men, as usual, were working in the field, and although she would have liked to be nearer to Jacob, Evi relished this time with *Mevreouw*. It made her feel as though she were wrapped in cotton batting, as though she were safe and protected from having to think about that day off the coast of Rotterdam.

In a strange way, although she had turned seventeen, she felt more vulnerable, more defenseless now than she had before the day she had dressed like a harlot and lured that first Nazi to his death.

"Evi," *Mevrouw* poured the tea and sat. "There is something you need to know…"

Evi sat up straighter.

"We had a visitor yesterday, while you had target practice with Jake," *Mvreouw* began, a softness in the planes of her face. "It was a man named Johan Steegen. Do you know him?"

Evi shook her head. "I don't think so."

"Well. He is a friend of your friend, Mila Brouwer. It seems that he was able to locate your Mam's barge, still afloat in the sea near Rotterdam, and bring it back to Haarlem."

Evi's eyes widened.

"The barge is back, Evi, in the same berth alongside the Spaarne where it has always been. *Meneer* Steegen says it is still in fair condition and does not appear to have been ransacked."

Evi thoughts flew to baby Jacob, but *Mevrouw* closed her eyes and shook her head. "There was no baby, Evi, no one living or dead on board the barge…But everything else – your clothing, pots and pans…everything seems to be the way it was left."

Mvreouw paused. "It is your home, Evi," she said finally. "You are able to return to it if you wish."

Tears sprang, faster than fireflies on a summer night, and Evi let them flow. She shook her head. "I cannot return…not now, not yet…"

Mevreouw covered the space between them and took her into her arms. "It is all right, Evi. I understand. *Behagen*, you may stay here as long you like…it is only that you needed to know…"

ZOE

The phone was ringing as Zoe fit the key into the lock of her apartment. It was past nine, the end of another long day helping Gerrit deal with the trials of too many people in too little space, and fearful of Gestapo intrusion.

She was tired to the core, but the phone still shrilled. She sloughed off her coat and reached for it.

Her mother's voice was so full of fright, so pierced with moans and muffled sobs, that Zoe could not decipher the words.

"Mam," she begged. "Slow down, *behagen*. I cannot understand. What is wrong?"

Her mother took a jagged breath. "Zoe…I've been trying to reach you for hours. Your father …the Germans took him!"

Zoe sat heavily in the nearest chair. "What? When, Mam? Why?"

Her mother sniffled, blew her nose, took a deep, wobbly breath. "Inciting rebellion. That is what they said." She blew her nose again. "They *beat* him, Zoe," she said, finally. "They dragged him by his arms out the door…"

"Inciting rebellion…" Zoe tested the words, trying to imagine what in the name of God her mild-mannered father might have done.

But it was not relevant, not at this moment. Instead, she steeled herself against the memory of her child minder dragged by the Gestapo out of her home.

"Where did they take him, Mam?" she asked, trying desperately for calm. "Do you have any idea where they might have taken him?"

Her mother once again dissolved into tears. Zoe gave her a moment.

"Mam," she tried again. "I need to know. Do you have any idea where he might be held?"

A new wave of sobbing. More nose blowing… "I do not know, Zoe, I do not know…Wait…wait…perhaps…"

"There is a barn," her mother managed at last. "A big old barn on an abandoned farm just down the street from the old feed store…"

"Yes, I know it…"

"Early in the war, it is where the Nazis held scores of Jews during the roundup here in Enschede –"

Her voice broke. "Well, for a while anyway, until they were…transported elsewhere…"

"I did not know that," Zoe said, her own dread mounting as she tried formulate a plan. "I am not certain what I can do, Mam," she said. "But I have some friends I can call on. In the meantime, *behagen*, please, try to calm yourself."

She listened as Mam's breathing slowed. "Is there anyone you can call to stay with you?"

But this brought another spate of tears. "*Mevrouw* Van der Wall is our nearest neighbor," she said finally. "But her husband was taken, too!"

Zoe frowned. *Van der Wall, too?*

"Mam," she said slowly. "You have no idea why they were taken?"

A long, tremulous breath. "Something about – identification papers," she said finally. "A few of the men here have been urging people to turn over their papers to the Resistance, then report them as stolen and apply for new ones…"

Zoe closed her eyes, instantly reminded of the dozens of ID papers she had stolen. She would not have expected her conservative papa to so actively support the Resistance.

"All right, Mam," she said finally, with as much calm as she could muster. "Please take care of yourself. Think of better times. Let me see if something can be done…"

MILA

Mila hunkered down in the privacy of her closet and tried once again to reach Pieter. But the call went unanswered, and she lay back against a row of long skirts and pounded a fist into her hand.

There was little doubt in her mind now that Pieter had, as Johan Steegen had suggested, gone back to Amsterdam to finish the failed assassination – without her.

The lack of detail about de Boer in the daily newspapers suggested that authorities wanted the public – and his would-be assassin – to know as little as possible about de Boer's condition or his whereabouts. But there were a limited number of hospitals still operating in Amsterdam, and Pieter was resourceful enough to figure out quickly enough where the man was being treated.

Wherever he was, the *verdomd* police captain was undoubtedly heavily protected – but if Pieter could not get to him while he was still in hospital, Mila had little doubt he would stay close enough to try to finish the bastard once he was released to his home.

Rising, she returned to the three days-worth of newspapers strewn on her bed to read a few of the stories she had only skimmed. A piece in the Telegraaf caught her eye.

'As neighboring Belgium is in the throes of liberation by advancing Allied forces,' the story read, 'the Dutch government is urging General Eisenhower's chief of staff to begin an offensive to liberate the Netherlands…'

The Reich, in a bid to show how well they were treating the Dutch, had responded with a show of largesse, allowing distribution of the Swedish food and medical supplies they had withheld since the twenty-eighth day of January.

Mila sighed. It was encouraging news. But how quickly would the Allies respond?

Restless, she gathered up the newspapers, crushed them into a heap and tossed them into a wastebasket. She paced once or twice around her bedroom, pausing only to ruffle Hondje's topknot.

Pieter was right to return to Amsterdam without her, she decided. What could she have done to help him?

On the other hand, if he found himself in trouble, who would he have to turn to? What would happen, *lieve God*, if he were discovered – or captured? *What then?*

The thought of losing him…of never seeing him again, was enough to flood her with resolve.

She threw a change of clothing into a shoulder bag, searched her handbags for as many guilders as she could find, and stuffed them into the bag as well. She put her identification papers into one section of the bag and the false Swiss papers Pieter had given her in another. She slipped on her most comfortable walking shoes and opened the door of her room.

It was past eleven and quiet, the household asleep. She would not be missed until morning.

Bu at the sound of the door opening, Hondje stood upright in her bed, tail wagging.

"Hush, now," she whispered, fingers against her lips. "I will return soon – and Reit will take good care of you in the meantime."

Hondje slid forward on his two front feet, his little backside in the air. Blowing him a kiss, she closing the door gently and tip-toed down the stairs.

EVI

A sudden rapping at the front door yanked Evi out of a restless sleep. Otto barked furiously. She sat up, pulling the blankets around her, too terrified to move from the sofa. *Lieve God, had she somehow led the Germans to the Beekhof farm?*

In seconds, *Meneer* Beekhof bounded into the room, his bare feet slapping at the wooden floor.

The pounding continued, but Evi thought she heard a woman's voice.

"*Behagen*! It is Zoe! Zoe Visser! I am so sorry to wake you!"

Evi met *Meneer* Beekhof's gaze, watched him move stealthily toward the door.

The pounding slowed, and the voice could be heard quite clearly. "*Excuseert, behagen*! It is Zoe Visser!"

At Evi's nod, *Meneer* undid the front door's three locks, peered out, then opened the door. "*Kom binnen*," he said. Come in.

At the sight of her friend, clearly frantic, Evi threw aside the blankets and ran barefooted to the door.

"I am so sorry to wake you," Zoe was shivering. "I know I must have given you all a fright."

Her words were directed at *Meneer* Beekhof, but she nearly collapsed into Evi's arms as she spoke.

By this time, the rest of the family had gathered behind them, Jacob rubbing sleep from his eyes.

Mevrouw put he hands on her Evi's shoulders, leading her and Zoe toward the sofa.

The last of the evening's fire crackled in the hearth, casting each face in eerie shadows. Papa Beekhof moved to light a lantern.

Seated, Zoe took a trembling breath. "I am sorry to alarm you. I was not able to contact Mila. Nor could I reach Johan Steegen – and so, Evi, I come to you. I need help."

Evi listened as Zoe told them about her father's arrest by the Germans, that Gestapo thugs had appeared at her family's door without warning and dragged her papa out the door, just as they had at the home of Daan Mulder,

"My Mam is near hysteria," Zoe said. "But it is possible she knows where they may be keeping him – for a while, at least, until they are able to move him – who knows where…?"

Zoe's voice cracked. She was clearly working to hold back tears. Evi took her shaking hands in hers.

"I have no firearms, and anyway, I don't know how to use them," Zoe said." I had thought once that I might learn, but they frankly frighten me – "

She paused. "There is no way to know if we can locate papa, or if there is any way to help him – and perhaps I have no right to ask…But I know that you have been learning to shoot, Evi, and I may need protection…"

She took a breath. "Will you come with me to Enschede – tonight?"

"I will go with you," Jacob's voice was firm. "This is way beyond the means of the two of you."

A vision of Mam surrendering her life to the sea at the hands of the Germans passed before Evi's eyes. For the first time in her life, she felt fully grown, as though she had slipped, without notice or fanfare, into the skin of adulthood.

"You will not go, Jacob," she said, just as firmly. "It is entirely too dangerous for you to be out. You are too easily recognized as American."

She looked around at the faces of the others, frowning and clearly skeptical.

"Evi, I – "

"I said no, Jacob." She stood ramrod straight, looked into his eyes. "You must trust that you have prepared me for this."

ZOE

There was no chance of sleep on the three-hour midnight train they were fortunate to board from Haarlem to Enschede.

There were few passengers, and no overt German presence, but Zoe quaked to think of the consequences if they were to be confronted by Gestapo officers – if they needed to try to explain their journey, if the pistol hidden in Evi's bag was discovered.

Despite herself, she shuddered, remembering as though it were yesterday, the Nazi pistol shoved into her face on her last trip home from Enschede.

Thus far, *godjzidank,* the ride had been uneventful, and quiet save for the clacking of wheels against steel. It gave her time to share with

Evi as much as she knew about when the Germans had come after her father and why. But they were weary and anxious by the time they debarked at nearly three in the morning, as much from stress and misgiving, Zoe knew, as from the lack of sleep.

The city streets seemed other-worldly in the dead of night, subdued, and weirdly shadowed, lit by a sliver of moon and the occasional street light, and devoid of any footsteps but theirs.

They moved slowly, looking ahead and behind, braced for a noise, for another human being, for a Nazi checkpoint – but there was nothing but the clouds of their own breath dissipating into the night as Zoe directed their route.

Finally, Zoe stopped and pointed across the street at the barn her mother had alluded to – a good-sized structure long in disrepair, nearly stripped of its once-red paint, and seemingly deserted.

Cautious, they looked both ways, crossed the deserted street and listened.

Nothing.

But then, one would expect, if there were people inside, that they were sleeping.

A padlock on the wooden door confirmed that something was inside – but there was no way to know, in the pre-dawn quiet, if it was hay, provisions, or human beings.

Evi pulled her blue knit cap down nearly to her eyes, and at her signal, staying in in the shadows, they moved into the adjacent alleyway.

Zoe half-expected – maybe half-wished – to see a sentry standing guard. But as far as she could see, it seemed deserted.

Evi stood motionless for a long moment. Then she reached into her bag, retrieved her pistol, and shoved it into her pocket.

"Go back, Zoe," she whispered, pointing across the cobblestoned street. "You cannot help me here. Cross the street, stay out of sight, and wait for me."

She paused. "I am going to test to see if anyone is inside. But we need to be prepared. If anything happens – if there is shooting – you need to save yourself. There is nothing you can do to help me if there is trouble. Catch the next train and go home."

Zoe stared, alarmed at the full impact of the danger she was putting this young girl into. *What in the world had she been thinking?*

"Evi, no," she begged. "! I cannot let you do this. I am so sorry. We will find another way –"

Evi shook her head. "It may be useless," she whispered. Very likely, there is no one inside. This will be only a test, Zoe. I will be careful, I promise."

Zoe searched the girl's face in the faint moonlight, but if Evi was apprehensive, she hid it well.

"And you must promise that if there is trouble, you will run as fast as you can."

Zoe wavered, finally nodded, and moved back into the shadows, feeling more helpless and more anxious than she had ever been.

She watched Evi move toward the barn.

Unable to bring herself to cross the road, Zoe crouched deep behind a bed of neglected hawthorn bushes and watched as Evi put an ear to the back door of the barn and listened.

In the next moment, as Zoe watched, Evi bent, gathered a handful of something – maybe small stones or gravel – then tossed it in a spray against the door of the barn, and backed into the shadows.

MILA

German officers were everywhere in Amsterdam, guarding entrances, stopping people at makeshift check points, marching in the streets in that chilling, stiff-legged gait that never failed to rattle her – the more so now because of the pistol Mila carried, buried deep in her shoulder bag.

Exhausted and hungry, she bought a raw turnip from a sidewalk vendor and sat on a bench in the gathering dusk to devour it.

At four in the afternoon, she was no closer to locating Pieter than she had been when she had stepped off the bus nearly twelve hours earlier.

Assuming he had discovered where de Boer was being treated, she was certain he would have taken up a post nearby. She had made the rounds of the hospitals closest to the site of the failed shooting, then widened her search to include the next nearest. But even her skilled flirtation with security guards and any medical staff she could corner did little to yield useful information.

At University Hospital, however, the increased presence of sentries told her she was in the right place. She had walked briskly past the cordon as though she belonged there, had even managed to walk the halls on every floor, looking for the presence of the Amsterdam *polizie* who would likely be guarding de Boer's room. But in the end, it had taken every shred of charm she could muster to avoid being interrogated herself.

"*Idioot*," she berated herself. How could she think she could possibly get close to de Boer's bedside, never mind discover where Pieter might be in a city as big as Amsterdam?

She was considering taking the next bus home in defeat when someone sat down next to her on the bench – a middle-aged woman, she saw, dressed in a long, grey coat with a black wool scarf wrapped around her face, and black oxford shoes…the same sort of practical shoes Mila had seen on the nursing staff all day.

"*Goedenavond*," the woman nodded without facing her. *Good evening*.

Mila hesitated, "*Goedenavond*."

The woman produced a bottle of water from her bag, sipped slowly as she glanced around her. "You are looking for someone in hospital?" she said.

Mila narrowed her eyes.

"I understand there is a fine new play in Brussels."

It was a current code sentence used to validate Resistance volunteers.

Mila nodded almost imperceptibly. "I have heard as much."

The woman did not look at her. "I am a day nurse at University Hospital. You were walking the hall on the second floor, peering into patient rooms as though you were looking for someone."

Mila hesitated, taking the woman's measure. It was never easy, knowing who to trust, even when they knew the proper code words. In the end, she relied on instinct.

"My uncle," she said. "I am looking for my uncle."

The woman looked straight ahead, took another sip of water. "Your uncle is perhaps a well-known figure in Amsterdam?"

Again, Mila hesitated. "He is."

"In uniform, perhaps…"

"*Ja…*"

"I have a grandson," the woman said, her expression stoic. "He is eighteen years old. He was arrested three weeks ago by the Dutch police for distributing underground newspapers."

She looked around her, took another sip. "The police captain demanded more guilders for his release than our family could ever produce…"

Again, a sip of water. The woman closed her eyes. "I fear we may never see him again."

Mila took her cue, looking straight ahead as she spoke. "I am so very sorry," she said." In these dangerous times, one cannot know where the sympathies of Dutch officials lie – even seasoned police captains…like my uncle."

The woman paused. "You might be interested to know that such a man with a recent gunshot wound was released from hospital early this morning under heavy guard. It seems he will continue recovering at his home in Diemen…"

Abruptly, the woman stood, tucked her water bottle in her bag, and crossed the road to a bus stop.

Mila looked away, looked down at her gloved hands. Resistance, *godjedank*, was everywhere.

She knew of Diemen. It was not more than five or six kilometers from where she sat. Once, it had been a busy haven for Jews loyal to the Dutch Royal House – but Hitler's Reich had long since sent the lot of them to their deaths....

If Reimar de Boer owned a home in Diemen, he had no doubt purchased it for a rock bottom price after the Jews had been evacuated...

And if the day nurse was to be believed, the traitor was once again in residence.

EVI

The back door of the barn creaked open a sliver. Backlit as he was from a dim light inside, Evi could see only a stocky figure wearing a wide-brimmed German field cap. The man briefly scanned the wooded area, scowled, and withdrew, pulling the door closed behind him.

So, there was someone inside. The question was, who besides this guard – and how many?

She scooped up another handful of gravel, tossed it haphazardly at the door of the barn and retreated into the shadows.

In the next instant, the barn door crashed open, and this time, the guard emerged with pistol drawn.

Adrenaline pumping, Evi raised the Colt, took careful aim, and opened fire. She saw the German go down in a heap, but in the next millisecond, another figure emerged with a rifle, and a searing pain ripped through her left shoulder.

She tumbled to the ground, gritting her teeth against the pain, every instinct telling her to grasp her shoulder and roll with the pain. But whoever had shot her was running now in her direction.

She heard Zoe cry out. The figure turned toward the sound, and in the split second that he looked away, Evi willed herself to roll onto her good shoulder, raise the Colt, and fire.

Then she lowered the pistol, gave in to the pain, and surrendered to a merciful blackness.

ZOE

Zoe watched as three men ran from the open doorway of the barn, pausing only to glance at the two downed German guards before sprinting towards the woods behind the barn. They wore civilian clothing, no coats, no hats, and nothing to distinguish them – but Zoe would have known her father's halting gait – the result of a decades-old old soccer injury – anywhere.

"Papa!" she called, rooted to the ground, caught between a wish to rush to her father and the pressing need to get to Evi, who lay motionless on the ground.

She did not waver long. Clearly, there were no other guards inside the barn, or her father and the others would not have been able to rush out as they had. But Evi needed her.

In the next instant, she crossed the few meters, knelt at Evi's side, peeled back her coat collar, and shakily reached for a pulse.

"Zoe?"

Evi was alive! *Godjidank*!

She glanced up long enough to see her father's face. "Papa!" she said. "The barn is empty?"

He turned at the sound of her voice and nodded. "Zoe?"

"Grasp this girl carefully under one arm and help me move her inside…"

To her relief, Evi moaned as they carried her in and laid her gently on a pile of dirty straw. Under the light of an oil lamp hung from a hook on the wall. Zoe bent to her friend. In the flickering light, she saw the bullet hole in the shoulder of Evi's coat and a widening patch of blood.

She looked up only briefly. "Run, Papa," she said. "*Godjizdank*, you are safe. Go home only long enough to grab Mam and get yourselves to Tante Inge's house in Haaksbergen."

Zoe gently patted Evi's cheek. "Evi, can you hear me? It is Zoe…"

She looked up briefly. "Do you understand, Papa? Do not stay at home. Go with Mam to Tante Inge's. You will be safer from the Germans there than in Enschede."

Evi's eyes flickered open, but she groaned, clearly in pain.

"Go, Papa," she said, and her father, coatless, shivered in the cold, kissed the top of her head and started off.

Zoe lifted Evi's shoulder as gently as she could, tried to bare the arm from its layers of clothing enough to assess the damage. She probed the wound as gently as she could.

Evi whimpered, groaned, and cried out.

Zoe looked up, glanced out of the barn doorway, fearful a contingent of German soldiers could turn up at any moment.

"I am almost there, Evi," she murmured. "I know it is painful, but please try to be still. I need to see how badly you are hurt."

She was not skilled in human physiology, but she knew enough from her veterinary studies to know that the shoulder contains the main artery of the arm, and a nerve bundle that controls its motor function.

Luck was with them, she hoped, in that she could not detect the presence of a bullet. Possibly the bullet had pierced the skin and exited. But there could be fragments left behind…

She tore a strip of fabric from her underskirt, wrapped it around the wound to stem the blood, then tore a larger strip she would try to use as a sling.

Evi's eyes were closed again. She dared not let her sink into concussion. She patted her cheek. "Wake up, Evi! Try to stay awake. We cannot remain here."

Evi blinked. "Zoe?"

"*Ja,*" Zoe murmured, supporting her upper body as Evi tried to sit. "You have been shot," she told her, doing her best to fashion the makeshift sling.

Evi opened her eyes. Zoe searched them for signs of concussion, but her gaze seemed clear and focused.

"You must try to stand. Evi," she said, "and walk, if you can. We must get out of here, and quickly, before more German soldiers turn up."

Evi's eyes fluttered and closed.

MILA

Naked tree limbs reached toward the sky, and withered leaves swirled around the lamp posts. Around her, her countrymen and women appeared to go about their lives as best they could under the watchful eyes of the Germans. But they moved stealthily, hurrying from one place to the next, eyes mostly downcast.

Mila sat on the wooden bench, debating what to do next.

All at once, she knew. She rose to her feet and went in search of a public telephone.

When she found one, she slipped inside the box, thanked the heavens for a dial tone, and searched her memory. With Pieter unreachable and Daan gone, she decided to call Leela Bakker at the Dans Hal.

It took three tries until the call went through.

"Leela," she said, finally. "It is Mila. Mila Brouwer. I need to find a contact in Amsterdam…"

Leela did not hesitate. "I have an aunt in Amsterdam…Her name is Liesbeth…" She gave Mila a telephone number.

Mila hung up, hoped the connection would not fail, fed in more coins and dialed again.

She told Liesbeth that Leela had referred her, offered the words that would identify her as a friend, and told her she needed a local contact.

Liesbeth was as prompt and perceptive as Leela. She gave Mila an address.

"It is a reputable cobbler's shop," Liesbeth told her. "Be sure to tell them you were referred by the Van der Leeves. I am sure you they will be able to meet your needs."

• • •

It was a short walk to the address she was given, a cobbler's shop as Liesbeth had told her. A bell tinkled overhead as she entered.

Inside, a middle-aged man in a grimy leather cobbler's apron bent over a shoe last. He looked up as Mila entered.

"Hallo," she said, smiling. "My name is Mila Brouwer. I am from Haarlem, where I believe you may have friends. I was referred to your shop by the Van der Leeves."

The cobbler took a moment before answering.

"I know your name. We have a mutual friend, I think, by the name of Pieter."

Mila nodded. "We do."

The cobbler wiped his hands on his apron. "Berend," he called over his shoulder. "Can you watch the front of the shop?"

A young man with sharp blue eyes and a neat, short beard, stepped from behind a curtained area. He wore an apron much like older man's.

"Follow me, please," the cobbler told Mila. "I may have just the shoes you are looking for."

She followed him behind a curtained area into a small office, where he shook her hand and offered her a chair.

"There is too much glass out front," he said, sitting behind a cluttered desk. "Here we have a bit of privacy."

He held out a hand. "My name is Klaus Jaansen. I have known Pieter for many years – since long before we found ourselves on the same side of a cause."

Klaus Jaansen leaned back in his chair. "I think I can guess why you are here."

Mila felt instantly comfortable.

"Pieter came to Amsterdam to hold a certain police captain accountable for Daan Mulder's abduction."

She nodded.

"We offered our assistance, but Pieter believed he could act on his own. This mission is personal to him."

"It is. I was here with him for the initial rendezvous. A random passer-by was in the wrong place at the wrong time."

"And I can only guess," Jaansen said, "that Pieter wants to accomplish what he came here for."

"I want to help, if I can," Mila said.

Jaansen paused, but briefly. "The target resides in Diemen," he said, confirming what the day nurse had told her.

He gave her an address. "My guess is that Pieter is somewhere in the vicinity. But it is not so safely walkable."

She was about to speak when Jaansen leaned forward. "The place will be guarded, of that I am sure…and I must tell you there is not much we can do to protect you if your plans should go awry."

He paused. "But if you are determined, we can provide you with a bed for tonight, and a map and a bicycle in the morning."

EVI

She must have passed out, because the first thing Evi remembered when she swam to the surface of a misty fog was Zoe bending over her. She did not know for a moment where she was – only that the pain in her shoulder hurt like a mad thing as Zoe worked to extricate her arm from her layers of clothing.

"Ouch! Oh, Zoe it hurts."

"You are a hero, Evi. You need to know that. You shot down two German guards. My father and his friends are free."

Evi blinked, her gaze darting around the old barn, settling finally on Zoe's ministrations.

She did not feel like a hero. She felt like the daughter of a woman murdered by Nazis who had managed a bit of payback. What was it Jacob had called it? *Even Steven...*

"You were shot in the shoulder," Zoe told her. "It is a flesh wound, I think. I do not see a bullet, although there may be fragments."

Zoe was tearing a strip of fabric from her underskirt. "There was fair bit of blood, but that is subsiding" she said, wrapping the cloth around Evi's arm.

Evi winced.

"I know how much it must hurt, Evi. But we need to get out of here. Now…"

She watched as Evi gritted her teeth and rose to a sitting position, then helped pull her friend to her feet. Supporting her as best she could, she peered out of the barn, assessed the quiet, and walked the two of them past the fallen Nazis.

"My book bag…." Evi said.

Zoe found it where it fell in the gravel and hoisted it over her shoulder.

The pre-dawn streets were eerily hushed, but the chilling sound of Nazi boots had never seemed closer…

• • •

"Try to stay awake," Zoe told her as they boarded the near-empty train. "I do not think you have a concussion, but it would be best to stay awake if you can until we can be certain."

Evi nodded, doing her best to keep her eyes open and her brain from registering her pain. "Talk to me, then," she murmured. "It will help me stay awake."

Zoe cast about for something to say. One thing was uppermost in her mind.

"I have been working with my cousin, the head of a hospital in Heemstede," she blurted. "We are doing our best to keep refugees safe in a makeshift space at the hospital."

Evi's gaze swiveled.

"Mostly they are hiding families who have Jewish children in their care," Zoe went on. But also there are some Jewish doctors…and some others…".

Evi turned to face her.

"There is one man in particular I worry for…" Zoe said, grateful for the chance to speak of it. "He is himself a German – but hunted by the Nazis for helping Jewish escapees flee the country after the war began."

Evis stared.

Zoe sighed. "He is a kind man, Kurt – a caring soul…the kind of man who reads stories to the children to keep them quiet while they must remain in hiding…"

"You care for this man," Evi said.

A sad smile. "I do… He was one of the people the Germans evicted from their homes in Haarlem – and now he is high on their wanted list…I worry, even if we can help him avoid capture, how and where he might flee."

Evi sat back. Zoe felt about this German the same way she felt about Jacob.

"Mam's barge," she said. "The barge we lived on. It is once again berthed where it was…"

She turned to Zoe, a flash of pain running from her shoulder to her wrist. "I cannot go back there, Zoe. I could never live on that barge again. But there it sits, day after day."

Zoe frowned.

"I tell you this because if ever – well, should you and your storyteller need to run, there is a key to the ignition in the right-hand kitchen drawer just next to the sink."

Zoe's mouth opened.

"You understand?"

Zoe nodded. It was a kind offer, however unlikely. Her heart went out to the girl.

• • •

The night sky was beginning to lighten. Evi looked out the train window as dawn broke over the tulip fields.

"Oh!" she cried, face pressed against the glass. "Look, Zoe, look!"

She pointed out the window at a sun-splashed patch of red and yellow.

Zoe followed her gaze. "Tulips!" she gasped. "There are tulips!"

It was early for even the first of the tulips – not yet the first of March. Evi sighed, recalling the nights when the half-frozen tulip bulbs Mam brought home in the barge were all that had saved them from starvation.

And yet, there they were, pushing through the soil, tulips, proud and defiant,

She squeezed Zoe's hand.

Zoe squeezed back.

Perhaps there was hope, after all…

• • •

Haarlem was awakening when they stepped off the train, Evi leaning hard against her friend.

A few hardy workmen in heavy peacoats traversed the quiet streets. A bundled-up old man moved morning newspapers from a wagon into a corner kiosk. A pale sun cast long shadows on the cobblestones.

"Let me take you to the *kliniek*," Zoe told her. "It is too early to find a medical doctor, and I can get a better view of your wound."

Evi debated. "It hurts a bit less, Zoe, and I want to get back to the farm. Jacob and the Beekhofs will be worried."

"I know, Evi. But an untreated bullet wound can cause all sorts of damage, and there is always a risk of infection. At least let me have a better look at it."

Evi considered – and nodded.

"Anyway, it is a short walk. Here, lean on me.

ZOE

It was not much warmer inside the *kliniek* than it had been on the street, but the power was on, and Zoe was able to turn on the surgical lamp over the examination table.

"Hop up here if you can, Evi."

Using her good arm, Evi hoisted herself up, grimacing slightly as she sat.

Zoe shed her coat, then freed Evi's arm from the makeshift sling and bandage. "The bleeding has mostly stopped, Evi," she said, gently palpating the deltoid muscle area around the wound. "And yes, I think the bullet must have entered and exited the soft flesh I do not see any evidence of it."

Evi groaned at her touch.

"It would take an X-ray to know for sure if there are any bullet fragments left inside," Zoe said. "But X-ray supplies these days are mostly reserved for the war-wounded. I do not have any slides just now. Perhaps you should see a doctor."

There were Resistance doctors who would not question the source of the wound. But Evi was eager to get to the farm.

"It is not hurting as much anymore. Just a few shooting pains now and then. I can manage."

Zoe felt carefully around the shoulder bone. "Does this hurt?"

Evi swallowed the pain. "Not…so much."

Zoe fingered the joint. "This?"

"Mmm…a little."

"What about your range of motion, Evi? Are you able to raise your arm – or move it in a circular motion?"

Evi tried. "Ouch!"

She paused for aa moment, then tried again, pressing her lips together to contain the yelp as she raised her am not-quite shoulder high.

"All right, stop, Evi. Do not force it," Zoe said. "At least until the soreness eases."

She reached behind her into a supply cabinet for the precious stock of antibiotics Pieter had been able to procure.

"I will inject an antibiotic to ward off infection. That much I can do – and I cannot cast it, but I can fashion a better sling. You must try to keep the arm immobile until you can see a medical doctor."

Evi sat still for the injection, and watched as Zoe created a functioning sling from a roll of surgical bandage. Then she slid off the table.

"Wait," Zoe said, looking Evi straight in the eye and taking her by the elbow of her good arm. "Evi…I don't know how to thank you for what you did tonight…"

Evi shook her head. "I did it for Mam."

Zoe felt tears spring to her eyes. "I know. But my father owes his life to you…"

Evi managed a half-smile. "I would do it again," she said. "Two more Nazis dead…"

"But your arm –"

"It is only a flesh wound. You said so yourself. It is nothing. It will heal."

Zoe sighed. I think so, *ja*. But you should see a proper doctor."

"I will," Evi promised. "But now, I need to get back to the farm. Jacob and the Beekhofs will be worried."

Zoe helped her on with her coat, helped her hoist the battered book bag over her good shoulder. "You cannot ride a bicycle with your arm in a sling. I will walk with you."

But Evi shook her head. "No need, Zoe. I will be fine. Just comb my hair into braids in the event I am stopped at a German check point – and pull my cap down low."

Zoe did as she was asked, combing Evi's hair into two thick braids, fastening them with lengths of surgical twine and pulling the blue knit cap with their cheerful yellow butterflies nearly down to Evi's eyebrows.

"There," she said, stepping back. "You look notably younger. Are you sure you do not want me to walk with you?"

Evi shook her head again. "Thank you for taking such good care of me, Zoe. I will be fine. I promise."

Zoe sighed, watching from the doorway as Evi began her trek. When she was well out of sight, she closed and locked the door and went to the telephone at her desk.

She found a connection, and dialed. The telephone at her parents' home in Enschede rang and rang and rang. Zoe hung up. *Lieve god* they were safely on their way to Tante Inge's…

She closed her eyes. She knew she should sleep. But her heart was with Kurt and Gerritt and the others in the basement of the hospital in Heemstede.

MILA

Mila left the home of Klaus Jaansen and his wife before seven in the morning, on a sturdy bicycle of unknown origin, with two apples, half a loaf of bread, and a pair of binoculars in her shoulder bag, and a hand-drawn map she had already committed to memory.

There was not a great deal to memorize, she reflected. The route was flat, as was the town of Diemen itself, situated as it was on the south bank of the River Diem and surrounded by patchy wooded areas. But she set out in the bitter morning, chilled even in her heavy coat, with her scarf wound tightly about her face and filled with a grim determination to find Pieter and finish off police captain Reimar de Boer with or without his help.

Where was Pieter, she asked herself for the hundredth time, pedaling into the gray morning. She could close her eyes and see his brilliant green eyes, the shape of his jaw, the calm intelligence in his face. He was somewhere nearby, she could feel that he was, intent on avenging Daan's fate by eliminating the German collaborator.

But where? How? And was she any more prepared than he to finish what he had started?

The bag was heavy on her left shoulder, weighed down by the Luger she had owned since her father had presented it to her in the year she turned sixteen. She had not seen a German checkpoint since she left Amsterdam, and she prayed she did not see one – but if she did, she was prepared to capitalize on her association with *Obersturmfuhrer* Franz Becker…

• • •

De Boer's home was an ordinary box on the corner of a street lined with ordinary boxes. It was set amid a mix of low brush and fir trees bordering on woods, and there was nothing to distinguish it except the two uniformed police officers standing sentry in front of it.

Only two?

Mila pedaled past the house with little more than a glance, turned a corner and pedaled past the rear, surprised to find no guard standing sentry.

There was a waist-high picket fence behind the house, and no one beyond it that she could see from the street. But it would take a proper vantage point to know for certain – and to get a sense of how the house was laid out, and where de Boer was located inside.

She circled the area on the bicycle, casually, as though she were out for the exercise, keeping an eye out for a rise in the terrain, or a building

– anything within range of the de Boer house that could offer a decent view.

She dared not appear in sight of the guards again. She pedaled past the rear. It was warm enough now that her breath no longer clouded in front of her.

She was not certain she could still climb a tree, though she had climbed a few as a child. But her attention was caught by a trio of evergreens on the corner of the street diagonally opposite de Boer's home.

Pushing the bicycle in among the trees, she hoisted her shoulder bag high on her arm and squeezed between the thick boughs, looking for a possible foothold. Sharp pine needles scratched at her face. She pulled her scarf up around her mouth and peered about, searching for a branch heavy enough to bear her weight.

Finally, she thought she might have found one, a short, sturdy limb near a crotch in the midpoint of the trunk. Grunting, she steadied her right foot on the limb, then held her breath as she heaved herself up and prayed.

She found herself perched unsteadily on the limb, clinging by her fingernails to the rough tree bark, and struggling to balance the weight of the bag as she brought up her other leg.

Her muscles trembled and she breathed in short bursts, scrabbling for a steadier perch. Then, somehow, she was settled into the vee of the trunk, her bag firmly perched in front of her,

EVI

Jacob was the first out of the farmhouse when Evi trudged up the long driveway, bone weary and grateful to have gone the distance without running into a German check point.

"Evi! What in hell happened?"

His face was white, his gaze focused on her arm in the sling under her coat. Evi thought if she had not been so weary, she might have leapt up into his arms.

"It is nothing, Jacob – a flesh wound, Zoe told me. She treated it. I will be fine."

"A flesh wound! You took a shot?" Jacob's eyes narrowed. He took the bag from her good shoulder and examined the makeshift sling.

From the top of the steps, the three Beekhofs watched.

"*Behagen*, Jacob," Evi said. "I am cold – and very tired."

He drew her toward him, holding her gingerly at the waist. "I never should have let you go off alone. God, Evi, you could have been killed."

He led her past the others and settled her on the sofa, covering her legs with a knitted blanket and kneeling on the floor at her feet.

Mevreow ran to put up the kettle, then hurried back into the sitting room. Willem sat on the floor next to Jacob, *Meneer* stirred a fire in the grate.

Evi looked at the four of them, waiting for her to speak, but all she wanted to do was sleep.

"I shot two German guards outside a barn in Enschede," she managed, searching Jacob's face. "I took a hit to the shoulder, but Zoe's father is free. The wound is not serious. It will heal…"

"Good God," Jacob muttered. "Are you sure, Evi? Let me have a look…"

He brought her forward, but Evi stopped him, her small hand firm on his larger one. "Please," she said. "I need to sleep…"

"Will you have some tea, Evi?"

"Later," she said, leaning back on the sofa.

"My bed," Jacob murmured. "Don't even think about it. You'll be more comfortable there."

She was too tired to protest when his arms reached under her, lifting her as if she were weightless.

The last thing she knew before she fell into sleep was the softness of a feather quilt falling over her, and the touch of Jacob's fingers on her brow.

ZOE

Zoe awoke to find she had slept for nearly twelve hours. Once, she remembered, she had been rattled awake by the noise of strafing German Stukas. But she had sunk back into sleep the moment the noise receded, and now the sun shone high in the sky, a tentative promise of spring.

In her dreams, she had replayed Evi's brazenness in Enschede, saw again her father's figure fleeing into the night. She tossed about, praying for her parents, for their uneventful trek to safety.

But something else had peppered her sleep, and she was anxious to discuss it with Gerritt. Reluctantly, she threw aside the patchwork quilt and stood up to face the day.

Later, she would bicycle to the Beekhof farm to check on Evi's condition. But first, she thought, drinking a cup of weak tea, she needed to go to Heemstede.

· · ·

Gerritt looked up from his paperwork at the sound of her tap on his open door. "Zoe. I was worried…"

Briefly, she told him of her father's capture by the Gestapo, of the trip she and Evi had made to Enschede and the price her brave young friend had paid to gain her father's freedom.

"I told my parents to go to Tante Inge's in Haaksbergen. I pray they will get there safely."

Gerritt listened wide-eyed. "And I as well." He leaned back and raked a hand through his greying hair. "Indeed, what will become of any of us if this war is not over soon."

He stood up and pulled out a chair. "Sit."

Zoe did.

"This morning, on the BBC," he told her, "I heard the Allies have crossed the Meuse into Roermond. It is a good sign, Zoe. They are getting close. But who knows when liberation will come?"

Zoe sighed. "We cannot afford to wait, Gerrit. We need to begin moving the strongest people to safety."

She took a breath. "I have an idea. The morgue, cousin. The ambulance bay. Where do the bodies go?

Gerritt sat back. "To the mortuary, of course – one of several mortuaries, whichever will prepare them for burial..."

She inclined her head.

His eyebrows rose. "Ah, yes, I see...But even if we could transport these 'bodies,' would the mortuaries agree to keep them in hiding?"

Zoe lifted her shoulders. "I do not know. But it is worth asking the question. As many as they can hide, Gerritt, especially those we know are being hunted by the Germans."

Gerritt sighed. "Doctor Aaron, perhaps...and Kurt Shneider..."

Zoe waited.

"Brilliant, Zoe. Let me contact one or two morticians...at least the ones I know to be patriots."

• • •

It was quiet when she stepped off the elevator in the basement – almost unnaturally quiet. The autopsy room was closed, as was the door to the morgue. Zoe bypassed them, opened a narrow door and, in the light of a single overhead bulb, took the short flight of stairs to the sub-basement.

She knocked as expected, the designated signal. The door was opened a crack. Zoe recognized one of the hiding mothers, the wife of a Haarlem bricklayer.

"Zoe," she said. "Come in."

The light inside came from an overhead bulb and a pair of a pair of two hastily commissioned lanterns. Her eyes scanned the room.

People sat on mattresses, napped in the quiet. Even the children seemed sapped of energy. Her heart broke at their suffering.

She nodded at those she had come to know, then made her way to the far end of the space, where Kurt, in the light of one of the lanterns, was reading to a handful of listeners.

He looked up as she neared, and she warmed at the smile in his eyes and the slightly crooked line of his jaw.

"I missed you," he told her, kissing her on both cheeks when he sent the little ones for a bathroom break.

She dared to rest a hand on his face. "We had a slight – emergency, I'm afraid."

He frowned.

"I am fine, Kurt. We handled it…And you? How are you managing?"

"As well as can be. It is hardest on the children…"

"Oh, how they love your stories."

He smiled in a way that sent shivers down her spine. "For as long as we are safe here…*ya*."

MILA

The mid-day sun was more brilliant than Mila had seen it for months, creating shadows on the landscape as she peered through the dense boughs in front of her. But it carried little warmth to her perch in the crook of the sturdy pine.

Her vantage point gave her a fair view of de Boer's house and grounds – good enough to follow the routine of de Boer's police guards who, she noted, checked the rear of the house every thirty minutes. But with the shades drawn, it was impossible to tell where de Boer himself might be resting – or whether the bastard was ambulatory or bedridden.

Shifting position, she reached into her bag and pulled out one of the apples. The first taste of it, sour and sweet, was a taste of heaven.. She wiped her chin with a corner of her sleeve and chewed.

She finished the apple, and tossed the core into her bag, watching as one of guards circled the grounds and returned. She looked at her watch. Twelve-fifteen. On time to the minute.

She ate a chunk of bread. In thirty minutes, the other guard made his circuit.

Her back hurt, and her legs began to numb. but there was little she could do to change position. Before the sentry made his next circuit, however, she felt a surge of excitement. A window shade was pulled up inside the house, likely to let in a bit of the afternoon sun.

Through her binoculars, she saw the receding figure of a buxom uniformed nurse – and behind her, a figure propped up on pillows in bed.

De Boer!

It was impossible to know for certain if she could pull off a kill shot from her distance. She estimated she was the best part of thirty meters away. She would have to be extra careful to control the recoil – and the curve of the trajectory.

But it was possible.

The street was quiet, a stray cat here and there, an occasional dog-walker.

She ate the second apple, eyes on her target, watching the scene through the bedroom window as though she were watching a movie. The nurse left the room again and Mila sat straighter.

Minutes later, the nurse reappeared with a tray, which she laid on a bedside table. The figure in the bed looked up and waved her away.

By the time a sentry passed by next, the afternoon sun was waning. It would not be long before the shade was pulled, and with it, the window of opportunity.

Mila sat tall, dug her thighs into the tree trunk. *It's a chance worth taking,* she told herself.

Slowly, deliberately, she reached into her bag and wrapped her fingers around the Luger. She felt its familiar heft in her grip, eased her forefinger against the trigger. Sighting, calculating, she took aim at her target. *One...two...squeeze!*

As the shot rang out, she felt herself jerked backward, two strong arms wrapped around her. She opened her mouth to scream, but a hand reached up and clamped itself around her mouth.

EVI

"We saw tulips from the train window on our way back from Enschede," Evi said, carefully drying a soup bowl. "Red and yellow tulips poking up from the soil."

"It's a wonder there are tulips left to bloom," said *Mevrouw*, drying her hands on her apron. "How many bulbs have filled Dutch stomachs this winter?"

"Nevertheless, we saw them," Evi winced as she reached to put the bowls on a shelf.

"Your shoulder hurts, *ja*?"

Only a little. It is better now, without the sling."

"We can bring a doctor here..."

Evi shook her head. "I can bicycle into the center if I need to."

"I don't know, Evi," *Mevrouw's* face was sober. "The Germans are on high alert. It is as though they know the war is all but lost to them."

Jacob had told her much the same thing. He had heard it on the BBC, he said, listening late at night with Papa Beekhof, The Allies had dealt the Reich a devastating blow, taking several towns in and around Limburg. German soldiers had begun to defect.

"It's the beginning," Jacob told her, his face alight. "The Allies will be here soon."

• • •

Jacob had been sitting at her bedside when she awoke after the harrowing night in Enschede. "Hi, Itty Bitty. How are you?"

She had managed a smile. "As fine as anyone who has taken a bullet to the shoulder."

"That's not funny."

"It was not meant to be funny. But I think I will be fine."

She leaned on her good elbow to pull herself up. "You are a wonderful teacher, Jacob. Even in the dark, sighting from the ground after I was hit, I killed those two Nazi guards."

She sat up, using her good hand as leverage. "You would have been truly proud."

"I am proud." His hand was warm on her face. "Good job, Itty-Bitty"

She willed him to come closer, but he took a step back. "Guess you don't need me anymore."

She had steeled herself, looked deep into his eyes. "I will always need you, Jacob…"

• • •

"If you think you are ready, Evi," Mevrouw said now, "you may go back the barge. Willem can go along with you. You will want to bring back some clothing, *ja*? And whatever else you will need."

She was not eager to be back on the barge. Mam's heart and soul were there. But of course there were things she wanted to have – Mam's hand-knit blankets, and her box of photographs – and some of her sweaters and boots.

"If you think it is safe…" her voice trailed off.

"You can take the back roads." *Mevreow* laid a hand on her good shoulder. "Willem will know how to go."

PART FIVE

Haarlem, the Netherlands
March 1945

ZOE

"There is some good news, Zoe," Gerritt came up behind her in the hospital's dim sub-basement.

She had been listening to Kurt's expressive voice reading *The Ugly Duckling,* marveling at his ability to keep even the youngest children rapt, no matter how many times they had heard the story.

They had worked out a system for bringing in food, for tending to minor emergencies – even for ensuring that the 'bodies' posing on gurneys in the morgue could walk about and exercise on schedule.

They had developed a signal – three quick blasts of an airhorn – to alert them if the Germans stormed the building. The door to the ambulance bay was a way out, though the bravest of them knew they might be running into the arms of the enemy.

Zoe turned to her cousin. "Any good news is a blessing."

Geritt sat beside her on a low wooden bench. "Two of the city's mortuaries have agreed to help when we are ready to evacuate our refugees. They will keep transport our 'bodies' once or twice a day – and they will keep a couple of marked vans in the ambulance bay with keys in the ignition so that anyone escaping will have a chance to outrun the Germans."

MILA

Mila struggled, falling backwards, landing in a heap on the cold ground, limbs entangled with her captor's.

"Let me go," she kicked and pushed, but powerful hands held her. Her mouth found an arm and she bit down.

"Ouch! Mila, it is I."

Her head swiveled. "Pieter?"

"I was waiting till dark. You beat me to the vantage point."

"Did I get him?"

"We cannot be sure." He helped her to her feet. "But neither can we wait to find out. We need to get out of here – now!"

But heavy footsteps barreled into the street and the WAH-wah of police sirens pierced the air before they reached the end of the street.

Mila blessed the falling dusk as they crouched between stands of trees and alleys.

"There is a canal on the other side of these woods," Pieter said, leading Mila through the brush. "I have a small dinghy anchored there. My plan was – *is* to take it to the north end of town not far from the railroad depot."

He picked up his pace as their distance widened.

"There is a ten o'clock train to Brussels," he huffed, as the sky above them began to flash red and blue. "We need to be on it," he told her over the noise of screeching sirens, "before the *polizie* move to shut everything down."

Mila followed in Pieter's wake, moving fast to keep up with his stride, nearly stumbling on the roots of an oak tree and feeling his strength as he steadied her. She was breathing hard by the time they reached a clearing and she saw, in the pallor of a cold moon, what appeared to be a bobbing row boat.

Pieter stepped in, then reached for her hand. The dinghy rocked under their weight. She fought to keep her balance and sat hard on the wooden bench. Pieter grabbed for the oars. In seconds, they were moving away from shore, the ebbing sound of police sirens giving way to the steady splash of oars in the water.

EVI

Something was amiss. Evi could feel it the moment she entered the Beekhof's kitchen. *Mevrouw*'s back was to her, leaning over the sink, but Jacob and Papa Beekhof, at opposite ends of the table, wore decidedly grave expressions.

"What?" she asked, searching Jacob's face, dropping a bag full of clothing on the floor.

Willem brought in a wooden crate and stopped short at the silence.

"What has happened?" Evi asked again.

For a long moment, there was no answer.

Mevreouw turned to face them, her mouth a grim line.

At last, Jacob met her gaze. "Do you remember," he said, "when I told you the Beekhofs had managed to obtain a Dutch ID for me?"

She nodded.

"Well, it seems the identification I have belonged to a guy who was deceased…a guy about my age named Hans Mittlinger, who was living in Amsterdam when he died."

Jacob's gaze met Papa Beekhof's for a second, then flitted back to hers. She could read the anguish in his eyes.

"Well, it seems…" he exhaled noisily. "It seems the guy was German by birth, but the Germans don't seem to know he's dead."

Evi scrunched up her face, looked briefly to Papa Beekhof, then settled her gaze on Jacob's face. "*Ja?*"

"So, Hans Mittlinger is being conscripted into the *Wehrmacht*…the German Army…"

Evi's eyes grew wide.

Jacob nodded slowly. "He is to report to the High Command in Maybach II, just south of Berlin, at 0700 hours on the eighteenth day of March."

Evi dropped heavily into a chair.

ZOE

They were deep in conversation in the dim light of the basement morgue.

"*Lieve god*, the children are gone," Zoe said. "We can only pray they can be transported from the mortuaries to safety…."

Kurt shook his head. "We will never know. But we did what we could. Now we pray."

Zoe sighed. She looked down half-heartedly at the list they were preparing for Gerritt.

"You and Doctor Aaron should be the next to go. You know that."

"Aaron, yes, but I will take my chances until the others have escaped."

Zoe looked at him and sighed. "How do you decide whose lives are more important than others," she murmured.

Kurt did not hesitate. "The hiding mothers. Some of them sent their own children abroad to keep them safe from warfare…"

The list was not yet half completed when the three blasts tore into their consciousness.

Zoe was the first to move.

"The airhorn," she said. "*Lieve god*, Kurt," she said, "They are here…the Germans. You must get out of here now."

"The others first," he protested. "I will help them toward the ambulance bay. How many will the van hold, do you think?"

Zoe shook him by the shoulders. "You are not hearing me, Kurt. You must go first. You are high on the list of the Reich's most wanted. The others will know what to do."

He hesitated, his face a mask

"Go now, Kurt – if not for your own sake, then for mine."

He looked at her and something electric passed between them. He reached for her, and she knew she must go with him.

She was propelling him out through the door to the ambulance bay when the first sounds of jackboots began clattering down the stairs and daylight flooded the morgue.

She had never driven a vehicle this large, but when the van was full of fleeing souls, she slid into the driver's seat, turned the key in the ignition, and sped out of the bay, tires screeching.

Heart hammering in her chest, she lowered her speed as she reached the main road, realizing, belatedly, that a speeding mortuary van might be a certain target for Germans on high alert.

Slowly, steadily, she guided the van through familiar streets, eyes darting left, right, straight in front of her, watchful for check points, for gathering German soldiers, for signs of anything out of the ordinary.

It was not until she pulled to a stop in the alley behind the Klaasen Mortuary that she realized she had been holding her breath. Gulping air, she jumped out of the driver's seat, raised the back door of the van, and flung open the mortuary door.

Shivering in the cold, in their hospital nightshirts, the evacuees filed into the mortuary.

"*God zegene*," Zoe whispered to each as they passed. "God bless."

Kurt was the last to disembark. "How can I leave you, Zoe? I cannot think of it. I may never see you again…"

She met his gaze, and a thought came together in her head.

"Stay in the van, Kurt. Get up on the gurney and under a blanket. If we should be stopped, you are a very ill patient – near to unconsciousness, you understand?"

Kurt's brows knit together.

"There is no time to explain. Do you trust me?"

The shortest of pauses. "With my life."

MILA

The latest edition of the *Telegraaf*, which Pieter had managed to find after they crossed the border into Belgium, was cause for muted celebration.

The Americans had successfully taken the Rhine at Remagen in Germany. Another blow to Herr Hitler. Not surprisingly, the German army had responded by executing thirty-six Dutch men and women pulled at random at a deserted fair ground in Amsterdam.

But Queen Wilhelmina had announced her plans to return to the Netherlands.

It could only mean, Mila thought, *that liberation could not be far behind.*

They had very nearly missed the train to Brussels. The station master had been wary of their soiled, damp clothing, and it was only after Pieter had convinced the man he was on holiday with his mistress – that they had had too much to drink and had slipped in a darkened garden in their haste to catch the train that he had eyed Mila with unconcealed longing and sold Pieter the tickets.

She looked with satisfaction at the newspaper. Below the fold on page one, a story under bold headlines reported the assassination of Amsterdam Police Captain Reimar de Boer in 'a bold second attack on his life.'

The assassin was still at large, the story read, but authorities were employing the latest advances in forensic science in an attempt to trace the bullet lodged in de Boer's spinal cord to the revolver used by the assassin.

Mila put down her tea cup in the small café in Brussels and passed the paper back to Pieter, pointing to the last sentence.

"Can they do that, do you think?"

"Trace the bullet?" Peter shrugged. "Perhaps. "The science is not exact. But *ja*, I suppose it is possible."

The Luger lay deep in the depths of the canal, but the chance that the bullet could be traced to her was altogether alarming. Mila wondered when, if ever, she would walk again on Dutch soil…

Oddly, it was little Hondje she thought she would miss the most…

"That means," she said finally, "I could not go home again if I wanted to."

Pieter took his hands in hers. "Not for a while. Would you want to?"

Mila looked around her in the March sunlight. Belgium, which had for so long been a vital link in the escape route forged by Resistance forces, had already been liberated. People here seemed to be going about their business if not altogether without care, than at least with their eyes looking straight ahead and not at the ground beneath their feet.

"Are we safe here, do you think?" she asked.

"Safer than we would be in the Netherlands."

"It is daunting to think we cannot return…."

Pieter removed his hands from hers and tenderly cupped her face. "Maybe one day, my love – if you want to."

The icy misgiving in the pit of her stomach seemed to melt away in the sunlight. She looked deeply into Pieter's green eyes, and she knew she was already home.

EVI

It was not quite dawn when Evi turned in her bed on the sofa, burrowed down deep into the covers, and then suddenly sat up straight, eyes wide open.

It was quiet in the house but for the remnants of the night's fire popping and crackling in the grate. But she was sure she heard voices…

Men's voices, low and insistent, and now beginning to fade.

Throwing off the covers, she slipped her feet into boots, threw on a sweater and the woolen pants *Mevreow* had sewn for her as a birthday gift. She grabbed a jacket, the one with Mam's blue knit cap tucked into the pocket.

First light was beginning to break when she opened the kitchen door.

She heard no voices now, but instinct propelled her through the wet grass and early spring growth all the way to the hidden tunnel at the end of the field that ended where the land met the river. Her heart beginning to hammer in her chest.

She had known, as surely as if she had been in on the planning, what she would see when she got there. But the sight of Jacob standing on the shore in front of a small motorboat, and Papa Beekhof stowing something inside, filled her with sadness and fright.

Jacob turned to untie the ropes. It was a moment before he saw her.

"Evi…"

She jammed her hands into her jacket pockets, did her best to keep her lips from trembling. "You were going to leave without me, Jacob…"

"Evi, it's dangerous -"

"Without saying goodbye…"

"I have to go -"

"I know that, Jacob."

"Then, why are you asking?"

She moved toward him, her voice a whisper. "Because I love you, Jacob…you know that. I cannot let you leave without me…"

Jacob crossed the distance between them, stopped to look at her for what seemed like forever, then reached out and crushed her to him.

"Oh, God, I love you too, Itty Bitty." His kiss was warm on her lips. "But I can't let you do this," he murmured into her hair. "In a small boat, through the North Sea, Evi, can't you see how dangerous this is? Maybe impossible."

Papa Beekhof put a hand on her arm. "Evi, *behagen*, Jacob is right. More than twenty-four hours by sea, my dear girl, and at that, only a faint hope of reaching the English Channel…

But Evi had never been so sure of anything in her life.

She drew back to lose herself in the familiar planes of Jacob's face. "Where you go, I go, Jacob Reese. I would follow you to the ends of the earth."

ZOE

Piercing sirens split the air from every direction, and the streets were clogged with Dutch police cars and all manner of German vehicles. Zoe kept the van at a slow but steady speed, avoiding the traffic as best she could, traversing the streets toward the river.

Finally, parking the van across the street from the pier, she slipped out of the driver's seat and signaled to Kurt to get out.

She grasped his hand, surveyed the landscape, and led the way down the windy pier to the *Blijde Tijding*.

She had never piloted a barge before any more than she had driven a mortuary van, but Evi had offered her an incredible gift. It was a risk, but a risk worth taking.

"Where on earth are we going," Kurt muttered in her wake. She did not take the time to explain.

To her great relief, the door to the barge was not locked. It swung open at her touch. She pushed Kurt in ahead of her, then followed him in and locked the door behind them.

Kurt glanced around, then turned his gaze on Zoe.

"The barge belongs to my friend, Evi Strobel" she told him, rummaging in the kitchen drawer for the ignition key Evi told her was there.

She held up the key. "Evi used to live on this barge with her mother," she said. "But now she has another life – and *godjizdank*, her generosity now may now help to us save ours…"

Kurt's face was a study in astonishment.

"There is a safe house I know in Middleburg," she told him. "We are safer on the water than on land, I think, and I know people in Middleburg who can help us cross the border into Antwerp."

Kurt reached for her, his face still unbelieving, and she allowed herself a moment in his arms.

Then she handed him the key. "Can you pilot this thing?"

"I once kept a sailboat on a lake near Stuttgart."

"Well, that is a relief. Then, go!"

He moved toward the helm and studied the controls. Zoe took a pair of binoculars from a hook on the wall and moved to the small rear deck.

A slight wind ruffled her hair, but the river was calm, the sky a deep azure, and the air warm with promise that the stubborn winter might indeed give way to spring.

She heard the engine sputter and cough, and finally spring to life. She felt the shudder of the old boards beneath her feet and the first sensation of movement.

In the near distance, a small boat cut a shallow swath through the water. Squinting through the binoculars Zoe thought she saw two figures in the boat, one of them wearing a bright blue cap with a yellow butterfly on the side.

EPILOGUE

Fairfield, New Jersey
April, 2017
She reached for a cut glass dish on the second shelf, then pulled back and winced in pain, massaging her left shoulder. *Idioot*, she told herself. *Wouldn't you think, after all these years, you would know better!*

She stepped on a stool, retrieved the dish, and filled it with homemade pickles, then glanced at the clock as she stowed it in the refrigerator next to a pitcher of iced tea.

From the yard, where her son, Thomas, was roasting chickens on a spit, she heard the lilting voices of his wife and Anneke's sister, Klara. They were busy cutting roses for the table, and as she turned to fill a vase with water, the door burst open and her daughter, Hannah, and her laughing gaggle of granddaughters and great grands bustled into the kitchen.

"Oma," called the youngest, "they had *stamppot* at the European Deli, not as good as your potatoes, of course, but we bought some anyway."

"And *stroopwaffels*," said Hannah, also not as good as yours, but we can never have too many sweets."

"I made six dozen *speculaas*," she started to protest, but her voice was drowned out by the sounds of seven women talking, laughing, unpacking bags of way too much food to fit in her crowded refrigerator.

She gave herself up to the noise and the bustle because she knew it was hopeless not to, but she heard it instantly when the front door opened at just after four, and Anneke called, "Oma, we're here!"

"*Lieve god*," she breathed, tears springing to her eyes as she rushed to the figures in the doorway. "Zoe...*lieve god*, I can't believe it..."

Zoe fell into her arms. "Evi...."

The woman she hugged was stooped and smaller than she remembered, but she would have known her anywhere, Evi thought, hugging Zoe tight. The decades fell away and the short, white curls were once again a lively brown and the frail little figure robust.

Now, as Zoe began to pull back, she saw the tall, silver-haired man at her side.

"Evi," Zoe said. "This is Anton - "

Zoe's son, Evi guessed.

"Oma, where are your silver candlesticks?" Hilde called.

"And your large Delft platter - for the chickens?"

And just like that, the greetings were done, and the guests piled in, and chairs were unfolded, and platters of food were laid on the table and the house hummed with busy, laughing people.

"L' Chaim," they shouted as glasses were raised. *To life*, Evi thought. *Indeed*. And it was not until the dishes were cleared and coffee and *speculaas* and *stroopwaffel* were on the table, and Zoe was deep in conversation with her daughters and their daughters, that she found herself facing the good-looking man who had stood at Zoe's side in the doorway.

Early seventies, she guessed, about the same age as Thomas. Tall and dark-haired, with flecks of grey in his brows, and a pleasantly ruddy face.

"Anton, yes?" she smiled.

"Yes, Ma'am. Anton Kuyper."

"Please, call me Evi. You are Zoe's son, *ja*?"

The pleasant face broke into a grin. "Oh, no, ma'am. Sorry for the confusion. I met Zoe - that is, Doctor Visser - in Amsterdam only a year ago. I was searching for connections to the Dutch Resistance in the Netherlands during World War Two."

Evi cocked her head. "Really?"

"Yes…I've been trying to find out more about for my own beginnings, and Doctor Visser thought perhaps you could help."

Her eyes widened. "And how is that?"

He leaned back in his chair, brows slightly furrowed, gave her a quick half-smile. "Well…all I know about my birth, really, is that it was sometime late in 1944 – or perhaps early in 1945 – and that I was found by a fisherman, screaming my head off, on an old. abandoned barge somewhere off the coast of Rotterdam…"

Evi felt the blood drain from her face.

Now the man leaned forward, concern on his face. "Mrs. Reese – are you alright?"

Evi worked to find her voice. When she did, it was little more than a whisper. "*Lieve god*…baby Jacob," she whispered finally.

She sat forward, grasped both the man's hands and looked into his earnest dark eyes.

"You are Jacob Rood," her voice was soft. "Your name is Jacob Rood."

Now the man sat perfectly still, his mouth falling open.

Evi took a shaky breath. "You were born to a Jewish mother sometime in the last week of January of 1945, I think. What I know from my own mother is that your mother died while hiding from the Germans, with you and other Jewish refugees, in one of the old limestone caves near Limburg…"

Evi became aware of a growing stillness in the room. But all she could see was the rapt face of Anton/Jacob. "My mother, who worked for the Dutch Resistance, rescued you and brought you home in that barge."

The words spilled out of her. "You were no more than two or three weeks old, and amazingly robust in spite of being malnourished – but there was something wrong with your hip – or your leg. We thought you needed medical help…"

The man who had been baby Jacob seemed to hang on every word.

She told him of Mam's resolve to get him to Belgium, where she could be sure no doctor would report him to the Germans for being Jewish. "You had been circumcised, you see…"

He nodded.

"And so, we headed south in the barge, toward Belgium – a route my mother had navigated many times, ferrying Jewish escapees toward the border…"

Her voice broke as she told him of the Nazis ambushing the barge, murdering her mother in cold blood – and of her own very narrow escape.

"We could both have been killed that day by the Nazis," she said. "In fact…I was certain you could not possibly have survived…"

"I would have died," he said, sitting perfectly still, "if your mother hadn't somehow concealed me – or if my father – I mean the man who found me and raised me - had not heard me wailing in that barge. He found me hidden in a small compartment beneath the controls…"

Anneke was the one to break the silence. "Oma," she said. "You never talk about those days – how you and Opa escaped from Haarlem, or how you came to America…."

Evi covered her mouth with her hands, rocked slowly in her chair. Then she rose and left the room. When she returned, she held in her hands a blue knit cap, with a yellow butterfly on its side.

Zoe gasped when she saw it.

"This is all I have to remind me of that day," she said softly. "My mother – my dear Mam, God rest her soul – made this for me on our last Christmas together. I wore it on the day Jacob and I left Haarlem…"

In the silence, Evi took a deep breath. "We left in a little motorboat on a chilly morning in March of 1945, hoping, foolishly perhaps, to make our way through the North Sea and into the English Channel…"

She felt the spring of grateful tears. "We were fortunate," she said. "The seas were calm, and we were spotted and rescued by a British patrol boat somewhere in the Wadden sea on our second day out in the boat."

She felt every eye in the room fastened upon her.

"By the time liberation came, in May of that year, I was already in this very kitchen, learning to bake challah with my mother-in-law, Jacob's mother – watching freedom come to the Netherlands on a tiny, black-and-white television screen."

She looked over at her eldest son. "I was already pregnant with you, Thomas, and learning to live as an American…"

She paused and looked at her oldest friend. "And you, Zoe? You went home?"

Zoe nodded, slowly. "Thanks to your kindness, Kurt and I made it to Middleburg in your mother's barge," she said. "I could swear, Evi, that I caught a flash of your bright blue cap that day as we prepared to move out into the Spaarne…"

Evi's hands flew to her face.

"In any case," said Zoe, "My Resistance contacts were able to move us safely across the border to Belgium. We stayed in Antwerp until after the liberation. Then we returned to Haarlem. Kurt had been a construction engineer in in Germany, and he was eager to help rebuild the broken city. "

She leaned across the table to take Evi's hand. "Your shoulder," she looked around at the sea of rapt faces.

"Your Oma," she said, "took a Nazi bullet in order to rescue my father from the Germans. Evi, tell me, *behagen*, that your shoulder healed properly."

Evi shrugged. "For the most part. It hurts a bit when I reach over my head. But I told you then and I tell you now, I would do it again if I needed to…"

She leaned forward. "And Mila, Zoe? Do you know what happened to Mila?"

Zoe sighed. "She telephoned me after she and Pieter safely reached Brussels, shortly before Kurt and I left Haarlem. They were preparing to make a life in Belgium, she told me…"

A pause. "But not long afterward, she was diagnosed with uterine cancer. She died in August of 1948. She was not yet thirty."

Evi heard the collective intake of breath.

"Pieter endowed a scholarship in her name at the University of Amsterdam," Zoe said. "The Mila Brouwer Woman of Bravery Scholarship…"

Evi nodded, deep in the grip of memory.

But by that time, Thomas had brought out a bottle of Jenever, the Dutch brew made from juniper berries, and they drank to the millions who died in Hitler's war and toasted those who had survived, and the noise level increased, and Alette, her youngest great-granddaughter, named for the woman who had come to Evi's aid on that terrible day off the coast of Rotterdam, asked to try on Oma's blue cap.

• • •

It was after eleven, and she was bone tired, by the time Evi finally closed the door of her bedroom. Zoe had been installed in Hannah's old room, Anton Jacob Rood Kuyper in Thomas's. In the morning, they would breakfast at Hannah's, then pay a visit the Holocaust memorial museum in New York City before seeing a musical on Broadway.

But for now, she needed to rest. She creamed her face, as hopeless a gesture as that was, she thought wryly, given the map of her astonishing life in her ninety-year-old wrinkles. She ran a brush through her silvery hair, changed into a nightgown and climbed into her bed.

She lay there for a moment, re-living every moment of the impossible, incredible evening, then sighed and turned onto her good right shoulder.

She leaned across the bed to touch the pillow where Jacob had rested next to her for more than forty years.

She closed her eyes and swore she could hear his voice, as clearly as if he were in the room.

"Good job," she could hear him whisper in her ear. "Good job, Itty-Bitty…I love you."

AUTHOR'S NOTE

Every novel has its genesis – someone, some issue, some tiny thing that sparks a connection with the heart of a writer and takes on a life of its own.

Winter's End came to me in the last months of the pandemic as I found myself reading about strong Dutch women like Hanni Schaft, Corrie Ten Boom, teenaged sisters Truus and Freddie Obersteegen, and others who fought for the Resistance, risking their lives to save Jews, Dutch citizens, and enemies of the Reich during the German occupation of World War II.

The character of Evi Strobel moved into my head and refused to leave until I told her story, and as I pondered what direction to take, Evi introduced me to Zoe and Mila and their exploits during the last harrowing months of the war – the Hunger Winter of 1944-45 – and I could hardly type fast enough to keep up with them.

I tried to be faithful to the timeline of the war, and to the mission of the Dutch Resistance, bending the facts only as necessary in the interest of better storytelling – and as I was unable to return to Amsterdam during the pandemic, I relied on my memories of that beautiful city, and Haarlem, where *Winter's End* begins. I take full responsibility for errors of time or place.

For months during the lockdown, I read chapters via Zoom meetings to a critique group led by Marla Miller. I thank Linda Rhoades, Victoria Waddle, Kelley Bowles, Debi McCarthy, John Trotti, Connie Deuschle, and posthumously, Randy Quiroz – and for graciously lending her medical expertise, Dr. Richelle Marracino, MD. Your insights helped build a better story.

I am ever thankful to my beta readers and personal cheering squad, Judy Girardi, Sherry Clark, Larry Markman, Larry Padgett, and, posthumously, Vern Kappius and Sandy Levine.

For their deft oversight, I thank Black Rose Writing publisher Reagan Rothe and his exceptional staff and, for another fantastic cover design, thank you to David Ter-Avanesyan.

Last, but not least, thanks to you, my readers, without whom any author is nowhere! Please connect with me at BarbaraPronin.com, find me on Instagram @writerbobbi, and/or on Facebook or Goodreads – and if you enjoy *Winter's End*, I'd be grateful for your review at Amazon.com, BarnesandNoble.com, on Goodreads, and wherever you buy or borrow books.

Barbara Pronin
May, 2025

ALSO BY BARBARA PRONIN

The Miner's Canary
Sing Sweetly to Me
Thicker Than Water
Syndrome

AS BARBARA NICKOLAE

Finders Keepers
Ties That Bind
Kiss Mommy Goodnight

ABOUT THE AUTHOR

Barbara Pronin is the author of seven mystery novels, including three as Barbara Nickolae, and two non-fiction books. When a short article about women of the Dutch resistance in WW II caught her eye, the character of Evi Strobel moved into her head and refused to leave until she told her story. A former Brooklynite who loves dark chocolate, Greek sunsets, and the L.A. (nee Brooklyn) Dodgers, Barbara lives and works in Orange County, California, where, when she isn't writing fiction, she struggles at her spinet piano and writes about real estate.

NOTE FROM BARBARA PRONIN

Word-of-mouth is crucial for any author to succeed. If you enjoyed *Winter's End*, please leave a review online—anywhere you are able. Even if it's just a sentence or two. It would make all the difference and would be very much appreciated.

Thanks!
Barbara Pronin

We hope you enjoyed reading this title from:

www.blackrosewriting.com

Subscribe to our mailing list – *The Rosevine* – and receive **FREE** books, daily deals, and stay current with news about upcoming releases and our hottest authors.
Scan the QR code below to sign up.

Already a subscriber? Please accept a sincere thank you for being a fan of Black Rose Writing authors.

View other Black Rose Writing titles at www.blackrosewriting.com/books and use promo code **PRINT** to receive a **20% discount** when purchasing.

Made in the USA
Middletown, DE
06 October 2025